Stymie

Also by Andy Plattner

Winter Money

A Marriage of Convenience

Offerings from a Rust Belt Jockey

Dixie Luck

Tower

Stymie

a novel in stories

Andy Plattner

MERCER UNIVERSITY PRESS

Macon, Georgia

MUP/ P709

Published by Mercer University Press
1501 Mercer University Drive
Macon, Georgia 31207

29 28 27 26 25   5 4 3 2 1

Books published by Mercer University Press are printed on acid-free paper that meets the requirements of the American National Standard for Information Sciences—Permanence of Paper for Printed Library Materials.

Printed and bound in the United States.

This book is set in Adobe Caslon and Palatino display.

Cover/jacket design by Burt&Burt.

Library of Congress Cataloging-in-Publication Data

Names: Plattner, Andy, author.
Title: Stymie : a novel in stories / Andy Plattner.
Description: Macon : Mercer University Press, 2025. |
Identifiers: LCCN 2024054747 (print) | LCCN 2024054748 (ebook) |
ISBN 9780881460285 (paperback) | ISBN 9780881460339 (ebook)
Subjects: LCSH: Stymie (Race horse), 1941-1962--Fiction. | Horse racing--United States--Fiction. | LCGFT: Novels.
Classification: LCC PS3566.L33 O44 2014 (print) | LCC PS3566.L33 (ebook)
| DDC 813/.54--dc23/eng/20241119
LC record available at https://lccn.loc.gov/2024054747
LC ebook record available at https://lccn.loc.gov/2024054748

Contents

MERCER UNIVERSITY

MERCER UNIVERSITY PRESS

Endowed by

TOM WATSON BROWN

and

THE WATSON-BROWN FOUNDATION, INC.

Groom

It was thought that after the war, Ben Held would marry Bonnie Dennert and they would find a place of their own. He'd returned to Newport, Kentucky, and his parents' shotgun shack on the river side of Second Street. Weeks passed; he remained silent on the matter. He could ask her father for her hand, but Ben knew she would want him to speak directly to her and answer for herself. She no doubt had to sit through any number of meals with her parents and her sister...*So, what's happening with Ben? He going to propose? Thought you two were...* He tried to imagine how Bonnie would respond. *Dad, Ma...he will, or he won't.*

He tried to picture her expression when he'd say to her they ought to be married, and soon. Perhaps she would be ecstatic. She might wrap her arms around his neck and hold on so hard he couldn't breathe. Or she might look up into his eyes and say, *Are you sure?*

She was nineteen and the casinos didn't bother about the age of a young woman if she happened to be with a soldier, and enough people knew Ben had been a soldier, even if he never wore his uniform anymore. Bonnie touched the dice for luck, sat on his knee at a poker table. They'd take an open-air omnibus over to Covington and from there would ride the trolley to Latonia Race Track. They preferred the highest of the ascending rows in the grandstand, this so she could take in everything, not just the races. Her parents would give her an afternoon off from the grocery store if she was going to spend it with him because they felt he would propose soon. The infield held colorful gardens, a glassy lake. This was said to be one of the most beautiful racetracks in America, in the whole world.

Perhaps everyone anticipated that something would be missing from Ben, and in this way, nothing was out of place. He knew that she was in love with him, and he was in love with her. She said he could talk about the women he'd encountered in France and Germany, though not endlessly. She'd heard so many things already. She might have her doubts, but she would marry him, and it wouldn't be a big wedding that involved the whole rotting neighborhood; it would be done at the office of the justice of the peace. When he imagined this, it made his heart turn. He knew that type of wedding would be right for them because things had to be on their terms, as much as possible. This was also the problem.

When he'd been away, he'd thought about what the people in this town would think of him. Though he'd never fled a battlefield, he'd felt panicked enough to have done so. Even if he escaped through a French forest, lived on the lam, something in him would forever be tormented by the idea that everyone back home had heard of what he'd done, and he would only be remembered as a coward. If you were a coward, nothing you ever did or said mattered. Other than the people who knew him, he wasn't likely to leave much of an impression anywhere else. The barkeep at the Kentucky Grill would buy him a round, and everyone at the counter raise a toast. But he'd eventually lose interest in their talk. And while he was staring off, not listening, he'd feel the looks of others.

He'd been home for a couple of months, living with his folks, and hadn't proposed to Bonnie. On a summer afternoon in July, he sat on the steps of the front porch of his parents' shack and looked out to the young beech trees that bordered the edges of the Ohio. From the corner of his eye, he caught someone heading in his direction. When he heard Bonnie call his name, he turned and there she was, moving down the grassy bank from the sidewalk that ran along Second Street. She wore a dress greener than a May lawn, a beautiful frock that went all the way to her ankles, and he'd seen it once before, right after he'd returned. On her head sat an odd-looking top hat, small and tan, with an aqua feather sticking up from the band. They hadn't made any plans for the day, and he'd been thinking he might walk up to her parents' grocery. He remained at the top of the wooden steps and she stood before him, dressed the way she was, in the best clothes she owned. "Good morning, Ben."

It was time. "Morning." He decided not to tease her or drag it out. He took out his packet of cigarettes and she held her hands together. He liked the acorns in the pattern of the dress. He wondered what exactly had made her decide that today would be the day. Sometime, he would ask her.

"Your folks away?" she said.

"At work. Here I am. Lookin' at the river."

She turned her shoulders in that direction. Her brown eyes traveled back to him. "You're watching the river."

He didn't need to ask about the difference. "Like I'm watching you," he said.

"Yes."

He said, "You want to sit here, next to me?" He made room. She put her right foot on the lowest step, but this was all she did. "Well," he said. He wanted to say, *You know what I'm going to say.* But he was the man and he needed to speak. "I think you and I ought to get out of here, Bonnie. I think it's time. I want to marry you and then I want to leave. Or we can leave and get married at the next place we go."

"Where will we go?"

"With the horses," he said. "The meeting here ends in a

month, the stables will split up, we'll catch on with somebody. Washington Park. I'd like to go to Chicago myself. We had a fella in our unit..."

She had not taken her eyes away from him. "Why should I leave?"

"Because I won't be here."

"I will be."

He decided to look past her, to the line of beech trees, the morning sunlight whitish against their trunks. "I'll be fighting with myself if I settle down. Then I'll be fighting with you. But if we can..."

"I haven't been proposed to before," she said. "But this isn't a good one."

He exhaled. "I can't imagine ever doing it again. You don't have to stay here forever. Come with me, you don't have to marry me. If you don't like it...I can't pretend...I don't want to pretend, that's the short of it. I don't want things to be any more difficult..."

"My life isn't going to be a burden to me, Ben. I won't allow it. If that's what you're worried about."

"In a way, that is what I'm worried about. We'll just be trudging on, one day, then another. Good god."

"That's the way it'll be wherever...you can't..."

"I know you don't want to leave, I understand. I want to go to Washington Park, and I want to see Chicago. Anthony Fiers, he's from my unit. He told me to look him up. I wrote down his address even. I'll go to work in the stables, shovel manure or whatever. Before the war, you and I went to Latonia. You told me Latonia was the name of a Greek goddess. She was married, who was it to?"

"Jupiter."

"Yeah, well nobody's gonna be naming any planet after me...I'm going to leave at the end of July. I want you to come with me. I want to be excited about everything. To start, we'll probably have to live near the stables, but I can work my way up. Maybe I can even be a trainer, work for old Colonel Bradley. I don't see what's so wrong with all of this...are you let down?"

"I guess I usually am in some form. By others, I mean."

"I knew what you meant."

"I can never be talked out of the way I feel."

"If you loved me more, would you go with me?"

"Yes." She said this right as he finished his question. "If you stay here, I'll be your wife. I'll look after you. I'll lay down with you whenever you want."

"You have till the end of July to decide."

"You, too."

"Right." At this point, he brought his attention to her hat. He was careful about saying anything unkind. "I've never seen you in that before."

While keeping her eyes on him, she reached up and touched at the tips of the feather. "Found it in our attic. Ma said it's not hers. So, of course, I became interested."

If things had gone differently, if he had said what he needed to in a different way, he would've asked her inside. Because right then, more than anything else, he wanted to. Enough with the talking. His parents wouldn't return for hours. Even if they did come home and Ben was in his room with Bonnie, his parents wouldn't say a thing because it was widely understood that he was going to marry her. When a soldier wanted his girl, he shouldn't have to wait. He said, "I'd like to do something with you today. I don't really care what."

"I took off from the store," she said. "I should get back."

"What did you tell them you were doing? Putting on that dress and all?" He shouldn't have said anything, and for the first time this morning she looked hurt. The way she looked made him want to say he could change his mind, maybe he could stay in town. He could work in the stables at Latonia when the meeting was going on and then, when the horses moved away, he could get something else, something in town until the following spring, when the horses came back.

"They didn't have to ask," she said. "And they won't say a word when I get back because they'll know. Anyway, I wouldn't be caught dead working in this...well, good-bye, Ben." She moved back one step.

"I'll see you around," he said.

"I'm sure you will."

* * *

When she walked away, he wanted not to notice because if she looked back, he wanted to seem just fine observing the river. When he glanced in the direction from where she'd appeared, there was the sliver-like shape of the green of her dress growing smaller. If he were leaving tomorrow, he would have chased after her. In a little while, he wanted to walk up to Fourth Street, to the Carnegie Library, and look at the newspapers. His father worked at the Weidemann Brewery, and his mother and her friend Amanda Osteen cleaned churches. At breakfast this morning, she'd murmured something about Corpus Christi. His father managed inventory for the brewery, but he didn't like the work and didn't like to talk about it. His father didn't like to work at all, and Ben wondered if this trait would eventually surface in him. He didn't want to be dissatisfied like that, however. His father didn't say much, didn't ask for much. Ben had tried to imagine both of his parents as children growing up, and it wasn't easy, especially when it came to his father, because he'd never seemed young and didn't encourage anyone to look at him that way.

This afternoon, he would go to the library, but tomorrow he would take the omnibus and then the trolley over to Latonia. He'd go early, an hour before the first race, and he'd walk over to the stables to see about work. He'd have to shovel out stalls, that's where everyone started, and he imagined it wouldn't matter because it would be good to be around the horses, which was what he wanted. Before the war, he'd attended the races at Latonia and the horses had thrilled him. They still could.

* * *

The next day, he caught a bus and then the trolley over to Latonia. At the stables, he introduced himself to one trainer, then another. He spoke of his plans, that he wanted to travel with a stable and do the work asked of him. The trainers weren't talkative, and they might've viewed him with some suspicion. A groom—that was a colored man's job, a drifter's job, an illiterate's job.

A man named Jenkins made him an offer. Report to work tomorrow at five a.m., see what the work is, see if you can do it. Ben's mind flashed an objection because the trolley for Latonia didn't start its runs until eleven a.m. Instead, he said all right. What he did then was take the trolley back to Covington, grab a bus for Newport. At his parents' home, he packed his duffel bag and left them a note on the table that said he'd be back in day or so, he had some things to tend to. They'd deduce he eloped with Bonnie. He returned to Latonia on the last trolley of the day, combed the neighborhoods for a flophouse. With a racetrack nearby, this was a simple deduction. The rooms of the house he found had newspapers for wallpaper. In his corner of the room were articles from the year before, and he found a box score, the Redlegs beating the Giants 5-1 behind trusty Hod Eller. Eventually, he lay back and tried to rest, which wasn't easy because the night turned swampy. There were four other men in the room with him and some of them seemed to know one another, and at one point he almost yelled out to them to shut the hell up. Moonlight shone on the curved glass of the clock near the doorway, and at least he had his army cot because he could always find sleep on that, even for just an hour or two. Part of him hoped he'd hate working at the stables, the smell of horseshit would be too much. Then, he could just get on with the life waiting for him in Newport. He would wind up marrying Bonnie and staying in town and sitting pretty after all.

Just past four a.m., he slung his duffel over his shoulder and headed for the silhouette of the spires atop the Latonia grandstand. The barn area was dark except for the tack room lights. At Jenkins's place, he could make out a colored man guiding down the shedrow a half-moon-shaped wheelbarrow with wooden wheels. Jenkins appeared right in front of him. He told Ben to store his bag, grab a pitchfork. Jenkins had five horses, four geldings and a mare, and two workers, both colored. One was the exercise rider, a small man Jenkins called Mops. The other man was bigger than Ben, maybe six and a half feet tall, and he was the one who brushed the horses and tacked them up for their morning workouts. By the time the sun came up, Ben's arms and neck were covered in sweat. The groom, Doc, wore overalls and rubber boots. He moved in a measured way and did not perspire. He showed Ben how to attach a shank, how to lead a horse from its stall. Everything one did around horses was purposeful. The horses had been conditioned to react to the cues of the man, yet they would always remain unpredictable.

By ten, each of the five racers in the stable had been out to the track for training, then returned to the barn for a bath and cooling-out walk. For the final trainee of the morning, Doc held the lead-rope over to Ben, and Ben began to guide the gelding down the shedrow. From ten paces behind, Doc followed. He lumbered, titled from side to side like a clock pendulum. Around and around the shedrow their little parade went. Doc kept an eye on him, and Ben knew Jenkins was paying attention too, trying to see what, if anything, he might be up to. No doubt he suspected Ben was a gambler or worked for one. Maybe Ben would slip something into a feed bucket. Or was just trying to get a line on a horse. For his trouble, Jenkins gave Ben four bits. Next morning, Ben showed up right before five, and Jenkins again put him to work.

* * *

The following day, after Ben completed his morning chores at the stables, he returned to Newport, caught a ride with a racegoer who had a motor car, a grand Pierce-Arrow roadster. Ben hadn't showered in days. The driver, a kid younger than him, said he'd lost a lot of money at the races and wondered if Ben had, too. After dropping him off on Second, the car rumbled away, heading further east. Ben carried his duffel by his side, and when he started up the steps of his parents' home, he could see them through the screen door, at the dinner table. He didn't look like anyone who'd just eloped, and he felt the eyes of his parents on him. On the pine table, they had plates of stewed apples, boiled potatoes, steamed kraut. His parents never looked happy while they ate, and because Ben was hungry, he decided to light a cigarette. "How y'all doin'?" he said.

"We're fine, son," his mother said.

"Sorry about the note. I was out looking for work. Found some, too. I'll be leaving town in a little bit." His father continued eating; his mother seemed to be reassessing the contents of her plate. Hers were a scrubwoman's hands, wrinkled past her age, with dried, fractured cuticles. He said, "Don't be upset with me. Mom?" He was worried less about his father.

"Yep," she said.

"I can't stay here, I can't live on the front porch like some old hound."

"I know that." His mother was a slight woman, and the quietness at the table that followed was not unpredictable. Until it was time to put out the cigarette, he used his hand for an ashtray and then went to the kitchen to fetch one. They had the same wrought iron stove as when he was a boy. On the stove stood a pot of soft-looking potatoes. He made himself a plate. Though he hadn't had a good meal in days, he overlooked the stewed apples. At the table, he began to eat heartily; the sight of this, he felt, would bring relief to his mother.

"I'm going to ask you to take off those boots," his father said.

"Shit?"

"Mm-hmm."

"Right." On the front porch, Ben unlaced his boots, then faced in the direction of the beech trees that ran along the river. He felt deep affection for his parents. He could try to explain his plans as best he could. But if they didn't understand, he shouldn't be angry at them. When he went back inside, the creaking of the screen door was the only sound.

At the table, he began to eat again.

"Where?" his father said.

"Nebraska, Lincoln. I wanted to go to Chicago, that was my idea. But the outfit I got on with are going further west. That's okay. I asked Bonnie if she's going with me, but I don't think she is. I don't think it makes any difference where I'm going, she doesn't want to. She might change her mind, but I'm not betting on it." He wanted to sound matter-of-fact. He wondered then if his parents had insight into how much he felt for her. "I know you all worry about me, but I'm safe, the war's over…I wanna keep my hopes up, this is what I can think of, the races. You know, Pop, you're the one who took me to Latonia for the first time." Neither his father nor Ben glanced in the direction of Ben's mother.

His father said, "I took you to Redland Field, too. Don't see you trying to be a shortstop."

"That's my backup plan…look, I'm not trying to blame anyone. I know a lot of guys want to find their place, they have the right girl and everything. I want to be excited. Everybody wants that."

"Not everybody," his mother said.

In a moment, his father said, "We have enough. This house. You didn't ask my opinion, son, but I'm going to give it to you, if that's all right. If you think you'll never tire of being poor, then go to Lincoln, Nebraska. Never been there myself, though we took the train once to Saint Louis. If you think money will matter to you, you need to do something other than clean up after horses. You know the answer to that better than I do."

"What, money?"

"Money," his father said. "Yes."

He was about to say I don't care all that much about it, but his eyes were on his mother and to say such a thing would upset her, mainly because she was his mother, and poor was all they'd ever known. "The races just make me feel alive, that's all," Ben said. "I gamble a little, everybody in this town gambles." Then, he held up his hand. "Not everybody. Are y'all worried about what you're going to tell your friends? That I went away with the circus?" He tried to grin.

"We're not thinking of that," his father said. "Ben."

"What?"

"Bonnie," his mother said.

"What do you think I'm gonna do, break her heart or something?" After he said this, he wished he hadn't.

"Haven't you made her promises?"

"What, do you follow us around or something?"

His mother pinned her eyes on him.

"I did propose to her," he said. "But I'm moving away and that's where I'll be."

"Away, Nebraska," his father said.

"That's right."

His father said, "If we write you, it'll be to 'Benjamin Held, Away, Nebraska.'"

"Something like that." He wanted to finish the potatoes on his plate. He ate so fast it was as if there were a car waiting for him outside. He thought of the Pierce-Arrow, supposed the kid had stolen it. He pushed back from the table. When he spoke again, he said, "I feel like going for a swim in the river."

"Warm enough for it," his father said. "Don't get a stitch."

"I'm not mad at anybody, I want you to know that," he said. He was now dizzy. He and Bonnie had gone swimming in the river together, they'd done this before he went away to war. They'd done it last week. He thought of her, her wet hair in ringlets falling to her shoulders. Right then, he wanted to stay, he wanted to stay here forever; the only consolation was that the feeling would pass. He wanted to confess his feelings for Bonnie, but he realized they already knew, and to them it probably just seemed like he was spiting himself, that his plans were a way of avoiding a decent life he had every right to. Other than the way he felt, what did they know? Look at this shack, he thought. Who are they to say anything? He wanted to go swimming in a few minutes, he'd take his duffel with him and get a piece of soap to wash his clothes. He said, "I'm leaving soon, that's all."

"We appreciate that," his father said. Ben wanted to say, Don't feel bad for me, don't ever feel bad for me. But he didn't speak again. He carried his plate to the kitchen.

Later that evening, as twilight arrived, he made his way down to the river. The water was tepid, and he splashed out from the shore and when he got far enough away, he faced in the direction of the beech trees. In the evenings, his mother liked to make coffee. They didn't have electricity as yet and she went by candlelight. He couldn't see any light coming from inside the house, but just the same, this was what he imagined she was doing.

* * *

At the end of the month, like he said he was going to, he left. He rode in a boxcar for Nebraska with Doc, Mops, and five horses. He felt that Doc and Mops were both wary of and bemused by him. Sure, there were white stable workers. And there might be a million better lives out there, though those people weren't necessarily staying alive. The three of them pulled out bales of straw from the supply they'd stacked in one corner of the boxcar and played cards for smokes. When Doc and Mops talked horses, Ben paid attention, asked questions. The horses had been campaigning hard, and they stood in the makeshift stalls without creating commotion. The races at Latonia had been too tough for them, but Doc said they'd win out in Nebraska, they always did. Ben felt like asking Doc and Mops where they were from, how they'd come to work at the stables, but he decided it would be better if they brought that up on their own. He told them he'd been in the war but hadn't said anything more about it.

In Nebraska he worked at Lincoln, and the following spring, when Jenkins wanted to once again try his luck at Latonia, Ben caught on with a different outfit, a stable heading for the newly opened Ak-Sar-Ben in Omaha. The open-air grandstand spanned the length of the homestretch; it filled daily with somber white men in straw hats and shirtsleeves. He noticed the young men, the ones his age who'd surely been in the war, dressed like the older ones. On July afternoons, as the tight-packed crowd fanned themselves with racing programs, it seemed as if they had turned into an immense flock of birds.

Ben became a stable foreman for Hank Iyelly, supervised a string of a dozen runners. He plotted how to start his own stable. Ak-Sar-Ben was terrific, and he loved it that the spelling of the track was the name of the state backwards. He scraped together enough to purchase a filly and a gelding from Iyelly, both maidens, and set out for Arlington Park in Chicago. He aspired to race his horses at the top level of the game. Bad luck followed. The gelding, Yard Dog, foundered and had to be put down. The other horse, Honey Blonde, cracked her shin during a morning workout. When the Depression hit, Ben was already back to rubbing horses.

In Chicago, he sat in the stands, marveling at the world's leading money earner Sun Beau, a fearless, rugged horse who broke the track record for a mile and a quarter in the Arlington Handicap while in nothing more than a gallop.

Equipoise, nicknamed "The Chocolate Soldier" because of his toughness and determination, paid a visit to Arlington in the summer of '32 and took three races in nine days, including the Gold Cup. The crowds were wild for Sun Beau and Equipoise and on the days when horses like this were running, Ben couldn't doubt the choices he'd made.

Whenever he had a good afternoon at the betting windows, he wanted to send his folks money. He'd slip a five-dollar bill in the envelope, along with the letter he'd written. Always reticent about complaining, even in a joking way, he'd reread a letter before folding it for the envelope. He had pride, sure. He didn't want them to worry, but if in a letter he came across as exceedingly cheerful, they would suspect he wasn't being forthright. The better idea was to talk about the spectacular horses he saw. He didn't write this in his letters, but a horse like Equipoise or Sun Beau also made him wonder—what would life feel like if he ever wound up working around a horse like that? During his brief stint as an owner-trainer, he'd felt pressure. He worried about making his bills, getting the feed man paid, and overall the business of racing subtracted from the wonder he felt about it. And he'd come to appreciate how important that was.

In 1934, he barnstormed up to Michigan to try out another new track, the Detroit Fair Grounds. The stable he worked for had a horse in the Detroit Derby, but Cavalcade came over from Maryland to win it going away. He heard the other grooms prattling on about the car factories and because they had unions, the pay there was five times what a stable worker could get. Ben, broker than ever, wondered if it was time to start worrying more about money. And cars were the future, there was no secret about that. He went down to the Ford River Rouge complex with a buddy, a white groom, Bobby DeWine. The factory stretched for miles, a small city made of shining metal, towering smokestacks, immense coal bins. On either side of the narrow river, freighters were lined up like taxis. The plant had its own steel mill. He and Bobby finally located a hiring office and were given identification cards to fill out. Bobby explained to Ben that he didn't know how to read or write too well, and so Ben filled out the card according to the information Bobby told him. On Ben's card, he wrote his name as Jack Sullivan and listed his birth date as July 4, with no year. They were told to check back with the office in a few days. Bobby wanted Ben to come with him then, but Ben said he wanted to think about it some more. He didn't see Bobby again and supposed the factory had hired him after all.

* * *

He made his way over to Havre de Grace in Maryland. When his trainer sent a horse to Delaware or New York for a bigger purse, Ben rode in the same boxcar or horse trailer, and he looked forward especially to those trips to New York because that's where the very top horses raced. He saw Whirlaway win the Futurity, and Devil Diver the following year. Calumet Farm and Greentree Stables had brilliant runners with the best bloodlines, and the kings of the jockey colony rode for them. Whirlaway, a bright, long-bodied chestnut colt with a thick, golden tail, moved so fast he seemed like a phantom. Devil Diver, a sweet-moving, inexhaustible Greentree runner with a rather long head, carried twenty pounds more on his back than good horses and found the winner's circle without drawing a heavy breath.

Ben hadn't started out barnstorming to see great horses, though he understood those were out there. He felt surprised at times how swept away he was by them; it was as if he wanted to be a young boy again and feel the way only a young boy could. Yes, cashing a ticket on that fantastic horse brought a certain feeling as well. Prosperity. Maybe he was simply a broken soul who required a different form of salvation. He could say he was broken because of the war, but he had always felt a certain way about horses, ever since his father had taken him to Latonia for the first time. Being in the war had solidified certain things to him about life. He could say that, too. Men were both intentional and random in their cruelty. The world overall was uninterested in him, what he felt, what he thought, so he had to make these things of interest to himself, but in doing so he'd moved out to the edges of life where splintered, unreasonable people found themselves. The way he felt about horses, that was the truth about him, no matter what it meant or would finally result in.

In the spring of 1940, in an attempt to get on with Calumet, he took the train from Baltimore up to Hempstead, New York, and Belmont Park. He told the foreman at Calumet he'd be willing to start as a groom, no problem. Calumet wasn't looking for help. Neither was Greentree, nor the Whitneys. He was already forty years old, a racetrack lifer. When he applied for work at those Belmont outfits, he began by talking about where he'd been, the jobs he'd had. Eagerly, he explained how he wanted to be around the best horses, how this had become a dream of his. The subject had him talking more than a groom needed to.

When he went looking for work in the stables at Jamaica Racetrack in Queens, he simply put himself out there as someone who needed a job. That's what it had come down to. He wound up being hired by Hirsch Jacobs, the winningest trainer on the grounds. In six months, Ben went from groom to foreman. Jacobs liked it that he never complained or showed up late. Ben knew this because Jacobs would gripe to him when other workers were guilty of either. Ben believed the work he did had value. When the foreman was on time and didn't bellyache about his chores, the grooms knew nothing less was expected of them. Ben got along with everyone, knew how to talk to anyone who did the work he had done. Jacobs trained claiming horses, runners of light value. He kept his horses healthy and fit and spotted them in races they could win. Jacobs was always looking for a deal, to buy a horse out of a claiming race and find ways to make it better. He worked hard, which Ben liked more than anything. He had a lovely wife and a shiny, metallic-blue Pontiac he drove to the barn each morning.

* * *

In the summer of 1943, Jacobs acquired a chestnut colt named Stymie out of a claiming event at Belmont Park. The trainer sent a groom, EJ Holman, to ride with Stymie in the van back to Jamaica. When they got to the barn, Stymie was given a bath and then EJ and Ben took turns guiding the weary chestnut around the barn. Stymie hadn't done much running in the race, finishing seventh of eleven runners. Jacobs had gone $1,500 to get Stymie, loose change for a horse already racing. Not one to wait for a return on his investment, Jacobs raced Stymie relentlessly. Every few days, Stymie faced the starting gate. The horse responded with a string of losses. The races were dead sprints and he got too far back early. Jacobs put him up for sale, for $3,000, and there were no takers.

Stymie had been claimed from the barn of Max Hirsch, who trained horses for the King Ranch of Texas. EJ played cards with a groom who worked for Max Hirsch and asked him how they'd handled Stymie. The groom laughed and passed EJ a flask, said, You are poor, little sorry-ass son of a bitch!

Stymie was a common, rowdy, stupid horse, and Max Hirsch had been embarrassed to run him in the King Ranch colors. And when Stymie had been claimed away, no one had been more pleased about this than his trainer. EJ reported this to Ben, who considered passing along the information to Jacobs, but when he imagined the reaction he decided against it. As a racer, Stymie was sluggish, hated competition, and didn't respond to punishment. He despised humans in general.

Once, while EJ brushed Stymie before a race, Stymie reared up and struck EJ with a front hoof, knocking the groom out cold. Ben grabbed at the shank, but Stymie chased him and Ben dove under the stall webbing. Jacobs trotted down to see about the commotion. When EJ sat up, he motioned for everyone to stay back. Then, he held his bleeding head to his knees. Jacobs eyed the defiant Stymie at the back of the stall. He said, "It's gonna be him or us, boys."

Stymie survived the heavy racing, the endless string of losses. He was not a run-of-the-mill juvenile, there was strength and resilience to him. The summer before, Ben had noticed Count Fleet, a two-year-old with a liver-colored coat. Very fast but found ways to lose. An odd-looking, nonchalant colt with a spindly barrel and too-straight pasterns. A big, beautiful head. His trainer put blinkers on Count Fleet and the horse responded with more focused efforts. Once Count Fleet had grown into his frame, he became a terror at the races. In the spring of his three-year-old year, he swept through the Triple Crown races, winning the last leg, the Belmont, by the length of the stretch.

Young horses always held their fair share of mystery and potential. Good breeding, of course, increased the chances for success, but pedigrees were fallible equations. Ben read up on

King Ranch's line-breeding philosophy, a practice of inbreeding to bring out the best traits in a bloodline. They'd done this with cattle and felt it would work with horses. Though he didn't resemble him, Stymie was a grandson of Equipoise. That gave Ben faith. Man o' War was the great grandsire on both sides, paternal and maternal. Stymie, it seemed, had been the result of an experiment. Was the colt's temperament the result?

Thoroughbreds were commonly skittish and spooky, anyone who'd worked with them for any time at all could verify this. Ben found life in them. He cared for horses. He bet on them, and he wondered what they could understand about him. He felt that a naturally gifted horse would quickly have it all clocked. That horse could key on its talent, run like the world was on fire. Other horses, he felt, needed to puzzle out what they had to do to bring out mercy in people. He felt that many horses could do this, but not all of them were willing. There was something in them, some form of wildness only known to animals, that wouldn't allow for complete human control. It was usually the thing that got them sent to the slaughterhouse.

After his war, when he left his hometown so he could barnstorm with the horses, Ben could more or less take or leave people. In the end, they would only disappoint, then horrify. He'd been in a war and the truth was impossible to avoid. He had the power to astonish others and had sickened himself with what he'd done in the war. It had been easy to shoot a man who already had his arms up in surrender. When he'd returned home, he'd known that there wouldn't be any getting back to things, there would only be getting on with things.

There was another one going on now, a bigger war ripping Europe to pieces. America fought on two fronts, and because America won its wars, Ben did not want to doubt the outcome of this one. Every army believed it could win. But he'd been in his war and knew losing was possible. Now, the weaponry and ammunition were more devastating. He didn't feel as lucky about the horses and his life with them when he listened to news reports about the battles because he could readily imagine the feelings of those fighting in them. There was no avoiding that.

War could be felt at home in every way. In fact, at the start of the year, horse racing in California was suspended. Santa Anita was taken over by the army and became the biggest ordnance center in the west. Tanforan was turned into an internment camp for Japanese Americans. Tropical Park in Miami was closed mid-meeting. Due to a temporary ban on pleasure driving, Hialeah Park's season was cancelled altogether.

* * *

In August, Stymie came sailing from the back of the pack to win a cheap claiming race. Then he ran again two days later, placed second. He ran six days later, then two days after that, then three days after that. He won again, a sprint at Aqueduct, another track in Queens, in the middle of September. In the fall, the races usually went to Empire City up in Yonkers, but the track had been closed temporarily and the dates reassigned to Jamaica. This helped Stymie as well because he didn't have to step onto a shipping van on a race day. Stymie grew more anxious during those van rides. At Jamaica, he won a sprint at big odds and following this placed in three straight races.

Stymie earned a local reputation as an iron horse. Though the New York season ended right after

Thanksgiving, Jacobs wanted to keep him in training. It was decided that the stable would ship to Miami for the winter. Both Tropical Park and Hialeah were reopening despite the ongoing war and the incredible losses suffered on all sides. Jacobs invited Ben and the rest of the crew to ship with the horses, and Ben accepted the offer immediately while also understanding the races could be cancelled at any time. He preferred to remain with Stymie. He believed that somewhere a racetrack always would remain open. And Jacobs would be the man to find it.

Stymie's final start of the New York season was the Jamaica Bay Handicap. The morning of the race, after the barn chores were finished, Jacobs summoned Ben to his office, asked him to close the door behind him. Jacobs took his place behind the squat desk. It looked like a military issue with its metal surface, stubby legs. On the desktop was a folded *Morning Telegraph,* a glass ashtray taken from Rinsky's Bar loaded with butts, an empty pencil cup, a black telephone as shiny as a beetle. Beyond where Jacobs sat, the wall held photos of his runners' winning races. On another wall, bridles hung from wooden pegs. It had been raining all morning, and because Stymie liked to race in the mud Ben wasn't worried about a thing. Jacobs reminded him of the schedules for shipping out and Ben listened. Jacobs said, "And I want you to talk with EJ again. He needs to be on that train with you."

Ben said, "Did talk to him."

"Talk to him some more." Jacobs, wide at the shoulders, had a potbelly, thin, greased-back hair, floppy-looking ears. He held an unlit cigarette between his fingers.

Ben wanted to choose his words. "Can we offer him something we haven't already offered him?"

"Like what?"

"More money?"

"Give a groom too much for a Friday night, Saturday morning he won't show. There's nobody knockin' his door down. Put him in his place and tell him he's coming with us."

"Tolbert is good, he can handle Stymie in Florida."

"That's not what I want. You ever run a business? You get people in the right places and don't let 'em go. You know what I'm talkin' about?"

"Me?"

Jacobs turned his palms up.

"I can't make him stay, Hirsch…I'll try."

"That's what I'm asking you to do. Here, want a Chesterfield?"

"Sure."

"Need a match?"

"Nope." Ben pulled out his own.

"Close that door behind you."

A five-foot-high wooden fence separated the barn area from the sidewalks, and on the stable's side of the fence there was a quarter-acre pasture for grazing. In one corner of the pasture stood a single red maple tree. In the fall, the leaves changed colors to red and gold, though by now the branches were nearly bare. The rain intensified. Ben stepped to where the water fell straight down from the edges of the roof and extinguished the cigarette. He went to check on Stymie. At the back of the stall, Stymie stood with his head hung low, like horses did when it rained.

***

Later, Ben returned to Stymie's stall. The rain drizzling from the edges of the metallic barn roof made a barrier of silvery beads. Beyond the fence that separated the stable area from the sidewalks along the street, opened umbrellas created a stream of large, dark bubbles. EJ approached from the far end of the shedrow carrying a metal bucket, a rope shank. Inside the bucket were a brush, rub-rag, hoof-pick. "He's comin'," Ben said, only wanting the horse to be aware of human presence. EJ, a muscular man with pepper-black skin, removed his porkpie hat right before he ducked under the webbing. In order to make room, Ben took a step away. Stymie stood at the back of the stall and didn't move. EJ positioned the bucket near the stall opening. "Be nice if he'd just walk over to us," Ben said.

EJ made a curved path for Stymie. Once he'd hooked the clip of the shank onto the ring of Stymie's halter right under the jowls, EJ guided the horse in Ben's direction. Ben stood inside the stall now. He accepted the shank from EJ and EJ went to the bucket. As he brushed at the point of Stymie's shoulder, EJ said, "I was listenin' to the radio yesterday outside the hardware store and the speakers cut out." He spoke quietly. "They was sayin' something sinking German submarines. You ever been on one of those?"

Ben, who also spoke quietly, said, "No, no way."

"Make you appreciate having nothing around you."

"No doubt...You know I gotta ask about going to Hialeah. Again. Make me look good if I could talk you into it. But I can't, right?"

"They're gonna close all these tracks down, Ben Held. Be down there without work, won't know anybody."

Stymie's muzzle wasn't a foot away, and Ben watched for signs of alarm in the eyes of the colt. In this way, he looked out for EJ. EJ had been too young for the big war and was too old for the current one. He'd joked he was lucky like that. He was detailed and did what was asked of him and Ben felt he would've made for a fine soldier. Stymie's eyes were like globes; they seemed alert, pleading, wise. "What would you do if they shut it all down? You're from Mississippi, right?"

"Hattiesburg, Mississippi, that's right. 'Cept for people, I love the South."

"Ever think you'd wind up doing something like this?" Ben said. EJ winced as he continued brushing. Ben thought about saying something about Miami in the wintertime. But what did he know, outside of where the war had taken him, was it would be the first time he'd been south of Louisville. "Well, you always got a job, you know what I mean?"

"I do."

In the distance came the sound of a raucous crowd. The Jamaica stands. Runners for the sixth going into the gate. The cheering intensified, then faded, and Ben could hear the voice of the race caller on the public address system. The crowd would tell him when the horses entered the homestretch.

EJ used a comb with a wooden handle to brush through Stymie's tail. Then, he cleaned Stymie's hooves, one at a time, by pinching at the tendon in back of the shin. He cupped a hoof in his hand and made quick strokes with a pick that always made Ben think of the number 7. He went to get a leather shank with the chain at one end. EJ replaced the rope shank with the leather one, then unfastened the webbing and led Stymie out to the black, spongy-looking pavement. By now, there was only a misting rain. Stymie's iron shoes clocked atop the asphalt as EJ and Ben walked at the colt's side. They passed a series of barns and then they could see the grandstand. On the roof of the stands stood a half-dozen American flags, still against the pebbly sky.

Other runners for the upcoming race walked ahead of Stymie and his crew. Though Ben wanted to focus on the race just ahead, he felt his thoughts wander—Where would they go if it all got shut down? Home? Grooms weren't so different than soldiers; the sons of poor families fought the wars. Right before they stepped onto the track to begin the walk around the clubhouse turn, EJ halted Stymie. He wiped at the lapels of his wool jacket, then stuck a short, unlit cigar in the corner of his mouth. He stared in the distance, to the packed Jamaica stands. EJ led Stymie in the direction of the sea of hats, dark coats, white faces. The rails that marked the oval racetrack looked loose and the poles that held them up weren't straight. On the track, Stymie's cleaned hooves sank into the mud. They marched around the bend toward the tunnel between sections of the grandstand. People called out his name. *Sty-may! We need you today. Don't fucking blow it, ya big bag of shit.* In front of the stands, a section of the outer rail was removed so the horses and grooms could pass into the tunnel. The tunnel was covered in shadows, and when Ben, EJ, and Stymie emerged from the other side, they'd arrived in the walking ring. The outside of the ring went twenty deep in racegoers trying to get a look.

Stymie and the other runners paraded around the oval-shaped paddock. Jockeys appeared, joined the cluster of trainers and owners. A rider stood at Stymie's flank. It was Brooks today. Jacobs, still looking for that perfect fit for his unusual colt, switched boys on Stymie more than he changed socks. The trainer puffed like mad on his cigarette, spoke a few words to Brooks, who, in response, solemnly nodded. Then, it was time. Brooks cocked his leg, Jacobs reached for it, hoisted him for the saddle. The grooms guided the horses back through the tunnel, and when they appeared out on the track voices yelled, *Don't shit yourself today! Try not to drop dead out there, Brooks. You heartbreak choke-up motherfucker. My kid needs another operation!*

Out on the track, Brooks guided Stymie away from the post parade and aimed him in the direction of the far turn. Stymie galloped and wings of mud flew out from under his hooves. Around the far turn, Brooks slowed him to a walk, and for a time the rider sat as regally as an owl. Then he gave the reins a slight tug, pointed Stymie in the direction of the starting gate. The gate was positioned in the homestretch, right in front of the stands.

Stymie lined up with the others, and when the gates opened the field sprang forward. Anxious jocks gunned their horses along. Brooks dropped Stymie close to the inside rail where they were showered in mud. The field of runners turned into the backstretch. Stymie was moving easily, with no encouragement. He lingered at the back of the field. Then, his head rose, a signal it was time. In the next moment, the arms of Brooks were flowing along with Stymie's mane. They passed one horse, then two more. Stymie already had the lead at the top of the homestretch. The crowd boomed, the stands quivered. Ben was amongst them, and on days like this, he could holler as loud as anybody. Stymie hit the finish far ahead of the others, and past the finish Brooks rose in the saddle, tightened the reins once again.

There were hats on the track and Jacobs, who stood in the mud near the finish line, grabbed at one, wiped at it with his elbow, then sailed it in the direction of the fans bunched along the rail. Brooks brought Stymie over by the trainer. When they were just steps away, Jacobs reached for the bridle. A security guard removed a section of the railing. The winner's enclosure was marked by slack, chain-link fencing and November-dead shrubs.

"Love to ride him in Florida!" Brooks said.

"Maybe, maybe," Jacobs said. A photographer knelt a few yards from Stymie, snapped the shot. Brooks slid down from the saddle, reached for the girth and pulled the equipment away.

I need you next race, Brooks!

I'll see you right here or else!

Ben strode alongside EJ as the groom guided Stymie around the clubhouse turn. At the barn, he grasped the horse's halter while EJ filled a bucket with water. EJ used a rag and wiped at the colt's legs and chest. Around the corner of the barn, Jacobs drove his big, long car. He got out and his wife extracted herself from the passenger side. They stood near the driver's door, and he lit a cigarette, extended it to her. Stymie was led around the barn, again and again. The sky beyond the neighborhood went purple, then turned darker.

Once Stymie had returned to his stall, the headlights of Jacobs's car came on. Beyond the fence, streetlights shone their cones of light down to the pavement. Music from somewhere, maybe the 623 Club. A young, hatless couple jogging up the sidewalk. The slums of Jamaica always had a little life to them right after the races. Ben wanted to grab dinner at the track kitchen. EJ said he was good.

* * *

At the kitchen, Ben decided on the Blue Plate. He'd bet his wages on Stymie, would get to cash the tickets tomorrow. He could check on the colt one more time before shuffling back to his own place, a cold-water one-room on 129th. The dining area of the kitchen had oblong tables large enough for families, but the kitchen was a few minutes from closing and he wound up with one to himself. A kid who exercised for Milky Way Farms stopped by, a guy called Nooner. He pulled back a metal chair, sat down across from Ben, and they talked about the race Stymie had won. Ben said it was a goddamn shame he hadn't had the time to get to the windows for the work he had to do because he felt Nooner was going to hit him up. When Nooner asked, Ben said he was going to

Miami and Nooner said he was going there, too, could pay him back then. Ben framed his plate with open hands, said, "This look like Gallagher's?"

Nooner hadn't been gone a minute when Irina, who worked at the register, stood at the far end of Ben's table. She stepped closer when he held out his cigarette pack. "Closing in a second," she said. "There's a war on." After using it to light her smoke, she blew out the match he had between his fingers. "You won the feature?"

"Yes, ma'am." He liked Irina, she seemed about his age, had soft-looking hands, favored cherry-red polish for her fingernails.

"Got your muddy boots all over my floor here. Such as it is."

"Have anything on him?"

"A little."

"I told ya."

"You tell everybody."

Ben laughed. "That's not untrue," he said.

"Listen, a horse like Stymie couldn't beat Alsab. Maybe in his dreams. Or yours."

"What are you doin' now?"

"Shooing you out of here. Bart's coming by to get me. He's probably out in the lot, waitin'."

"Gonna see you next spring?"

"Pro-ba-bly." She reached for the closest ashtray, stubbed out her cigarette. "That horse looked good today. Who knows, maybe you're not full of it."

* * *

At the barn in front of Stymie's stall, Ben spotted EJ along with a woman in a light-colored beret. She wore a snug pea jacket and gloves. Ben could hear their voices and approached tentatively. The woman had dark skin and her lipstick glowed in the moonlight. EJ said, "Ben, you know Liza?"

Ben didn't, but he gave a nod in her direction. If she weren't wearing gloves, he would've put his hand out to shake. "We were just headin' out," she said.

Ben said, "You see the race today?"

"Liza's a seamstress. Makes uniforms for the army." EJ stood at her side, facing in Ben's direction. Dried mud came up to the shinbones of both men.

"We're all going to Florida," Ben said. "Well…what do you think of Stymie?"

"Dim in that space," she said. "Elroy talks about it, that I do know."

"Gonna be a great one," Ben said, though his tone didn't have the usual conviction. He was glad a colored woman wasn't afraid to speak to him. Ben was a good foreman, he felt all right about that. "I was in the army, back…those uniforms were kinda scratchy though, when I think about it…but they were warm." He nodded in appreciation to Liza, though she'd only have been a child then. He said, "I left for the races right after that war. We gotta go where we gotta go, right, EJ?"

"That's right, Ben."

"Well, hell then." He stepped forward to put out his hand to shake with EJ.

"All right," EJ said.

"Ma'am."

"Good-bye."

With this, Ben did an about-face, went back up the shedrow. He had a hike to his flat and the damp air had him walking with his hands shoved in his pockets, his arms tight at his sides.

His apartment was on the third floor, and after closing

the door he felt chills shooting down his shoulders. He wet a towel at the kitchen sink and used it to clean dried mud from his arms and neck. A Kentucky bath. In the darkness of his room, he stretched out in bed with a half-pint of Old Crow at his hip. He had the images of EJ and Liza in his mind and he thought sure, to plead his case, EJ had brought her back to the barn when nobody else was around. EJ probably was saying to her, Look at this horse, we gotta stay with this horse, even while knowing damn well you had to be around a horse all the time to know what it was capable of. Liza looked like the kind of person who would listen, anyway. At least she'd gone back to the barn with him after the race. It wasn't hard to imagine she'd have questions. Where would we stay? What kind of work will they have for me down there? For a horse, I'm giving up my life here...for a horse?

Ben was like EJ, but then he couldn't be, and Ben understood as much. Ben could chase after ridiculous things. In the dark, Ben felt like smiling about that, the choices he'd made. But smiling-wise, it didn't feel like much of one. He was tired, ready to sleep. He thought of how closely EJ and Liza had stood together. She made uniforms for the army. Winter was coming.

Dade Taxi

Stymie and the other horses in the Hirsch Jacobs stable were shipped from New York to Miami for a winter campaign. Three railcars for eleven horses, four men, and four dozen sacks of feed, twenty bales of straw, ten of hay, and six trunks of equipment. At Hialeah Park, the grooms lived in a tack room in the same barn where the Jacobs horses were stabled. Ben took a kitchenette in a by-the-month motel, the Green Wave, at the corner of Palm Avenue and Fifth Street. The walk each morning to the track took fifteen minutes.

Each morning, stable work began at five; horses were given a light breakfast of whole oats, cracked corn, molasses. Then, one by one, they were tacked up and ridden out to the racetrack for a training session. At the barn, Ben and the grooms cleaned stalls, prepared bath water. Horses were cooled out, returned to stalls bedded down with fresh straw. By mid-morning, the work at the barn was complete. If Jacobs didn't have a horse running in the afternoon, Ben would be free to watch a few races from the grandstand.

He preferred the upper section because he could behold the track, the barns, and all that encompassed the sun-drenched world of Hialeah, Florida. This was where he met a cab driver named Kelly Brighton. She took a seat in the same bleacher row, a few spaces down from him. He noticed her ocean-blue coveralls, the floppy, blue-and-white-striped train conductor's cap with *Dade Taxi* stitched above the long brim. She explained that the company had a fleet of seven Nash 600s, each driven by a girl like her. She would be leaving the meter off for the rest of the afternoon. At the conclusion of the races, they rode in her taxi to The Seashell Tavern. They completed the night in his motel room. She kept her brother Brendan's house in Sunny Isles while he was out on a carrier in the Pacific. She liked horses and she liked to bet her money.

Her blue Nash had a Grade A gas ration sticker pasted in the lower left corner of the windshield. When the radiator smoked, she added water from the corked jug she kept in the trunk. One time, she hit a pothole on Dixie Highway and the glovebox flipped open. Her driver's papers were in there, and he looked right to the age listed because he'd been wondering. Twenty-six.

He spotted a few No. 3 ration books, and it turned out that none of them were in her name. We buy and trade, she explained. At a red light, she returned the license and the books to the glovebox, whacked it shut. In her taxi, she drove him to Surfside, Miami Beach, Hollywood. On a couple of occasions, they grabbed fishing poles from her brother's garage and enjoyed an evening at Ocean Beach. They cast their lines into the surf, shared a towel and looked out to the path of moonlight that went all the way to the horizon. Afterward, she was too bushed to drive Ben back across town and they spent the night at her brother's house. She returned him to his motel in the morning, in time to change and get to work. He tried to convince himself it was all a lark, good fortune he needed to simply appreciate. But at times he felt as if he were falling for Kelly. He would feel this in the early morning hours, when he'd first awaken. He'd feel it whether she was at his side or not.

Another unexpected occurrence: Stymie, the best horse in the Jacobs stable, couldn't find the winner's circle at Hialeah. In New York, he had survived an improbable season of racing and became a horse people recognized. But in Florida, Stymie kept losing. There were poor starts, bad rides, flat finishes. He ran primarily in sprints; the Hialeah track surface was on the cuppy side, and favored speed horses. Ben talked to Kelly about the colt's enormous potential and extraordinary toughness. She liked to gamble, but she was better with her money than he was, especially when it came to not wagering on Stymie.

In late February, Stymie stretched out to a mile and an eighth for the first time in the Flamingo Stakes and finished a credible third. Ben and Kelly watched the race from the grandstand, sitting side by side in a spot not far from where they'd first met. He wore the pink-and-white-striped shirt she'd bought for him at Spooner's Department Store. As soon as the horses crossed the wire, he left her side, descended the grandstand steps. He stepped onto the track, joining Stymie and the colt's groom, Tolbert, for the walk back to the barn. Later, Kelly picked up Ben in front of the track kitchen and they aimed for the Green Wave. Stymie had gone off at odds of 20-1 and the third-place finish had surprised some horseplayers. Kelly and Ben sat up in bed, and he couldn't decide if he was happy with the result. When they'd first shipped down to Miami, a race like the Flamingo seemed like easy pickings. Kelly listened, as she always did, for a little while. Then he agreed it was time to stop talking about horses.

* * *

A week after the Flamingo and just a couple of days before the Jacobs stable was to ship north for Jamaica, Queens, Ben awakened in his motel room with Kelly at his side. Through the walls, he could hear voices: two young-sounding men, arguing. They'd checked in the evening before. "Can you tell…hear?" Ben said, in a whisper.

"Sounds like *Cuba*, what they're saying. Probably blue tickets, the both of them." Kelly turned in bed and flipped on the radio, then laid back again. "Ferensi" by Artie Shaw.

When Duke Ellington started, Ben said, "Getting close to time…"

"Let the guy tell us."

In fact, the record spinner did. After "Moonglow," he said, "So sublime…It's now four-thirty-nine…" Kelly threw back the covers like they were a cape. She went for the bathroom, flipped on the light. He could see the back of her slight, nude body, her blond hair falling past her shoulders. On the nightstand on his side of the bed were the Lucky Strikes. Water ran in the bathroom. He finished one cigarette and started another before the door opened.

"Yeah, yeah, 'I've Heard That Song Before'," she said. The saffron light from the bathroom streamed all around her. She'd pulled up the bottom half of her sky-blue overalls, wore a loose-fitting ebony t-shirt. "Where's my hat?"

"You had it on…"

"Here…" Kelly stepped across the room, reached for the switch by the door, and the small room filled with light. She swiped her cap from the floor, then sat on the bed, tilting his hip towards her. "Helen Forrest needs to get out from under Harry James's boot. Gimme one of those goddamn things." He held out the already-going cigarette. She tilted her chin upward, exhaled. Upon returning it to him, she crossed her arms. Her eyes were blue-green, her skin so fair he could see veins above her temples. "Are you joining the world this morning?"

He said, "I'm beat. I slept ten minutes."

"Brendan didn't want to enlist," she said. "The day he

was shipped out, he and I concocted a plan to dress him as a woman, take a road trip, pretend we were sisters. I sat him in front of the mirror, slapped on cosmetics. He didn't want to fight, but he did."

"I sure understand that."

"Loves his country. We all do."

"Right."

She smirked. "Our last day together's gonna be over before you know it."

"You have to say it like that?"

"That's the way it's gonna turn out, big boy. Unless…you been thinking about what I said?"

"You say a lot of things."

"You can get a job at Tropical Park after the meet ends here. Get another motel. Closer to me. I'll give you everything you want."

"You can do that for me in Queens, too."

"The offer is for here only."

Ben said, "Stymie's gonna run good. He's in at a mile and an eighth…allowance race. Today's his day."

"I have to leave in a minute." Kelly looked down to him in a kind way. "I'm doing my shift and I'm going to the races. I like your horse. He's been wanting to run long, it's easier company…"

"I do like you, Kelly. An awful lot."

"I'm only gonna ask you so many times." She leaned down, kissed his cheek. Then she stood, slid her hands into the deep pockets of the overalls. "We'll have dinner at my place tonight. I'll show you how easy it's gonna be. I can give you a ride to work if you'll get up in a minute." He didn't take his eyes from her. She touched her fingertips to her mouth. "Guess you're walking."

She left on the light, and he considered the empty room.

Cinnamon-colored carpet, table by the window that looked out to Fifth Street. By the window hung a painting of a sunrise or sunset, they could never agree. In the painting, the sun tipped just above the horizon line of the ocean and the sky was all pink and blue around it. The radio played "Let Me Off Uptown." He thought of a magazine photo he'd seen of Anita O'Day…a sleeveless white dress, shiny curtains as the backdrop. "Massachusetts," with Gene Krupa's outfit, was probably her best. He stretched his arm past where Kelly had been, lowered the sound and listened for the voices from the next room. They'd gone quiet. They'd probably heard Ben and Kelly talking—how much could they tell? Everyone had to be on the lam from something, otherwise why would they be in a motel like this?

Ben dressed for work, opened his door to a predawn, olive-green sky. As he strolled for the stables, the breeze touched his face, his bare arms. Palm Avenue led straight to the Hialeah entrance. He walked along the shoulder of the road, could see silhouettes of the towering, slender palm trees, the ten-story-tall grandstand. A sedan came flying in his direction, a white Corsair with all the windows down. Someone from inside it yelled, "Ya fucking cracker!" The fast-moving wind flapped his shirt collar.

At the security gate to the barn, he showed his badge to the drunk-looking guard. He strolled past one rectangular barn after the next, listened to the birds chattering and then the sound of a barking dog. Some of the stables here had mascots. A goat, a parakeet, an English greyhound. One horse owner was always accompanied by a leashed monkey.

At Jacobs's barn, Ben moved down the line of stalls, arrived at the illuminated tack room. The grooms had a coffee pot going, and keeping his head bowed, Tolbert brought up a mug for Ben. Ben gave a nod to Macky, then Flask. Late at night, grooms took part in crapshoots and poker games. Ben said, "You fed yet?" Tolbert had the muted manner of a man who'd just lost every cent on a sure thing.

"I got it," Ben said. Toting his mug of coffee, he went the length of the shedrow once more, then used a key to open the room next to Jacobs's office. In the middle of the dark room, he gave a tug to the string and on popped the light. He scooped oats into a wheelbarrow, then corn, and poured in a pint of molasses after that. For mixing, he had a sawed-off broomstick handle.

Stymie occupied the first stall in the row and remained in the shadows until the feed was dumped into his bucket. Then his muzzle dove in. Next came Holy Dreamer, then St. Raphael. Double Rah Rah, Prime Speed, Sergeant Eric, Evade, Red Rifle, Good Family. They'd shipped down here with eleven, had nine left. Just a handful of wins among them. Anyway, the weather had been a dream. Ben guided the wheelbarrow back down the shedrow, parked it in the feed room, pulled the string and the room went dark.

* * *

Stymie returned from his morning session, a light gallop twice around the track, and Ben held the shank while Tolbert washed the colt's legs, cleaned his hooves. Tolbert hot-walked Stymie while Ben scrubbed buckets. He felt good about today. Stymie, the onetime weary and miserable racer, never tired of it now, and this had made Ben wonder if animals could understand the concept of being indestructible. He'd put his paycheck on the race today, and if Stymie got beat, he wouldn't have a dime to line up a room in Jamaica. He'd manage.

Once all the chores at the barn were complete, he

stepped though the barn area for the stable gate. The track kitchen, one story and rectangular like a barn, loomed just ahead. Inside, he ordered a fried mackerel sandwich, macaroni salad on the side. He fished four bits from his trouser pocket. Gretchen, the cashier, kept a stack of racing programs next to her register. She placed one on his tray, didn't ask for the dime.

Colored grooms filled the seats at the table nearest the exit and other colored grooms had gathered around it. Remaining tables were occupied by white men in white t-shirts. Exercise riders, maintenance crew, jockeys. The room held murmurs, laughter. In the mornings, optimism was plentiful. Ben considered the cover of the program, the drawing of the entrance to Hialeah Park on the newsprint. Stone pillars and, beyond them, two rows of palm trees, stretching to the horizon.

FORTY-THIRD DAY OF RACING, MARCH 4, 1944

The bottom of the program read,

BUY UNITED STATES WAR BONDS AND STAMPS

Every race had horses with military-related names: Col. Hockwald and Proud Shot in the first; in the second were Navy Bomber, Battle Fit, Doctor Jeep. And so on. Weapon's Pride, Allied Forces, Conquering Army…it remained peculiar to him, running races at this paradise with another world war going on. The races were a way of proving they all lived on a thrilling, civilized planet. The man on the battlefield was someone he'd never be again. He wanted this more than anything. He'd carried a rifle, aimed it at any form rushing in his direction. Following a battle or any type of encounter with the enemy, he'd try not to show what he was feeling. Remains of fellow soldiers brought terse reactions from him and the other men in his unit.

He flashed back to a morning when his battalion was marching along a deserted road outside Soissons. They spotted a smoking, tailless German Fokker D VII in the sky, and then two figures falling from it. One parachute opened, the other one didn't. The troops sprinted in the direction of the opened parachute. The surviving German soldier they came upon surrendered immediately. It turned out that the other landed in a ditch. A big blond man, an officer, with bullet holes in his blood-caked topcoat. The fall must've broken every bone in his body. The men in Ben's outfit decided to fold the officer in half and tie the laces of his boots together behind his head. Ben did the lacing and cinched them as tight as possible. The living German got the heaves, went to all fours. Someone came up, booted his balls. Then, a buddy of Ben's, Teddy McManus from Murfreesboro, Tennessee, shot the German in the back of the head.

Ben added salt and pepper to the fried mackerel; the track kitchen got the next-days from the clubhouse dining room so the kitchen-mackerel was predictably tangy. He thought about the things he might've taken home from the war, something from a checked-out Fritz. A bayonet or helmet. Tags. He'd come back in his own sergeant's uniform, which he'd worn on the train to Cincinnati. Home again, he washed it in the river. After that, he folded it, and placed the uniform in a cardboard box. He left the box with his parents. Kelly's brother, Brendan, was with the light carrier USS *Belleau Wood*. Ben had been in that battle, believed he would die in it, had only wished for his death to be sudden.

He finished his sandwich, left the macaroni. He looked over the program, had two Luckys along with his Coke. He'd learned over time that when images from the war came back to him, he shouldn't try to think of something else. He'd learned not to ignore what he remembered, and he let what he remembered tell him things, remind him of all that he would never be able to do anything about.

Under a canary-colored sky, he walked along Palm Avenue. If he stayed in Miami, how much of all this would change, the things he did and thought about every day? Kelly wasn't promising him the moon and the stars, but if he stayed here, he would have her to look forward to, perhaps for as long as the war lasted or at least until what was left of Brendan was sent home. He understood she liked him, wanted to be with him. She made the moves for them, decided where they went, when it was time to undress and give him what she wanted to give him. In his motel room, he peeled down to his underwear and t-shirt and laid down for a nap. The first time she'd brought up the idea about him staying in Miami, he'd laughed a bit and said, *No way. Forget it.* His answer was something she'd expected because she kept smiling at him. This had been a few weeks ago. Since then, she hadn't pressed it too hard. His main thing was Stymie. Ben's life might be changed because of a horse like this, even if he couldn't articulate how exactly. He didn't own Stymie and wasn't involved in the decisions regarding the horse's racing schedule. If he stayed here, at best, he'd wind up with a job like the one he had now. And Stymie would be back in New York. If Kelly's brother came home alive, Kelly would want a house for herself, not the paper-thin walls of a motel room.

He awakened, reached for the radio. "Peanut Vendor," a tune he'd heard a million times and still loved. He left the door to the bathroom open while he showered so he could hear "Pistol Packin' Mama." He dried off, combed his dripping hair. By the time he got back to the barn, Tolbert was in the stall with Stymie, a shank in one hand, a brush in the other. Ben wanted to ask him about the game last night: Craps or poker? Loaded dice or marked cards? Tolbert seemed morose, probably didn't have a cold nickel left to play on Stymie today.

Ben said, "What do you think about Miami, Tol?" Tolbert removed a mane comb from his back pocket. Ben knew the groom had heard him. "Would you stay here if you could?"

"I can. Don't want to."

"How come?"

Tolbert held out a section of the shank to Ben, then started to comb out Stymie's golden mane. When he finished, he pulled a hoof pick from his back pocket. "Everyone down here's a thief."

"You keep telling me that."

"It keeps being true."

"Everybody's got a story. You stay long enough, maybe you'll have one…betting Stymie today? You know he's gonna win. Third in the Flamingo last week, this field's way easier than that one."

Tolbert moved on to Stymie's rear right hoof. "I know."

Stymie's head, the white blaze on his face, was within arm's length for Ben. Stymie didn't like to see a hand moving in his direction, no matter the intention. Once the colt's feet were picked clean, Tolbert reclaimed the rope shank and Ben went to the tack box to get the leather one. They knew Stymie preferred to be led around with the noiseless rope shank, but Jacobs insisted the horse be led over to the stands with a cleaned leather one. His was not some gypsy outfit. Ben stuck two one-dollar bills in the pocket of Tolbert's shirt that hung from the open tack box door. He returned carrying the shank and the shirt. Tolbert held the bucket over to him.

The three of them walked through the barn area for the track, with Tolbert leading Stymie. Some of the grooms and runners for the feature were ahead, and beyond them lay the racing oval and the vast Hialeah stands. Ben and Kelly had gone fishing one time right at twilight and they'd spotted a freighter out on the horizon. He said that from this distance the freighter made him think of a racetrack grandstand. Kelly looked like she might laugh, say, *Well, of course it does,* but after watching him for a second, her expression softened and she said, I never really thought of it that way, Ben. The grass in the Hialeah infield had remained emerald-green all winter. The lake was part of a sanctuary for hundreds of pink, oddly elegant flamingoes. Blue-purple bougainvillea plants grew over the grandstand façade.

On the lawn inside the saddling ring stood the owners and trainers of the horses. They might as well have been holding croquet mallets. Ben peeled away; he wouldn't have any work to do until the race was over. He went past the security guy who watched the entrance to the saddling ring, moved directly for the betting windows, emptied his pockets. He went up a long flight of steps to the second floor of the grandstand. He knew Kelly would be waiting for him. By now, the horses were on the track for the post parade. Despite the good race in the Flamingo, Stymie stood at 5-1. The resplendent colt was on his toes, prancing sideways. Ben wished he had a million dollars right now but only so he could bet it all. That's how certain he was about everything.

While the horses were in the warm-ups, Kelly placed her cap on her knee. She fluffed her hair with her fingertips. The infield lake held a few tiny islands and the flamingoes, as pink as Coney Island cotton candy, were gathered at one end. The horses stood behind the gate, which was parked in the middle of the homestretch. Then one by one, they stepped in. The crowd hummed, then sparked as the runners were launched. From the rail, the little chestnut colt Fire Sticky darted to the front; Slide Boy angled over from his outside post to chase. Stymie dropped back to trail.

Arcaro gave Fire Sticky a long rein and they cut out a solid pace. The field turned for the backstretch. Atkinson guided Slide Boy out from the fence to challenge. Stymie remained in last, more than ten lengths behind. A half mile to go, Stymie's head rose like a periscope and Adams knew to loosen the reins. The leaders barreled around the far turn, dirt rising in their wake. Just inside the top of the stretch, Stymie bulled his way between two faders. He still had four horses to catch. Fire Sticky didn't give in to Slide Boy, and with an eighth of a mile left the race seemed down to them. Knocking into other horses had lit Stymie's rocket. He'd zoomed into third and when Slide Boy stalled, Stymie darted by, also lugging in. A hundred yards out, Fire Sticky led by two, but his fight was deserting him. Stymie nearly ran up his back, but Adams swerved out just in time and right at the wire Stymie flashed by him. Ben's insides leapt; his whole head tingled. Stymie's wins gave him moments he'd only dreamed of finding.

Kelly clutched his arm. "Damn, I think he finally won one."

"You bet he did!" Ben leaned over and kissed her temple. "Get me at the kitchen, okay?"

As Ben descended the steps, the race caller's voice came on the public address, "Ladies and gentlemen, the unofficial winner of our feature today is number four, Stymie. Number one Fire Sticky was second and number eight Slide Boy third. There is a steward's inquiry into the running of the race. Hold all tickets."

Ben turned in Kelly's direction, saw her shoulders drop. He said, "He didn't foul anybody!" A steward's inquiry, there wasn't a thing either of them could do about it. He had to keep moving. A minute later, Ben stood out on the track next to Tolbert as Stymie galloped back in their direction. Neither man spoke; the race had been roughly run down the stretch, anyone could've seen that. Stymie's jock Adams glanced at the oddsboard and grinned. He brought the horse to a stop in front of Tolbert and Ben. The soft dirt of the Hialeah surface stuck to Stymie's legs and chest, and standing out on the colt's neck were berserk-looking veins like lightning bolts.

"Take the pig down!" a voice from the stands called, a woman's voice, but it was like she was making fun of a man saying it. Up in their booth atop the stands, the stewards had the best view. But one could never be sure of their angle. "Ladies and gentlemen," the race caller said. "After review, the stewards deemed it that no disqualification is warranted. The results stand official. It's four-one-eight. The winner, Stymie, is trained by Hirsch Jacobs and is owned by Mrs. Hirsch Jacobs, ridden today by Johnny Adams. Running time for the race…"

* * *

Once Stymie was returned to the stall, the grooms gathered at their tack room and Ben could hear their voices. He knew Tolbert had bet that two dollars on the nose and would have his money to play cards tonight if he wanted, even if the game was run by cheats.

Dusk arrived, and Ben made it to the track kitchen ten minutes before closing. He explained to Gretchen he hadn't had the chance to cash his tickets on Stymie yet, even took the opportunity to show them to her. She let him have a bottle of beer on credit. He had a cafeteria table to himself, took the folded racing program from his back pocket. Page after page reminding of war bonds...Gretchen, still at the register, gave him a pen when he asked to borrow one. Inside the back cover of his program, he wrote:

> Ben Held
> c/o H. Jacobs Stable
> Jamaica Racetrack
> Jamaica, Queens, New York

When he handed the pen back to her, he saw she was watching him. He gestured to the beer on the table. "Message in a bottle," he said. "See you tomorrow?" She shook her head, though he knew she'd be here. He carried the beer outside, to Kelly's Nash. As she swept off the lot, they were beaming, like they'd just made love. He liked the big numbers on the speedometer and the way her small, strong hands looked on the steering wheel. Soon they were traveling north on Dixie Highway, listening to The Merry Mac's "Jingle Jangle Jingle." He plucked the program from his shirt pocket, touched the button on the glove box and the lid flopped down. "Before I forget," he said, placing it atop the khaki-colored ration books.

She wore her hat cocked to the side. Maybe she'd been drinking. "Forget?"

"So you have it, I wrote my name and address on the back page...you ever want to find me."

"You wrote your name?"

"The track address...Jamaica Racetrack."

"Ben Held, Jamaica Racetrack. Got it."

At a traffic light, he noticed the flakes of peach-color left in the sky. "In case you get sick of all...these perfect days."

"I got beefsteaks in the backseat there, wrapped nice in wax paper. Took me coupons and a tip to boot. Special." The light dropped to green. "You know, I never see you with any coupons."

"I eat out a lot."

"Can't push a ration book through a betting window, can you?"

"Nope."

"You guys were crazy trying to sprint that horse earlier in the meet." The street seemed like a parking lot, shiny cars going nowhere. Ben and Kelly listened to Charlie Spivak's "I Left My Heart at the Stage Door Canteen," and he drank from the bottle he'd been holding. She turned off the highway, went a block, and made another right. Cars lined both sides of the street. One-story houses, small yards, driveways. Palmetto trees, elephant grass. "Grab that bag from the backseat, will ya?" Kelly said, after easing over to the curb. Her brother's house was painted cardinal-red and had a little curved sidewalk that led to the front door.

Inside, she gestured to the couch. "Make yourself to home." He carried the bag into a walk-in kitchen; from the hallway, she called, "You know where the bar is. Go on, get me a whiskey soda. No ice!"

He made drinks, carried one in each hand and took a seat at one end of the couch. There were holders for ashtrays built right in the arms. The living room had cream-colored walls, tangerine carpeting, a dark recliner, an opened beach umbrella with blue and white panels. The drapes were light green, made with heavy material, like something that rolled open in front of a theatre screen. He'd been here before, just not this early in the day. When Kelly reappeared, she wore the black t-shirt from Dade Taxi, had changed into pink pajama bottoms. He held up her whiskey and soda. "You're beautiful."

"I'll drink to that." She took a place at the other end of the couch. "What're you thinking about?" she said.

His eyes had been going around the room. "Coming home…to this."

She stared in the direction of the drapes. "It's nice," she said. "Living…he's a salesman. A few years older than me. Back east, our family just stayed in apartments. My folks bunk over in a cottage in Miramar now."

"What's your brother say about the war?"

"You wanna know which side to bet on?" When he didn't answer, she said, "Cigarette?" A book of matches—the cover had green palm trees and the words *Green Wave*—was jammed in the pack he handed over and she worked one free. "The last letter he wrote me said, 'Don't worry about a thing, sis, Hirohito and Hitler are in a world of shit.' Hell, he's a third-class petty officer. What does he know? Do you like steak?"

"Sure."

"What's he gonna be like when he gets back?"

"Just get him back, that's a start. He might be different."

"Like you? A bum?"

"We keep Stymie in longer races, he'll never lose."

"Jesus."

"I have a theory, you know that. See, I looked up his pedigree. Came from the King Ranch in Texas. They inbreed their cattle, they think it makes strong traits even stronger. Its revolutionary."

"Sorta sick."

"How much did you make today, anyway?"

"I bet thirty bucks on the nose. All my fares."

"You're killer diller at the windows."

"I don't bet with my heart, I told you that."

"Mm-hmm."

"My daddy played, I told you. But he never quite figured it out. A salesman, too. Anyway, I know all…your theories." She held up her drink in a toast. "So, what do you say?"

"About…?"

"Don't act dumb. You gonna be my boy?"

He didn't want to ruin this. He wanted to feel her under him, that would be true a month or even a year from now. He knew what she was saying to him. "You have a lot to look forward to, Kelly."

"You've always been like this?"

"After the war, I wanted to put my faith in horses." He wanted to make her smile. It would be their last night together, that seemed nearly official now.

"I want a man around who doesn't want anything…but me."

When Ben spoke again, he said, "Well, I'm hungry."

A second later, she leaned to him, reached for the back of his head, kissed him on the eyebrow. She said, "Here, take this pack of matches and go start a fire in that grill. Take it outside, the briquets are in that pail outside the door. Don't have to use a lot of them."

The house had a back room that was screened in, and outside that door Ben found a little can of lighter fluid next to the pail of charcoal. Kelly switched on the patio light. The grill had short legs, a shallow drum. He placed three handfuls of briquets in the drum and tossed a lit match at them. He decided to sit in the grass and watch the flames prance. She brought out a plate and serving fork. "Here. Burn mine. Your keys."

He reached where they'd fallen to the grass. The hotel keychain had a silver "5" on one side; the ring also held the feed-room key. "I stick out like a sore thumb," he said.

"Half the girls on this street are alone." The tines of a

serving fork were jammed into one of the steaks. "I'm going to finish the potatoes."

While on his knees, Ben guided one beefsteak, then another, onto the grill. In the backyard of the house next door, a tarp covered a motorcycle. The ropes looked loose. He turned the steaks. In a few minutes, she pushed open the screen door, said, "Come on, those are done."

"In a second," he said.

The small kitchen table was set with two plates, silverware, and a serving bowl of mashed potatoes and butter. "Both of the steaks are the same," he said. "How about a glass of water?" She went to the small kitchen and he heard tap water running. Then she turned on the radio; Billie Holliday, there was no voice like that. She brought him water. In a while, he said, "What kind of fares you get today?"

"Mmm, the usual. People...asking me to take 'em here and there. Saying 'what's a girl doing driving a cab?' I had two different fares with dogs. Generally speaking, I don't like animals in my cab. But they feel sorry for me and tip like mad. One lady, 'Oh, darling you can't possibly handle that suitcase.' But I did."

He wondered if the path of the conversation would've been different if they were in his motel room. Of course, there wouldn't be any steak barbecue. He said, "You're strong."

"I can lift a goddamn suitcase. When's that tin can of yours gonna run again?"

"As soon as we get back to Jamaica, I'm sure. He might make the Kentucky Derby."

"Don't make me laugh."

"Yeah, well, maybe that's a little tall...but you'll hear about him."

"You know I don't care, you know that? I don't know...maybe I'll just go to New York with you. You have a house on the water there, right?"

"I bet I won't find another girl like you when I get back to Queens."

"Then you won't be looking hard enough." She dropped a used match onto her plate. Her voice became quieter when she said, "You don't deserve good things?"

He wasn't going to answer that. He didn't want to talk about what he deserved because he deserved what there was. When she got to be a little older, she'd see it, too. He said, "I was better off the second I stopped worrying about that. Since you asked."

"That's a very negative outlook." She seemed childish then, not old enough to order a drink.

He stood and stretched. "I left my name and address on that program. I like you, Kelly. I thought about staying, I really did."

"We're at opposite ends, huh, Ben?" He didn't believe this to be the case. His sense of her was that she'd be happier on the road and with someone like him. But that would be a tiresome life for someone who didn't believe in it. Kelly rocked back in her chair and said, "Have another drink. I've had enough, don't make me anymore. I'll get these plates and everything… I bet Brendan gets a TV after the war. They say everybody's supposed to… Stretch out on the couch if you want to."

"Kelly."

In a moment, she said, "What?"

"You're a great girl. But at some point, I'd be turned out. And my big horse would be gone."

"And you know how that's gonna play out, too. You just won't admit it."

"No, I don't. That's the point. I can't say for sure."

"You racetrackers tell yourselves you can't be bought.

Only when you look up, you got nothing to show for anything. Wake up, old scout."

"Why'd you even bother with me?"

"Because you're grateful."

"Do tell."

"Anyway, it's not even your horse. You just clean its ass."

"This isn't you here, this house. You're pretending."

Her voice was quiet when she said, "What do you know?"

"How do you feel about me?" he said. "Tell me."

"You just don't want anything," she said.

"That's not true."

"I have no business being with a man like that. Falling for…it seems quite clear to me now." She cleared her throat. "I'm gonna clean up," she said.

* * *

Ben extended himself on the couch, leaned his head against one arm, let his ankles dangle over the other. He rested his eyes, listened to the sound of dishes being collected, water running in the sink. Nothing else was going to happen and he thought about getting out of here. He'd bet all the money he had on Stymie but hadn't had the chance to collect. No cash for cab fare, he'd have to hitch. He let his mind wander; as if he could do anything he wanted, including taking her if he felt like it, and she would be all right with that. Then came the sound of her steps padding down the hallway, a door closing.

He reached for his pocket, brought out the winning tickets on Stymie. Once the tickets were returned to his pocket, he closed his eyes again. And then he awakened sometime later to a darkened room. With the partially opened drapes came a silvery blade of moonlight. He heard music…from down the hallway.

At her bedroom door, he knocked. Kelly sat up in bed, under the covers, a paperback opened against her bent knees. Presently, the radio by the bed played the news: American bombers had begun daylight air raids on Berlin.

She showed him the cover of what she was reading—*Saratoga Trunk* by Edna Ferber. "Know it?" she said.

"Of it."

"This main character, Clio, is pretty vindictive."

He took a seat on the edge of the bed. By the closet door stood a full-length mirror. He imagined the reflection of a young man in a suit, a salesman, a man with neatly combed hair, shined shoes. Secrets.

"It'll be over soon. Berlin is falling." He nodded, and she switched off the radio.

"Brendan is in the Pacific…I'm gonna take you back to the Green Wave, that's your punishment. Don't worry. Set my alarm already."

"I wish things were different," he said.

"You walked all the way back here to tell me that?"

"Come with me."

"No. Everything is here. Heck, I made a killing today. Y'all had him in the right spot. At last." She opened the book. "So maybe you're not hopeless."

Kelly was more wonderful than even she could ever understand. If he said it now, she might accuse him of something. He said, "While I was here, I'm glad I had you to look forward to."

"Get some sleep," she said. "Go on." Her eyes were on the book, her voice softer. "I'll get you up, I promise."

* * *

He awakened to a conductor's cap, her face peering down at him. There was light from the kitchen, but overall things were shadowy. "Ready?" she said. "I gotta start my shift...you okay?" He'd been pulled out of a dead sleep.

"Sure." He coughed, felt his chest tighten.

In her Nash, she flipped on the radio, caught "Ration Blues" then "Sweet Slumber." The headlights carved into the darkness ahead. He felt like telling her he loved her. It didn't matter, and he wanted to say it, perhaps because he knew it wouldn't change a thing. He took a cigarette from his pack and held it over. She waved him off.

He said, "We'll be back next winter. Maybe it'll be all over then, the war. How will I find you?" When she didn't answer, he said, "I guess you'll find me."

"Next year, I won't be looking for any horse groom. Heck, I might see you walking down the street and I won't even blink."

"I'll act like I don't know you, too," he said. She could put him off at any point on the highway if she felt like it. Her radio played "Moonglow." Second morning in a row. He thought of them fishing at night at Ocean Beach. He thought about the ride ahead, in the rail cars with the horses. Tolbert would bring a deck and they'd play for pennies.

At the lot of the Green Wave, she wheeled the Nash around so they faced the highway. "Take care," she said. "I mean it."

"You, too."

"Wait." She reached across him, popped open the glovebox. She stuck her hand under the little stack of ration books. "Take the program with you. Yesterday's. Here. I gotta get to work."

He had the program in his hand as her taxi darted away. In another moment, he tapped his pockets for the key to his room. The key turned out to be in the pocket with the tickets he'd bought on Stymie. He inspected these again in the brightness provided from the nearby streetlight.

He opened the door to his room with the key, and his eyes caught the painting on the wall. He imagined how dawn might look through the motel window. Anyway, he saw that light every morning, right at the barn.

Banned

1.

In October 1944, the War Manpower Commission sent representatives to Jamaica Racetrack. When called in, Ben took a chair in Jacobs's windowless office and responded to their questions. The shorter of the two men from the commission had a scarlet, boiling face. He said, "Everyone should be a part of the push now. There are mills, and farms are sore for men. No exceptions, not even…racetrack people."

Jacobs, seated at the desk, said, "Horses need to be taken care of."

Ben said, "Y'all still running those prison camps out at Tanforan?"

The taller commission man said, "That's an Assembly Center for Japa—"

"It was in a magazine. I saw pictures, people were living in horse stalls."

"The press gets it wrong."

"A photograph is lying?"

"A photograph never says why."

"A photo—"

Jacobs said, "Listen, boys…long season."

The taller commission man stood in one corner. He said, "When all these tracks are closed, useless men will be exposed, these shantytown neighborhoods will be cleaned out. And we're not talking only about the coloreds."

"You can go, Ben," Jacobs said. "Close the door behind you."

Once he'd left the office, shut the door, Ben lingered. What he thought he heard Jacobs say was, *What do you want, fellas?*

In the days that followed, Jacobs didn't bring up the visit from the Manpower Commission officials. November arrived and there weren't any plans for shipping to Miami. Jacobs sent Stymie down to Maryland for a couple of races, the Riggs and the Pimlico Cup, and he finished third in each. The Jamaica meeting ended right after Thanksgiving. Jacobs laid off half of his workers, and a skeleton crew remained. Along with Ben, a groom and an exercise rider cared for a dozen horses.

On a Sunday morning a little more than two weeks ahead of Christmas, the horses completed light workouts. The stalls were cleaned, and Ben had taken to raking shedrow dirt. A spotless shedrow meant there wasn't a blade of straw in the way of winning. He noticed Jacobs at the far end of the barn, faced in the direction of the red maple tree near the wooden fence that ran parallel to the sidewalk. The branches reached forty feet into the air and the leaves were gone from the tree.

Jacobs said, "Talk to me!" Then, head down, he started for the stable office.

The trainer was seated behind his desk when Ben reached the doorway. "Work all done? Good. The government's about to shut us down."

"Us?"

"The game, the sport."

"They called you? The govern—"

"No. Lenny Pope, racing secretary at Belmont. Announcement's coming, it'll be before Christmas, I think. I'm sending a few horses to Virginia, Middleburg. Turn 'em out. Big Wages, Stymie, Yukon, Stinging Bee. I'll be home with my wife and daughter, so I'm gonna let you go for a little while, Ben. Until I need you again." He pulled open the top drawer of the metal desk, held over an envelope. "A month's pay. Go on, take it." Once he did, Ben stepped back.

"Are war prisoners going to live here?"

"What?"

"People, like in Tanforan? German soldiers, maybe?"

"No, Ben. I don't think so. But who knows? I knew you wouldn't like this."

"I don't."

"End of the war is close. You hear the news. They might cancel all the goddamn stuff for a while."

"They won't cancel Joe Louis."

"Maybe not Joe Louis." Jacobs tilted to one side and passed gas. "Look, I want you…when we're all back here. I don't need a foreman for my family."

"You lettin' the other grooms go?"

"Tomorrow's the last day for everybody."

"Want me to tell them?"

"I'll do it. Where do you think you'll go?"

"I don't know. We could lose the war, too, you know."

"Jerry's army is fertilizer. It's Tojo I worry about. Anyway, you and I don't have a lot of say in how it's all going to turn out. Give me a number so I can find you."

"Can't think of one," Ben said in a murmur.

"When's the last time you spent any time away from here?"

"I went to Kentucky after my mother died…in forty." In those days, he'd just started working for this stable. "She was in the ground by the time I got home."

"Tomorrow morning. Bring me an address…something."

The next morning, Ben tapped on the closed door to

Jacobs's office. Then he stepped out from the shedrow and his eyes followed the wooden fence line up the street. "Decided?" Jacobs said. His face poked out from the doorway.

"What about if I go to Virginia, with Stymie and the other horses?"

As Ben spoke, Jacobs interrupted. "I already have people there. Husband and wife. They're gonna hack the horses around. Keep their legs limber. But there's no place to run them. I'm not glad about the ban. Maybe Stymie will be."

Ben produced a slip of paper, which Jacobs slipped in a pocket of his trousers. "That's my father's address in Newport, Kentucky, the people he lives with..."

"Gimme one of those cigarettes," Jacobs said. The sky looked milky and flat beyond the bare limbs of the red maple tree. "Got enough money?"

"Yep."

"Look at it this way. When I see you again, it means we won the war."

* * *

On Tuesday morning, in his one-bedroom flat near the corner of 161st and 132nd, Ben, as always, awakened before sunrise. He made coffee, then his routine changed, and he began to pack his clothes. He took his one suit from its hanger, felt something in the kerchief pocket. He removed a button: *I Have Seen the Future.* He'd been to the Futurama Exhibit at the 1939 World's Fair in Flushing Meadows. A vision of highways, shining cities. A world sponsored by car companies of Detroit. He returned the button to the kerchief pocket. He unplugged his radio, wrapped the cord.

He went along the sidewalks outside the barn area of the racetrack on his way to the Locust Manor platform. He spotted a woman with a baby wrapped in a blanket; she crossed without looking while singing "Over the Rainbow" at the top of her lungs. A mother drunk like that early in the morning—he wanted to yell something to her about how that kid was going to turn out.

The Locust Manor platform offered a view of out-of-commission train cars and the zigzag of tracks of Railroad Park. He stood with his hands in his pockets and suitcase at his feet. Three kids horsed around on the backless bench behind him. He glanced around for their parents and then he said, "You guys okay?" They all grinned and nodded fast. He faced Railroad Park again. A thick mist hung over everything beyond it.

He rode the Long Island train to Grand Central, and inside the terminal were the constellations painted on the ceilings, the complex layout of stars against the ocean-green of outer space. He had an hour and a half until the first leg of his trip, the 9:16 for Baltimore, so he stood at a newsstand, dipped through a dozen magazines before settling on *The Morning Telegraph* and *Big City Detective*. He chose one end of a polished pew, flipped the pages of the detective magazine, couldn't decide whether to telegram his father. He thought of how he might explain in a few words what was going on. *Racing's banned. I'm coming home. Temporarily. BH.*

When his mother died in the summer of 1940, his father had sent him a telegram; a kid from the racing office brought it to Jacobs's barn.

> YOUR MOTHER IS GONE.
> LAST WEEK. HCH.

He hadn't been sure what to do, so he'd shown the telegram to Jacobs, who encouraged him to go see his family.

He'd ridden the trains back to Cincinnati. He thought they'd have her laid out, either in the boarding house where they lived or maybe at a funeral parlor. Since the flood of '37, Ben's parents had a second-floor room in Foster and Barb Drayton's house on Isabella Street. Once Ben got there, his father had explained she died of influenza, and she'd already taken her place in Evergreen Cemetery in Southgate. There wasn't much else to say. The following day Ben put on his World's Fair suit, his only suit, and because the city trolleys didn't run all the way to Southgate, he took a taxi. His father explained where he could find the marker, which would be a white cross. Her name was painted in neat blue letters: *Leslie May Held, 1881-1940.* He hadn't brought flowers. He stared at her grave and thought of his mother as a young woman, when they lived in the shotgun shack down beyond Second Street. She'd grown up in Southgate and it made sense to lay her to rest at Evergreen. The Helds never had any money—he felt that poverty at her gravesite, wondered what clothes she'd been buried in, the type of box that held her now.

Ben had returned to the Draytons' home, found his father upstairs in a rocking chair. His father was in his sixties then and hadn't worked much at all since the Depression. Ben said, I'm going to send you something so you can get her a proper headstone.

His father said, Son, we're in no hurry for that.

Ben wanted to object. He said, I guess all there's to do is go back to Jamaica.

Stay for a minute, his father said.

Ben said, Is Bonnie still around?

Married, his father said. I guess all I give you is bad news.

Is she around?

Married to some bum, his father said. Barb's the biggest busybody in the world, she'll know.

Ben said, You care if I take off for a little bit?

His father said, Go ahead.

Downstairs, Barb Drayton rested on the couch by the front door. She'd fallen asleep while sitting up and he spoke to her as quietly as possible. He apologized and then asked about Bonnie. Barb said she hadn't heard about Bonnie in a while. She said, Oh, Bonnie. It's not Dennert, it's Ringgold...right, Bonnie works, I think at The Wheel Café, you know, across the river. That husband of hers does nothing, of course. I don't know why she's drawn...

Ben thanked her. He set out on foot. He passed the speakeasys, the gambling clubs on Monmouth. On the Cincinnati side, The Wheel was up on Sixth Street and when he stepped in, Bonnie was the first person he laid his eyes on. Behind the counter, holding a coffee pot. When she spotted Ben, her shoulders dropped.

She took her dinner break early, sat with him in a booth at the back. She said she was still married. Had heard about his mother. She also told him about the closing of Latonia Racetrack over in Covington, how it had all been razed by the oil company that now owned the land. He wanted to tell her where he got the suit he was wearing, the things he'd seen. The Brooklyn Bridge, World's Fair, Empire State Building. More than anything, he wanted to listen to anything she had to say.

Bonnie talked about her husband. Ben didn't mind this because he was interested in knowing about the kind of man she'd marry. She talked about working on the Cincinnati side of the river, how it was the same and different all at once. After a while, she said, When're you going back?

Tomorrow, he said. Can I walk you home?

I have hours left on my shift, she said. He'll come get me.

2.

He'd barnstormed for the past two-plus decades, Lincoln Fields, Ak-Sar-Ben, Arlington Park, Detroit Fair Grounds, Havre de Grace. Finally, Jamaica. Since his mother's death he hadn't been back to Newport. Without horse racing, he didn't have any other place to be. There would be familiar faces, the streets he'd grown up on. It wouldn't be like when he came back from the war. He'd have stories he wouldn't mind telling.

In a coach full of soldiers, he rode from Baltimore to Cincinnati. Some private plopped down next to him, said, "Whaddya think, old scout?" Ben had an opened *Morning Telegraph,* and he brought the paper so the soldier could see.

"Racing entries," Ben said. "While they last. Where you from?"

"Western Hills, chief," the private said.

"I'm from Newport," Ben said. "Home for the holidays."

"Drink?" the soldier said, holding up a metallic flask.

"Why sure."

Just after three a.m., the train rolled into Union Terminal in Cincinnati. Inside, the soldiers were greeted by their parents, their women, their children. It was all terrifically hectic and seemed unbearable. Ben kept his suitcase at his side and considered the colorful mosaics that adorned the walls and ceilings. One sequence offered the story of America: Indians, settlers, railroad workers, steamboat captains, in the background a winding, cobalt river. The center of the ceiling was like a half-sun, surrounded by bands of orange, gold, and yellow. He thought of how his own mural might look: Stymie. A marching battalion of men. Latonia Racetrack. Bonnie. Swimming in the river.

A pew that held a sleeping soldier had just enough room

at one end. Ben faced the terminal entrance. In his heart, he didn't believe horse racing was over for good. The war being fought in Europe now was the worst ever, tens of millions of lives were gone, nations wrecked beyond repair. Horse racing! It had been going on this whole time. He knew the explanation: All of life could not be about war. In his suitcase, he had a photo of Stymie. He thought about taking it out but understood he didn't have to.

The soldier sleeping on the bench murmured and then his boots were moving, kicking. Somewhere in the terminal, a radio played Christmas music, piano renditions. "O Holy Night," "O Little Town of Bethlehem." He didn't need a taxi to Newport, wasn't going to knock on the Draytons' front door before sunup. This wasn't any emergency. He took a little walk through the terminal, returned to the pew where he'd been, and the soldier was gone. Dawn. He pushed open a glass door, stepped into icy air. The station entrance faced east. To his left were the hillsides, warehouses; straight away, in the distance, the gauzy skyline of Cincinnati. He couldn't see the river from where he stood, but he knew it was there. Past that, to the south, were the towns on the Kentucky side. Covington, Newport, Bellevue. Familiar, but now a daydream. He went along the curved sidewalk that led around the out-of-commission fountain and then turned to consider the hands of the huge clock on the terminal façade: half past six. In order to be closer to the river, he angled his course. He could see more clearly the houses packed tight on the northern Kentucky hillsides, the creamy sky above them. He went along Western Avenue, then south on Gest. As he approached Sixth Street, he thought about going east for a few blocks, showing up at The Wheel. See if she still worked there. Anyway, if she was married or not, Ben didn't want her to see him like this, discarded, drifting. The streets here were like those in Jamaica, trashed with newspapers, smashed bottles. An abandoned baby-carriage in the middle of the sidewalk, which he guided further from the street and parked at the entrance of an unopened print shop. On Fourth and Elm, on the roof of a five-story building, he spotted a billboard: *Let's All Back the Attack. Buy Bonds.* A taxi slowed, he waved it on. By the time he made it to the foot of the L & N Railroad Bridge, the sun had climbed above the hillsides. As a kid he'd played on the tracks, and he'd held hands with his mother when they went along the pedestrian sidewalk.

The sidewalk was made of steel grates and concrete. He glanced out to the steaming river as he crossed the bridge; saw that the gray waters were high, carrying broken tree branches, a section of wooden steps. He tracked the steps until he couldn't see them. The river carried a coal barge in the direction of the horizon. He moved to one side, made room for a family of four, a father, mother, and two small children, all dressed in dark clothes, dark caps. After that, he lit a cigarette and stared out at the river again.

On the Newport side, he walked up York till he reached Sixth, then made a right and went a few blocks until Isabella. He made another right there, and by the time he spotted the Draytons' house, he was feeling the cold in the base of his spine. Up the steps, three taps on the storm door. It opened a slice: Barb Drayton. "It's Ben," he said.

"I know who," she said. She motioned for him. The front room had hardwood floors, a sofa by the door, empty of furniture otherwise. She wore a clay-colored apron over her nightgown, black socks, no shoes. She padded down a short hallway, for the kitchen. There, his father and Foster Drayton sat at a table, and neither of them looked up until she said, "Look what."

Ben puffed his cheeks, waved his hand in front of his

chest. His heart was beating faster now. His father's eyes seemed glassy, and he kept blinking. "Well, I'll be. Ben's here," he said to Drayton.

"You hungry?" she said.

"Yes," Ben said.

"No hat," his father said. "As usual."

"Toast, eggs, potatoes," she said. Ben placed his suitcase by a kitchen chair. He removed his coat and laid it over the case. He combed his hair over with his hand. The table had skinny pine legs, and when Ben took the open place he was sitting across from his father. His father wore glasses now, with oval-shaped black frames. Barb Drayton placed a plate in front of Ben; the slices of toast were in a stack and within arm's reach. She brought him a cup of coffee.

Once he started, he ate fast. He said, "I had a long train ride. I'd like to lie down soon, if it's all right." He saw the three of them staring at him.

Ben said to her, "Another cup of coffee?"

Mr. Drayton said, "You ever get married, Ben?"

"He didn't," his father said, right away.

Vaguely, Ben felt like defending himself. He said, "No, he didn't." Barb Drayton brought the coffee pot.

She murmured, "Where you comin' from, sweetheart?"

"New York."

"New York?"

He said, in his father's direction, "I didn't know if you'd still be here."

His father's white hair was combed straight back, it went beyond his ears. "We're here," he said.

"Can I stay with y'all for a couple of days? Till I get a place of my own?"

His father said, "What happened in New York?"

"Closed."

"Of course, you can," Barb Drayton said. She held her hands together in front of her and peered down at him.

"They're about to ban horse racing," Ben said.

"Typical," Drayton said.

"They've cancelled horse racing," she said. "What does that mean? Has the war gone south?"

Ben imagined the three of them without him, having breakfast. What they knew of the war was what they heard on the radio, what they read in the *Times-Star*. "Resources," he said. "Gas, cars, trains—a lot of people come to the races now. You should see Jamaica Racetrack on a Saturday afternoon in July. It looks bad, people enjoying themselves at the races, yelling for horses and everything while there's a world war going on. People dying...Europe drowning in blood. I'm sorry. I'm tired."

"They kept running races at Latonia while you were in France," his father said.

"I know they did, Pop. Care if I go lie down?"

"Remember where your father's room is?" Mrs. Drayton said.

Ben climbed the narrow staircase, the suitcase at his side. He lay on the unmade bed, told himself he'd get up in a minute and straighten it. Soft-blue light streamed in from the window that faced north. Was that the bureau from the old house—had they somehow been able to save that from the flood? On top of the bureau were stacks of paperback books. The window next to the bureau looked out to Isabella Street. He closed his eyes and listened for the sound of voices drifting up from the ground floor because he knew they'd be talking about him. Surely, they had talked about him. A man his age, working in horseshit. He thought of a summer afternoon thirty years ago; he and his father had caught a trolley for Latonia Racetrack. Ben might've been fifteen years old and his mother said he was too young for the races. His father wore a light-colored suit that was loose on him. Latonia was surrounded by green hillsides. The dirt track was sun baked, and the dust rose in the wake of the running horses.

When Ben opened his eyes, his father sat in the rocking chair near the open door. "How long you been over there?" The chair had armrests.

His father glanced up from a book. "Just took a walk."

"Where to?"

"Down to the foot of the bridge. You walk all the way from Union?"

"I did. What're you reading?"

"Agatha Christie."

"Is that the bureau from the house?"

"It's not. Myself, I like to walk. Do it every day. I might live for a very long time."

If that's all you do, Ben thought. But he let it go. Prior to the Depression his father worked at Wiedemann Brewery; after it, he took small jobs around town, just enough to keep himself going. People looked after him. Ben's mother had done this, then the Draytons. In his own way, Ben did, too, when he had money to send from a winning bet. Was his father just a lucky man? No, Ben would not go that far, he wouldn't say that.

"I'm gettin' my own place," Ben said.

"You said that already. Are you all right?"

"I'm good."

"Bonnie Dennert is divorced."

"What?"

"You heard me. You're gonna ask at some point. Now, you won't have to." His father appeared pleased.

"I don't know why I'm here."

"You said they cancelled…"

"I could go to work on one of the breeding farms in Lexington. I thought about it. But I thought I'd try here."

"Feelin' sorry for yourself?" Ben didn't say anything. "What do you do up there exactly?"

"Work with horses."

"What do you do every day? That's what I'm asking you son."

Ben's eyes went to the water stain in one corner of the ceiling. "Get up before five. I live a few blocks from Jamaica Racetrack, so I walk to work. I have coffee with the grooms and then we feed. We get the horses tacked up."

"Buncha nigs, I guess."

"Yeah, we're all nigs. We clean tack, clean stalls. Get the barn moving, as the trainer says. On days when we have a horse running, I stay there all afternoon. Then I go home, maybe go out, get dinner at some joint in the neighborhood. It doesn't sound like a lot, not when you talk about it like this. But I like it. I know you think work is a scam." He didn't want to get into anything with his father. He thought his father might thank him for the money he'd been sending. "Most everything is."

"You musta had a long train ride."

"What's Bonnie doing?"

"Pompilio's. Been there for a couple years."

Ben pushed at the pillow so he could better prop his head. "They haven't made the announcement about the ban on horse racing. My boss told me it's coming. He's gonna call me when it's time to go back. Look, let me show you something." He pulled himself up, went for the suitcase, laid it flat on the floor, worked open the clasps, dug into his clothes. He extracted a manila envelope, and from that he eased clear an 8x10 photo. He brought it over to his father. The photo images were halved horizontally; the upper half showed Stymie close to the finish line of Fort Tryon Purse, the jock Adams riding low in the saddle, the horse's chest all plastered with dark-colored dirt. The lower image came after the race, Tolbert the groom holding the shank, standing at Stymie's head. Hirsch Jacobs and his wife were just in front of Tolbert. Beyond them, the gamblers jammed along the chain-link fence, a bank of white faces in hats. "That's the best horse in our barn right there. I think he's nearly the best horse in New York. He will be."

"You in here somewhere?"

"Just behind the groom and the hat the woman is wearing."

"Stymie," his father said. He held the photo over to Ben. "Never heard of him."

Ben said, "I'm just tryin' to tell you I'm doin' okay."

"You just said there's no more horse racing."

"Not my fault. Temporary, anyway."

"Go back to bed for a while, son. You look beat. I'm just gonna sit here. I'll turn the radio on in a little bit."

Ben slid the photo in the envelope, returned it to the suitcase. He stretched out on the bed, and he guessed it felt all right to be in the company of his father. When he awakened again, it was twilight. He found his father and Foster Drayton downstairs in the kitchen, playing cards. They noticed him, then went back to the hands they held. "I might take a walk," Ben said.

"It's on Washington, Pompilio's."

Always was, Ben thought. "Some Italian food."

"You do that. We got an extra key, Foster?"

"Take mine," Drayton said. "It's over in that drawer. Next to the sink. Bring us back a little something if you think of it."

"Italian," his father said. The old men smiled at one

another.

Ben stepped outside, flipped up his collar, felt the snowflakes touching his face. Tucked inside his buttoned-up coat was the envelope with the photo of Stymie. Every block, he'd have to whisk the snow out of his hair. He went east on Eighth, passing block after block of row houses, then turned north on Washington. He could see the lights of the speakeasys, the casinos, in the distance. Before he entered Pompilio's Italian, he wiped at the shoulders of his coat. Inside, he grinned in the direction of the bar counter, just in case he spotted someone familiar. Along the wall opposite the bar stood a row of five-cent slot machines with watermelon-striped covers and chrome handles, a half dozen of them. A couple of guys were playing, yanking on the handles harder than anyone needed to. He went out to the dining area, and before him appeared a tidy man in a buttoned-to-the-throat black shirt and scarlet apron. Ben put up an index finger, was shown to a table in the middle of the dining room. "I'd like to look out at the street," he said.

"Go right ahead. I'll send over a girl."

He'd been waiting at his window table for a couple of minutes and then a waitress slid a paper menu in front of him and walked off without asking if he was ready for a drink. She returned with silverware and a glass of water. "Is Bonnie here tonight?" he said. "Bonnie Ringgold? Bonnie Dennert? That's what her name was when I knew her."

"Not sure." She drew her shoulders back, sized him up.

"Spaghetti plate with red wine for fifty-nine cents." Her expression didn't change, and he pointed with his thumb to the window. "I used to come here."

"Anything else?"

"No. Thank you."

His food was served on a platter; the wine was filled to

the rim of the highball glass. He began eating. He didn't look up until he felt the presence of someone. Bonnie, her hands folded in front of her white apron. He chewed, swallowed. "My pop said you were runnin' this place now," he said.

"Deena told me somebody asked…I stood over there for a minute looking…I thought, is that Ben?"

"Can you join me?" He wanted it to seem like he hadn't been gone for long. But this wasn't how he felt.

There were empty tables, plenty of them. She glanced to his hip, the envelope. "I'm in the kitchen tonight," she said. "We're short." A moment later, she dropped into the chair across from him. "Your dad okay?"

"He's older," he said.

"What choice does he have?"

"I'm stayin' with him, just for a little while. Till I get a place of my own." Her skin looked glossy to him. Her eyes had always been a touch close together. Her curly black hair was long, past her shoulders; the strands of gray made her quite elegant. "Come on, what time do you get off, I'll wait for you. How are your folks?"

"Mama's gone, you know that. She died in '41. A year after yours."

"I don't know if I knew that."

"Doesn't matter," she said. He felt that she would be glad to see him. She might feel this way for a little while, anyway. "She had a stroke. Next day she was dead. Daddy's down in Falmouth, living with his brother, both of 'em as busted as banjos."

"I surprised Pop. I mean, hell, I write him, he knows where I live."

"What, you bring something for me?"

While keeping his eyes on her, his hand found the envelope at his side. "I didn't know if you'd be here. I asked

Pop if you were married or anything...he said he didn't know."

"Nonsense." She might've been just as nervous now.

"It's a picture of me...kinda. I wanted to show you what I was doing." She wedged the tips of her thumb and index finger inside the envelope and extracted the photo. "That's when Stymie won the Fort Tryon Purse. A coupla months ago. Beat a pretty good field. See, they're about to end horse racing. Until the war's done. I guess we shouldn't be racing at all now anyhow."

"This is a picture of you?"

"There's my head. Part of it." She touched her index finger to the photo. "I'm the foreman for Jacobs's barn. I make sure the grooms are doing their jobs. I'm not a groom anymore, but if a guy comes up sick or missing, I step in. I usually don't get in the win photo, but I was excited. Stymie broke a little bit of a losing streak in this one. You oughta see him," he said. She eyed him at this, and he felt himself grimace. "I'm in New York, with a terrific stable."

"I know your father's glad to see ya."

"I don't have bookies chasing after me...just got some time to kill..." He said, "It's almost Christmas. I wanted to see you. I thought you might be in town."

"Where else would I be? Ben Held," she said. "Goodness."

"Where you live? Can I walk you?"

"Not near the casinos," she said. "If that's the direction you're going. I usually walk with one of the other girls but she isn't here tonight."

"Learned some lessons. I still bet a race now and again..."

"Your food's getting cold."

"Room temperature, that's all. I think I'll stay here for a little while. I'll wait for you."

"If your pop told you I was married, would you have asked for me?"

"Yeah, of course." He picked up his fork. "Not sure I would've brought the picture, though."

She returned the photo to the table, near his arm, not unlike how the waitress had done with the menu. "That's a horse with people standing around it."

"I'm in there."

She stood. "I can get away in an hour."

"I'll be here," he said, after her. "Promise." He watched the hem of her dress as she moved between empty tables, made for the kitchen door. It swung open and then closed. He set the 8x10 against his water glass, as if he were reading a newspaper. When he turned his attention to his spaghetti, he ate fast. He touched his fingers to a paper napkin, and he worked the photo of Stymie back into the envelope and placed it by his hip again. He had two highball glasses of wine and cigarettes, then went to coffee.

When Bonnie returned to his table, she'd already put on an ankle-length coat. In front of him, she pulled on her gloves. He wondered what she could tell. "If you need a hat, go to the bar and ask for the hat box," she said. She tugged on a little Mercury number, totally out of style, then touched at the sides of it.

"I don't wear hats generally," Ben said, "Those guys look like they have somewhere they have to be."

"Noted. I'll modify my expectations. My place is a few blocks from here. Then you're going to have to walk back over to Isabella. Go on now. I'll wait for you outside. Leave a decent tip."

He extracted a dollar bill from his pocket, then another. He worked on his coat and carried his envelope over to the bar counter. Beyond the cannonball-shaped bartender stood rows of bottles, a movie-poster-sized mirror with a pewter frame. A handwritten sign said *No Women at the Bar* and Bonnie must've said something to the guy on her way out because at the sight of Ben he brought a beer case atop the counter. Ben opened the flaps, tilted it. Fedoras, a couple of tweeds, a Marine service uniform number. Three men in gray suits sat at the bar, hunched forward. The brim of the Carlsbad hat Ben chose was bent. Outside, Bonnie said, "Now it looks like you're waiting for a stagecoach. How on earth?" They stood on the sidewalks of Washington Avenue, the snow falling. "We go that way. Don't let your thing get wet there."

He stuck the envelope inside his coat. She wouldn't say specifically where she lived, probably so he couldn't get ahead of her. When a couple of hefty guys in tuxedos jogged around them, he reached for her sleeve. "I don't know why I'm here," he said. "I don't know how long the ban is going to last, the trainer doesn't know. They haven't even announced it yet. Maybe Jacobs just wanted to get rid of me. I could've stayed up there, waited it out…Manpower be damned." He'd taken his hand away at this point. "But I think I came down here to see you, Bonnie. It's starting to make sense. Sometimes, I just don't figure out things right away. Eventually, I do. Sometimes I need to say things…I'm saying something now. You're looking at me like I'm nuts or I'm plowed. I had a couple glasses of red, that's all. I think I came down here to tell you I want you to come back with me."

"You had the answer to that question twenty-five years ago," she said.

"I wasn't ready for you then."

"You weren't in love with me, Ben. Not enough, anyway."

He wanted to defend himself. "Things change and they

don't," he said. It was all he could think of.

"My apartment is still six blocks away."

"Let's walk then."

They went a half-block and she murmured, "Jesus Christ."

"Bonnie," he said. "Bonnie."

"What?"

They passed a block of row houses, all the windows dark. Somebody, maybe a gambler who'd lost everything, had gone around kicking over trashcans and the snow made a layer like icing over the spilled garbage. The streets were so quiet Ben could hear the snow falling, or thought he could. Then a car without the headlights barreled by, a black Nash. "We go right here," she said. "Indiana Alley, that's where I live."

He said, "I spent last winter in Miami. Hialeah. With Stymie. Jacobs's stable."

"You don't say."

"Lived in a motel, the Green Wave. Bare bones. Had a table, two chairs, a bed. Window where I could look out and see the highway. Maybe you would've liked it."

"You're bum-rushing me."

"I've just realized something, that's all. That's it."

"Yeah, I think I'm realizing something, too." Past Park Avenue, they made a right and ahead were other figures on the sidewalks, people in heavy coats passing under streetlights. He tried to imagine that he and Bonnie were married and that he'd never left. They would be walking through the falling snow for their little apartment. He'd stayed here like he was supposed to and he'd married her like he should've. When they got to their place after an evening walk, they'd sit at a kitchen table with a wobbly leg and have drinks. He'd have talked out the war, it would have taken time, but that finally would have been over, there'd be nothing left to say. Night after night, she'd have listened. And in the years that followed she would've done most of the talking and he would've been glad for that. More than anything, he wanted to hear the sound of her voice and find comfort in the kindness of her face. She'd aged rather beautifully. Life had always felt hard, he didn't mind and hadn't expected anything else. But that's not all it had to be. If they'd been married for the past twenty-five years, he'd have told her that tonight. He'd offer her this present, the both of them understanding he'd never be able to give her anything more. He'd make love to her, and it would be the easiest thing in the world to do.

"Your photo," she said. He hadn't noticed; the envelope had fallen onto the snow. She ducked back a step and reached for it. She brushed the envelope with the side of her gloved hand.

"Oh, okay, thanks." They went another block, then a half a block and she turned in to an alley covered by a fluffy layer of snow. They followed a single set of paw prints that led right to her door. "Pepe," she said. "A mutt I feed. I guess he couldn't wait. Look." The paw prints went further down the alley. "Shoot." The entrance to her place had concrete steps, wrought-iron railing on both sides.

She dug out a key, said, "Are you coming in?" He stayed in the doorway until she turned on a lamp atop a triangular-shaped butler table. Next to that, a pigeon-colored sofa. As she shed her jacket, she seemed to be surveying her space. He held the Carlsbad hat in his hands, ran his fingers along the damp felt of the brim. In the kitchen, she pulled the string that hung from the bulb fixture on the ceiling. She stood in a peculiar, yellow-green light. His apartment in Jamaica had been almost as large as this one. He knew he'd upset Bonnie, wanted for her to say it would be all right to take off his coat.

"Your pop waiting up for you?" she said.

"No, he's probably asleep. I'm supposed to bring them something to...him and Foster...they'll forget about it."

"Are they going to ban all the sports?" she said.

"I don't know."

"Maybe they should...until this is done."

"Horse racing is a phenomenon," he said. "Right now, it's the most popular thing in this country. I hear that on the news all the time. With the war on and everything. Where we race, Jamaica, you can't get in the place on a Saturday. Is that the right word?"

She'd folded her coat over the back of one the chairs. Her gloves and little Mercury hat were on the table. "Phenomenon? I guess so." She frowned, said, "You might say its popularity is phenomenal."

"I'm not going to apologize for saying I want you to move to New York with me. I probably could've done it a little better."

"Maybe you already knew what the answer was going to be, Ben."

"Don't answer me tonight, please," he said.

"Want a beer?" she said. "What kind of beers do you drink in New York?" She had two bottles on the table, a church key in her hand. "I can make you a sandwich. Cucumber tastes good with a beer. I read that Mrs. Roosevelt has a beer and a cucumber sandwich every night before she goes to bed. I might make one in a minute." Ben noticed books on the floor near the sofa. He imagined her stretched out on the sofa, reading one in the quiet of this place. Neither of them could be comfortable right now.

"Please say anything you want to me," he said. "In New York, you know, people move fast. Right at stuff they want. I've lived there for a few years now. How do you think the war's gonna turn out?"

"Me? I'm not planning to learn Japanese. Everything I've heard and read says Europe is gone. I don't know what's going to happen. Hard to believe one man started all this. But we're…mighty…I just want FDR to live forever. He hasn't done a radio talk since the summer, I know he's sick. When I think about everything, I'm scared to the soles of my feet."

"We should be." The chair creaked when he leaned back, and he sat up. "Remember when I came back? What was I like?"

"Quiet," she said, right away. "Mysterious."

"Was I angry?"

"Trying not to be, maybe."

"I felt ashamed. I was a good soldier. When the Manpower guys come to our barn now, they look at me like I'm a dog turd."

"You did your duty."

He spotted a lidless cigar box on the floor at the foot of the couch, a pen resting atop a collection of ration booklets. "A good soldier is ashamed. That was part of it, me leaving…. What're you reading, Bon?"

"Stuff, poetry. Christina Rossetti."

"The Christina Rossetti?"

"You know her?"

"No idea."

"Poet. Overdue. Taking it back tomorrow before I go to work."

"You still write poems?"

"Not exactly. I still like to read them though. I'm not a poet per se, but that's all right."

He said, "If it's still snowing, won't the library be closed?" The lighting in the kitchen seemed weak, which he was glad for. He knew that he hadn't all of a sudden gotten good-looking. "This is what I do at night in Jamaica," he said. "You know what I mean?"

"Go over things," she said.

"Yeah," he said. "I go over things. I think about the races. I think if I could show you Stymie you'd be pretty excited."

"Maybe he'll run in Louisville."

"He coulda been in the Derby this year, he just wasn't ready. Ran in the Preakness though."

"Maybe he can run in the Derby next year."

"Derby's only for three-year-olds. You only get one shot for that."

"How's the beer?"

"Good."

"The restaurant spots me. The barkeep brings bottles to the kitchen for us. I've got a case or two of empties I need to take back, actually. Maybe you can do that for me. In the morning."

"Sure."

"Were you planning on spending the night here?" He knew better than to answer. "Or were you planning to walk through the snow to return to your sleeping father? You can bunk on the couch."

"Okay, thank you."

"Ben," she said.

Things felt too solemn then. He said, "You worried that people might talk? You, an unmarried woman."

"All the people who gather in the alley each morning to see what I've been up to? Come on," she said. "Drink your beer. I'm going to make a sandwich." She went to the sink to do this. He watched her shoulders as she sliced a cucumber. She returned to the table with sandwich halves. "Take one. I put a little salt and pepper on it. Just take a bite."

"Man, it does taste good with a beer." He raised his bottle. "To Eleanor," he said.

"Yes," she said. "To Eleanor Roosevelt."

3.

Sometime that night, he fell asleep on her living room couch. He awakened hearing men's voices in the alley: *Don't know what way...don't got any money for that...you saw that goddamn game was rigged!* The curtains were drawn, so the snow might still be falling. The door to the bedroom, already ajar, opened further and Bonnie moved in his direction. She sat on the arm of the couch, by his ankles. "I'm up," he said.

"I'm used to it out there...middle of the night...people," she said. "Getting lost after losing."

"Joints ever close?"

"The bakery down the street, you remember, Herman's? Ah wait, that was after you. Anyway, they got three nickel machines, as soon as you walk in."

"You play?" His voice felt thick.

"I liked the Primrose, over in Wilder. Me and one of my girlfriends, Monica Deering, used to get dressed up and go over there. We like the carpet places. Cleveland guys took over, it's the Latin Quarter now. My ex, he talked about getting in with the Cleveland mob...'the family.' He wished for a lot...why're you here, Ben?"

He placed his right hand behind his head. "I've been thinking about it," he said. "Lyin' here on your couch, listenin' to these idiot gamblers. How many casinos are there?"

"Too many to count."

"I need a job," he said. "Maybe I can work a stick at a roulette table...at the Latin Quarter. Bonnie, I'm in love with you. I have to say it. There's no point in not saying it. I've always been in love with you. Always. I wanted you to come away all those years ago, but I wasn't ready for you and you knew it. Now, I am. I wanted to be free…a trapped man is no good. I'm not trapped now, what I mean is I'm not worried about it anymore."

"What about your father and his dinner?"

"He'll forgive me. Look, I want to marry you."

"You're being ridiculous." When she spoke again, she said, "I'm going to go back to bed in a minute."

"Bonnie," he said. He didn't say anything else.

She closed the bedroom door after her. When he needed to take a leak, he pulled on his boots, stepped outside and unzipped his pants while facing the alley wall. He watched the steam rise while he pissed, which seemed to go on forever. He went back inside, to the couch, and fell asleep. The next time his eyes opened, the sun was up, Bonnie was in the kitchen, and he could smell coffee and something in the oven. "Hello," he said.

"I made a water pie for your father. Take it to him."

"Okay. I'm gonna…" He went for the open bedroom door. In the bathroom, he found a brush with white flakes in between the bristles and knocked at the bristles with his hand before running them over his hair. When he returned to the kitchen, he decided to sit at the table with her.

She wore a light-blue robe, buttoned up. A cup of black coffee had been set out for him. "Don't ask me to marry you again. I guess you were in a dream state or something or you wanted to get in my underwear. I'm surprised you didn't try." She regarded him coolly.

"You going to library today?"

"I think so."

"When?"

"Old Main opens at nine."

"What's wrong with the one here? Can't be four, five blocks away."

"On Sixth. There's nothing wrong with it. It has books, walls, a roof."

"That's what I'm saying."

"Old Main's got the very best collection. The one here's a Carnegie library. That's fine. He gets rich off the backs of steelworkers and covers himself by donating bookshelves. His soul is squeaky clean, no doubt. A hero."

"Sorry I asked."

"Some of the girls, you remember Loretta and Marcella Sandhus? They went up to Youngstown to work, you know factory work, they're patriots, too. War or not, I guess I'm just a waitress. Anyway...I prefer the one across the river."

"I think I'll go there today, too. Maybe I'll get a library card."

"Do you understand what I'm sayin' to you, Ben?"

"You have feelings for me, I can see it in your eyes." When she didn't answer, he stared in the direction of the drawn curtains. "I'm sorry. I remember how I used to talk to you. Probably like you weren't even there."

"Isn't that what you're doing now?" He didn't answer. "The legs on that chair aren't sturdy."

"Last night, I just wanted to show you that photo of me and Stymie, that I'd turned out okay...we can have a lot of good things, you and me."

"The pie needs to cool, then take it to your father. Don't let them cut into it until tomorrow."

She removed a tray from the oven, placed it atop the stove, shed the mitten, reached to the cupboard for a plate. When he stood behind her, she stopped. His hands were on her shoulders, and she didn't turn. "I'm tired. But I want to," she said, her voice quiet. She turned around and laid her head against his collarbone. He kissed at her temple, then her jaw. He inhaled her stale breath. "What's happening, Ben?" she said.

"I don't know."

When they were in her bed, he tried to remember what they used to do, but he understood that was ridiculous, like the years hadn't passed and he hadn't learned anything else. He said, "Don't get under the covers. Let me see you."

"I'm so…old."

"So am I."

It was different, he thought that they both could tell that, but being with Bonnie was something he knew. He made love to her and as he was about to climax, he pulled out of her and she whispered, "Don't worry about that…come back." Neither of them got up from the bed afterward. "I can actually smell the horses on you…or maybe I'm imagining it."

"Can I meet you at the library later?" His voice a whisper, he said, "I have to have you again. You said that pie needs to set."

Mid-morning, he left the Carlsbad at her place and began his walk for Isabella Street. He carried an oval-shaped, salmon-colored hatbox. Inside it, a sheet of wax paper covered the pie. He'd gone a block and a half when a bone-thin brown dog ran right up to him. Ben brought the hatbox over his head because it looked like the mutt might go for it. "Pepe?" he said. "Are you Bonnie's?" The dog's ears went up. It took mincing steps as it crossed snow-covered Eighth Street.

The streets were quiet, tire tracks worn through the snow on Washington, sidewalks packed firm by footsteps. He'd get to a casino at some point, in a way wasn't looking forward to it because he could never win at those games. He'd come back after the war to a city ignoring Volstead. Newport was full of working German and Irish families who weren't going to give up their beer. It wasn't hard to imagine that ignoring one law made the people free to disregard others.

When the big flood hit in '37, the rollers said it was

Jesus, washing away the sins of the city. The water went back and, right after that, more casinos surfaced. And some real nice places, he remembered Bonnie saying that the one time he'd surprised her at The Wheel. Growing up, he'd learned how to gamble, so he knew the slots were for suckers. When he'd gone away to war, he'd been the best poker player in his squad. After he came back home, there were so many sharks around…he couldn't kid himself about trying to make a living at it. He thought of his father playing cards with Drayton last night, the living room nearly gone of furniture.

He unlocked the Draytons' front door. In the doorway of the kitchen, Ben held up the hatbox for his father and Foster Drayton to see. They each had a newspaper section.

"Paper's three days old," Drayton said.

"I'll pick up a new one today," said Ben's father.

"Bonnie sent water pie. But it needs to rest."

He made his father's bed, pushed off his boots and went over to pick out a book. Agatha Christie, Edgar Rice Burroughs. He stretched out with *Brave New World*; the cover was in orange trim and had a penguin logo in one corner. He'd read it years earlier, maybe at a homeless men's shelter in Detroit. He turned pages, moved back and forth through the novel, settled at the start of chapter 10:

> The hands of all four thousand electric clocks in all the Bloomsbury Centre's four thousand rooms marked twenty-seven minutes past two. "This hive of industry," as the Director was fond of calling it, was in full buzz of work. Everyone was busy, everything in ordered motion…

He shut his eyes and waited for the sound of an old man trudging up the steps. The silence closed in around him.

When his father didn't appear, he went looking for him. Downstairs, his father and both Draytons were seated at the kitchen table. A soup pot sat on the stove, and the kitchen reeked of cabbage. Everyone held a fork, the pie plate seemed to have been passed around.

"Good?" Ben said.

"Little slippery. But I do believe she added some whiskey," his father said. "Wonderful woman."

"I gotta go. Look for a place. Want your key back?"

"Nope," Foster Drayton said.

The walk to the library would take an hour at least, and he'd been going for only a block when the sun broke through and brought a lemony light shining down on the street. Past Pompilio's, a handful of men had one guy circled, and they were pushing at him. "Blue ticket, blue!" Ben stepped into the street to get around it. An electric trolley car turtled up Washington, packed with passengers, a pasty face in every window. He crossed the L & N using the pedestrian path; on Fourth Street on the Cincinnati side, a trolley was approaching from behind, he could tell by the sound, the hum of electricity in the wires above him. Anyway, he was close enough now to walk the remaining blocks.

Old Main stood just past the corner of Sixth and Vine, and when Ben stopped at the entrance, he stared up at the three engraved faces on the façade: Shakespeare, Ben Franklin…the other he wasn't sure about. He stepped inside the remarkable, cavernous library. In order to find out the location of the reading rooms, he went up the wide staircase to the information desk. The walls were covered by alcoves of books and these alcoves went upward, floor after floor. Pages, male and female, ascended and descended spiral staircases. Prior to the Depression, the library had been an opera house. The towering ceilings were there for acoustics. The sounds in the library were of footsteps.

He went from one reading room to another, and he started to feel good about getting there first, but then he spotted Bonnie in a spacious leather chair in a room near the main entrance. Beyond her boots, the sunlight beaming through the window produced a stretched block of light on the floor. He figured that even if she noticed him, she'd ignore him, just for a little while. A sign on the wall read,

Rules for Visitors of the Library

1. It is positively forbidden to spit on the floor or on the heaters.
2. Readers must not put their feet on the furniture.
3. Visitors are not permitted to talk in the reading-rooms, except in communication with the attendants.
4. Readers must return all books or periodicals to the attendant from whom they were procured.

Ben accepted the book Bonnie held out for him, went over to take an empty chair. She returned to what she was reading, and what she'd given him was the book he'd seen at her apartment the night before: *A Pageant and Other Poems.* He started a poem, "O Resurrection."

My life is like a broken bowl,
A broken bowl that cannot hold
One drop of water for my soul
Or cordial in the searching cold

He felt she'd picked her chair so when he glanced at her, he would notice the sign with the rules. He turned the pages of the book, returned to "O Resurrection." That page was dog-eared—a poem Bonnie loved? She used to write poems. She was young then and so was he. If they'd stayed together, their children now would be the ages they were then. Their sons would be off to this war and their daughters would have factory jobs. But they didn't have children to worry about. He felt certain now they belonged together.

The sunlight reached his knees. When she stood over him, her eyebrows arched. He reached for his coat, and she walked directly for the entrance. Outside again, in one quick motion Bonnie pulled on her hat. She gave a sniff and said, "Hungry?"

"Hell yes."

"Here, gimme that book, before you do damage to yourself."

"You said it was overdue."

"I checked it out again. This is for you."

The Maltese Falcon. "Great," he said. He opened the book to the middle.

"They have a rare book collection in one of the ground-floor rooms. We could see that sometime if you wanted. My friend Kiley, she works at the information desk, she'd let us."

"Yeah, rare books… Why didn't you just give me this in there?"

"I wanted you to suffer a little bit. You know, from poetry." He decided to kiss her. When he pulled back, they squared themselves. He pointed his thumb at the façade.

"Who's that other guy up there?"

She pointed to one, then the next and said, "Franklin, Dante, Shakespeare."

"I didn't know Dante."

She smiled a smile that she couldn't seem to help. "Come on, by the time we get back, we'll have a huge appetite!"

"Hey, I think I saw Pepe. Brown mutt, like a paper bag,

kept running right up to me, not far from your place. I said his name and he turned and ran."

"Pepe's a black dog," she said. "With a strip of white down the middle of his nose."

Further down Vine loomed Fountain Square and its centerpiece, a bronze fountain forty feet high, a sculpture of a heroine with her arms open. In the warmer months, when the fountain was operating, water flowed from her hands. The provider of much-needed rains, he knew that much about it. They stood before the still fountain and he said, "*The Genius of Water*."

"It's *genus*," she said. "You're from here, you shouldn't make that mistake." He wanted to ask about the difference, but she took his arm. They walked south, block after block, along the glimmering sidewalks. Beyond the river, the hillsides of Kentucky looked to be covered in powdered sugar.

He said, "I ever tell you about the literacy test they gave some of the soldiers?" She didn't respond, and he said, "I saw a copy, some private from New Hampshire had pocketed it…"

"I think you said something."

"One of questions was 'Is irony connected with blast furnaces?'"

"'Is a stone soft?' That was one, too, right?"

"We ought to try to find it. Old Main'll have it, won't they?" She shrugged, and he said, "Yeah, *The Maltese Falcon*, that'll be all right. I saw the picture a couple of years ago, in New York."

"I keep expecting to see Peter Lorre walking down Washington Avenue, looking for the right casino," she said. "Max, the barkeep at Pompilio's, says he saw Jimmy Durante at The Lookout Club. I guess you catch sight of a lot of famous people in New York."

"The pictures are the only place I look for them," he said. It felt like he had a lot of questions for her. When did they start using girls at the desks, as pages in Old Main? Why didn't she want to do something other than work in a restaurant? What kind of things did she write these days? Was it better that they hadn't spent the last twenty-plus years on the road together? In Newport, they crossed Second, then Third.

Inside the apartment, on the kitchen table, sat the box of ration books he'd seen the night before; next to it, the photo of Stymie. Still in his coat, Ben dropped onto the couch. "I need a job," he said.

"I have peanut butter and I have Spam," she said. "Or you can have a peanut butter *and* Spam."

"Peanut butter, please."

"Me, too."

The door to the bedroom was open, and he could see the bed was made, the tan covers smoothed out. He pictured her making the bed and he knew that a couple of hours ago he'd made her happy. "You toasting the bread?"

She closed the oven door. "Just for a minute. You'll see. Get something at one of the casinos. Stay away from the Cleveland ones, you go there, you're gone…"

"I got a little money…maybe I'll just read in the library every day until that runs out."

"They'll tear it down after the war. Bond issue last month. Too hard to keep the place up apparently. It's impractical…come here," she said as she set the plates on the table, then the bottles of beer. She moved the box of paper and the photo to the counter by the sink. She hadn't sliced the sandwiches into halves, and she shrugged again after sitting down with him. "I'm not writing a book or anything. Those ration books are from last year. A friend of mine, a guy I was dating actually, just for a little while, he was into collections for one of the clubs. He wound up with a bunch of these, but they expired before he could make a deal on them. He wasn't real clear about it. He kept saying how worthless they were. I told him I'd take 'em. I like to write. I liked him, he had really big, powerful hands. He was so in love with me he didn't know what to do with himself. But sure, yeah, it's kind of this game where I write a story, on the blank sides of the stamp pages. The story has to fit in the book, see. Usually, it's just stuff I see and what I hear."

"You should write a whole book."

"I don't want to write a book. My friend, Kiley, she wants to write a novel. She said she has most of it planned out. What I like to do is to write out something and then a little while later, like a month or even a year, go back and look at it. I was considering your photo there and thinking about that. All the smiling people, what are they all going to do next…everybody's going to go out and celebrate tonight. Drinks will be hoisted, people will be laughing, and they'll wake up the next day feeling awful, like fools, like they'd gotten excited over something silly. They know a war is on. This is not a one-for-all country." She scratched at a charred piece of crust.

"You can't win a war with a slogan like that. If you let me live with you, I'll pay half the rent," he said. "I'll pay all the rent if you want."

"How's the sandwich?"

"Okay."

"You'd wake up with me one morning and think, 'This is not all that great.' You'll look over and see that I'm ugly or that I'm getting old. I don't need to be evaluated."

"Maybe you'd be the one who woke up and think that when you look at me."

"Give it a week. Okay? Go back to your father, find a job. I'll be here. I promise."

"I'd like to carry those empties to work for you this afternoon."

"All right."

"And I'd like to see the rare books." He decided to finish his sandwich.

She said, "I toast the bread in the winter. In the summer, I don't do that for peanut butter."

"You didn't toast the bread for the cucumber…"

"Eleanor Roosevelt doesn't."

"How about we go lie down for a little while? I know," he said. "All these questions."

"Questions? I was going to say I feel like doing that, too."

* * *

That afternoon, they went together from her place to Pompilio's. She held open the entrance door to the restaurant because he was carrying her empties. "Just take those over to the bar, set 'em on the counter. See ya, Ben." She aimed for the swinging doors of the kitchen. On the sidewalk again, he paused at the window he'd been looking out from the night before. He thought maybe she would step back out into the dining room to see if he was still there. She didn't. He made his way to Isabella Street and let himself into the Draytons' house, found everyone seated around the kitchen table. Boiled potatoes and green beans. He didn't object when Barb put a plate in front of him. He said, "I might need to stay here for a week. I'm glad to pay."

Drayton spoke, said, "He can have our room. We'll sleep under the stars."

"Quiet," she said. "We have a fold-out cot up there…in

the attic."

She explained that the light for the attic was inside the door at the top of the third floor. The fold-out cot could be behind a rail of dresses covered in clear plastic. This was where Ben found it. Army-issue, wooden legs, olive-green canvas. A shiver ran through him because he realized it was his own cot…wasn't it? That cot had been a primary keepsake of the war, but then he remembered he'd taken it with him when he'd gone barnstorming. It got stolen…right, that was right. In Omaha.

He unfolded the cot next to the bureau in his father's room. Tested it, laid himself out flat, then heard footsteps, someone softly tapping on the partially opened door. Barb, with a pillow and a blanket. "Need any sheets?" she said.

"There are Quonset huts at Newport Catholic."

"New schoolrooms," she said. "Cheaper for the diocese. He's so glad you're here," she said. "Your father."

That night, Ben dozed and finally turned wide awake in what seemed to be the middle of the night. At dawn, he considered the saffron light against the window. He said, "You up?"

From the bed, his father said, "I'm awake."

"Bonnie says 'hi,' Pop."

"Hi to Bonnie."

Ben skipped breakfast, shaved and brushed his hair, and before eight a.m. was on his way down to Third Street. He went to the alley to knock on the side door of The Merchants Club. He remained in the alley for a minute, then tried across the street, Underhill's Fine Dining. Not open. Kentucky Grill, not looking. However, the doorman at the Five-Three said The Blue Derby might be short a man.

The Blue Derby hired him. He'd work the chalk during the afternoons, and if he could handle that there might be more. He started the next day, met the bookmaker in his office right at noon and was handed sheets of entries for the races at New Orleans Fair Grounds, Cranwood, Hialeah, Oaklawn. The horse-betting parlor had a wall covered with blackboards; four across, three down. Each read:

Track:		Race:
Horse	Jockey	Odds
1-		
2-		
3-		
4-		
5-		
6-		
7-		
8-		
9-		
10-		
11-		
12-		
Field-		

His job was to keep the boards filled with horse names and updated odds; he'd finish one set of sheets, be handed a few more. He printed words in caps, and he had to stand on a step ladder to get to the boards in the top row. The club's bookmaker, a slender, balding man named Denny, came out from his office to check on things, directed Ben to change the odds on certain horses, invariably lowering them, or sometimes he'd take the chalk from Ben and do it himself. He was self-assured and clearly obsessed with numbers. Ben marked the board until the last races were run at the eastern tracks, and then a guy everybody called Andy Eggs took over.

The races out in Arizona and California were only beginning. The job paid a buck ten an hour and after Ben was done for the evening, Denny would stand him the dinner special and as many draft beers as he wanted. Ben ate and drank at the restaurant bar and then it was back to Isabella. It seemed like an easy enough routine to fall into. He passed Pompilio's each night on his way home, lingered in front of the big window that looked out to the street.

On a Friday evening, he stayed for a few beers at The Blue Derby. While still a half block away from the Draytons', he could see someone sitting on the stoop. Bonnie, in her Mercury hat, her arms folded atop her knees. "You lost?" he said.

Shadows surrounded her face. "Early night. All the lights were off inside the house, and I didn't want to knock on the door. You left the book I checked out for you." But she wasn't holding any book.

He started up the steps and she tilted to make room. "Come on in," he said, after unlocking the bolt. When she was close enough, she reached for his arm.

"Don't turn on the lights," she said. Inside, he closed the door. "I saw you outside the restaurant last night. We were busy." She touched his face, her fingers still in the gloves. "Has it been a week? This morning, that's the first thing I thought of."

"Whether it's been a week?"

"Not that," she said, in a whisper. "Where?"

"Your apartment?"

"What can they hear? Where are they?"

"Upstairs."

"Kiss me." Then she said, "Right now."

They stayed by the door; she unbuttoned her coat and then the front of his coat. He lay down on the floor and she spread her knees on either side of him. He listened for the boards to begin creaking and then he didn't worry about it. He felt her and that's what he knew. He could taste the aroma of her on his tongue. When she stopped, he caught the light from the stairs. "Too late," he said, in a whisper.

Foster Drayton in the living room doorway. He wore thin pajamas and his feet seemed as large as boat oars. "Who is that?"

"It's Ben. You know Bonnie, right?" Drayton brought up his hand. Bonnie didn't return the wave, and Drayton went for the kitchen. "Don't get up," Ben said. "Lemme walk you home."

She raised her hem, began to neaten the dress. Ben wiped his stomach with the sleeve of his shirt. He tended to his buttons.

Coat on, he went to the kitchen doorway. By the sink, Drayton drank from a glass of water. Ben said, "I'm gonna walk her home. Sorry about that."

"That Bonnie Dennert?"

"Yes."

"I told Barb that's what it sounded like. But she wanted me to check."

"I'll probably be moving out."

After he swallowed, he said, "Well, it's been good having you here."

4.

Bonnie waited outside, at the bottom of the steps. In silence, they traveled a block and then he said, "So far, I like my job at the Blue Derby..."

"Truly humiliated. What about your things?"

"I'll get 'em." The light inside Pompilio's reached beyond

the curb. They walked through the glow of that, and he said, "I've hardly thought about you at all."

"He'll think I'm a used-up whore," she said.

"If his wife had found us…even then. Everybody knows how I feel about you."

That night, they slept together. He awakened in the middle of the night. More than anything, he wanted a beer. He spotted the cigar box on top of the icebox. He knew that he shouldn't, but he brought it down. The ration books were postcard-shaped, with thin cardboard covers and pages of stamps as delicate as newsprint. *Reginald Van Sleet,* that was a name written in cursive on a few. On another, *Terri-Ann Van Sleet.* The pages of stamps had images of tanks, fighter planes, aircraft carriers. The books were full of stamps; on the inside back cover of one book, *apt 206a* written in lipstick. The back cover of each had a list of instructions.

> This book is valuable. Do not lose it.
> Each stamp authorizes you to purchase rationed goods…

He skipped to the end.

> …give your whole support to rationing and thereby conserve our vital goods. Be guided by the rule:
> "If you don't need it, DON'T BUY IT."

Inside one book, he found Bonnie's handwriting, the small letters, on the backs of the stamp pages.

4:15

One thing I looked forward to after I came home from the war was having a bottle of beer at the Cascade Club.

The men there had a ritual of throwing beer bottles at the Southern Railroad cars heading west for Iowa City. They'd hear the train coming and hurry to finish their beers. Then they'd all run around back. Whoever had a beer bottle would chuck it at passing rail cars. Then we'd watch the train as it rumbled for the horizon. When I came home from the war, the first thing I told my dad was that I wanted to go down to the Cascade and I wanted him to come with me. He didn't want to. So, I went down there by myself, in my uniform, because I liked that uniform. There were only a couple of people at the club and nobody I knew. The barkeep noticed my uniform, stood me a bottle of beer. When I heard the train coming, all he was doing was eating a pickled egg and turning the pages of a magazine. I carried my bottle around to the back, and I let a few cars pass. Then I fired it and watched it smash. It felt like I'd waited my whole life to do that. When I got back to the little house on Carmel Street, I had dinner with my folks. My mother asked me how long I was going to stay in town. I don't know, I said. My mother had made cornbread and salt pork. My father didn't like a lot of talk at the table when we were eating. She said, So, what's Europe like?

He finished half of the beer he'd opened, stuck the bottle on the top shelf of the near-empty icebox. In bed, he felt her stir; she went to the bathroom, then out to the kitchen. He decided to get up, took a place on the couch that would allow him to see what she was making. He said, "Come over here." He patted a cushion, the fabric like burlap. When she was at his side, he said, "I read one of the things you wrote."

"I don't know what happened to me last night."

"I feel the same…am I here? Am I going to wind up with

Bonnie, after all this time? Dreams can be…"

She swallowed and said, "You mean one of my stories? Which one?"

"About somebody who threw a beer bottle at a train."

Her eyes were huge and shining. "So, tell me what I missed out on. For these past twenty years or so."

He knew that she wanted him to say only what was true. "Poverty. I've lived in tack rooms. I've been so hungry I've eaten handfuls of horse oats. You boil 'em. They're still bad but you can get 'em down. The trainer I was working for ran off without paying the help, so I spent one February at a homeless men's bureau in Detroit, Michigan. Read everything…played checkers…caught pneumonia. A couple of the boys talked about going to South Dakota to mine for gold. One day I woke up and they were gone…You stayed with me, you would've watched me lose money betting. In '24, I got a check for the military compensation law in Congress or whatever, more than six hundred bucks. Not sure whatever happened to it…I would've kept telling you everything was fine. I'd have said, 'Bonnie, I love you. Let's go to bed.'" He smiled in the direction of the kitchen sink. "It's been different since I've been in New York…"

"The one you read is a story my ex-husband told me. Something that happened to a friend of his. I added and subtracted some details."

"Where is Kenny anyway?"

"Gone, went to work in Indiana, wanted to be a union man. He had his moments when he was here. But not many of 'em. Roulette… Maybe he's doing okay these days. Maybe I don't have a good effect on my men."

"Maybe you're drawn to a certain type."

"Yeah. Poor." She kissed his cheek. She whispered in his ear, "Don't push for more than this, okay?" She leaned back.

"Anyway, the guy we need to apologize to is old Drayton."

"Probably has other things on his mind. I'll have coffee with you, then I'll get going. Be back in a couple of hours. Have to go to work. Simpler if we don't apologize. Can I ask you somethin'? 'Member you came to my parents' place on Second in the green dress? When we talked about getting married? How come you decided that day was the one, do you recall at all?"

"I remember the day, yes."

"Don't have to talk about it."

"No, I know. Yes, I remember. I waited for you to come over to my house, see? But then I kept waiting. It was summer. One evening, after work, I walked down to the river, the L & N, and crossed over. I didn't want to have dinner with my folks. I returned to the Kentucky side. I told myself to keep going back and forth, over the bridge, because I wanted to know what to do about you. I'd look out to the water, for a sign, I guess. That old river didn't care about you and me, but I liked to think...something was still possible. I figured then that whatever happened between us, it would pass, it wouldn't matter, not much. I knew what the river was saying was right. That's when I knew it was time."

"I should've done it myself."

"No."

"No?"

"It was better I did. If you had, I probably would have said yes."

"Don't say that."

"You asked, Ben. I probably would've said yes just to get everyone off my back. It turned out the way it should've," she said. "I'm not bitter."

"You're the only one," he said.

"Are you bitter, Ben?"

"I didn't mean bitter. I meant you're the only one. No matter what happens."

***

He left to get his things, and when he returned with his suitcase, she served him a bowl of black-eyed peas. He said he could unpack later, and she said she might do it for him before leaving for her shift. He worked his job, took his dinner and two beers at the bar. At Bonnie's apartment he reached his hand to the sill for the key. She'd unpacked his case, hung his suit in the closet. He didn't lay his eyes on her until he awakened, which was before sunup. She slept on her side, facing him. He wanted to kiss her, wake her that way, and make love to her, and go back to sleep himself. He eased himself out of the bed. He couldn't find the box of ration books anywhere. On the middle of the kitchen table was *The Maltese Falcon.* He stretched out on the couch and opened the book to chapter 1.

> Samuel Spade's jaw was long and bony, his chin a jutting v under the more flexible v of his mouth. His nostrils curved back to make another, smaller v. His yellow-grey eyes were horizontal. The v *motif* was picked up again by thickish brows rising outward from twin creases above a hooked nose, and his pale brown hair grew down—from high flat temples—in a point on his forehead. He looked rather pleasantly like a blond satan.
>
> He said to Effie Perine: "Yes, sweetheart?"

5.

Ben and Bonnie bought a Christmas tree from a Negro with a flatbed truck in James Alley. They liked the tree, and the next day Ben wanted to buy one for the Draytons but the Negro wasn't around. In Federle's Hardware Store, Ben spotted a pine bookcase for Bonnie. He rode with the bookcase in the back of a pickup driven by one of Federle's sons. He positioned it by their Christmas tree. He felt her kiss his cheek after she climbed into bed. He could smell whiskey on her lips, knew she was happy with the gift.

Pompilio's was closing early on Christmas Eve, but they both still had to work. Ben found himself at The Blue Derby just before noon. He spotted Denny at the bar, an opened newspaper on the counter. He motioned for Ben. "I'll find something else for you."

HORSE RACING SUSPENDED, EFFECTIVE JANUARY 3

> Washington DC—At the request of James F. Byrnes, the director of War Mobilization and Reconversion, horse racing in the United States will be suspended as of January 3, 1945. Byrnes released a statement yesterday, here is the wording of that statement:
>
> "The operation of race tracks not only requires the employment of manpower needed for more essential operation, but also manpower, railroad transportation, as well as tires and gasoline in the movement of patrons to and from the track, and in the movement of the horses and their attendants.
>
> "The existing war situation demands the utmost effort that the people of the United States can give to the support of its armed forces in the production of needed war materials. The operation of race tracks is

> not conducive to this all-out effort. Therefore, with the approval of the President, I urge that the management of these race tracks take immediate measures to bring the present race meetings to a close by January 3, 1945, and to refrain from resuming races at all tracks until war conditions permit."
>
> No other sports were mentioned in the announcement and Byrnes' office did not offer explanations other than what is included in its statement.

"Jacobs," Ben said. "What he said."

"Hell, you told me that's why you were in town."

"I'm from here. Can I hang on to this?"

"Yeah, all right. Let's get to the boards, anyway. We might be busy. You comin' in tomorrow? You guys are switching, right? Andy Eggs is doing the early tracks, Tropical and the Fair Grounds. Only western track going is Sportsman's out in Arizona."

"We'll still get horseplayers, Christmas or not." He moved away from the bar, then stopped in place and read the article again.

He worked the boards all afternoon, skipping the special. At the apartment, Bonnie had already set out their dinner: spaghetti and a corked jug of red wine. They hugged, she placed her hands on his shoulders and looked into his eyes. "I heard, one of the customers," she said.

"Come on, I'm dying." When they were sitting across from one another, she held up her glass and he held up his.

"Christmas, darling. So, how did you hear about it?"

"Denny. The article. I knew…been thinking though. What if it's like with booze and they're gonna take it away for good? Like Prohibition. They decide it's in the way? They can do whatever they want. And make up any reason they like."

"I don't disagree."

"Why horse racing? Why not other…that article I read, it bothered me. We have no say, Bonnie…" He started to eat his food. "I'm beginning to think being in love with you is the only freedom I have."

"Oh, god," she said, her voice quiet.

"What?"

"The news or whatever has nothing to do with you and me."

"Why wouldn't it? You and me can move to Canada or Mexico. You don't think they can't take anything away for good?"

"They can…during Prohibition, I saw a cartoon in some paper where they had four Germans hanging from a tree limb. Their names were Pabst, Schlitz…they take away what they want and then make up a reason why. It looks terrible, these people going to the races and yelling their lungs out or whatever. A world war going on…they worry about how something appears. Politicians. 'Unsinn!' Like my old gran used to say, 'Nonsense'."

"They locked up all these Japanese people at Tanforan… I have dreams about German POWs living in stalls at Jamaica. I bring them feed and water…and then I shoot them."

She said, "It's all right. Just a dream."

"The guys from the Manpower Commission looked at us like they were sucking on a shit lollipop." He let go of his fork while it was still in his spaghetti. She said his name and then, a moment later, said it again. "I'm all right. I mean what I say when I say how I feel about you."

"I know."

"Prohibition didn't last. They'll open the tracks again."

She raised her glass of wine, took a sip. After that, she picked up her fork. He said, "We'll win the war, everything will go back...I'm...I don't know. I guess I'm upset, I want you to be with me. No matter what. We win the war, I'll work at The Blue Derby. It's not mobbed up, it's too small-time for that. I'll live here with you."

"It's Christmas time for me, too. You shouldn't try to press..."

"You feel something for me, Bonnie. I feel you when you're under me. You came over last week to..."

"I kept thinking...one day he'll be gone again. But he's here right now. And I know he wants me. Tell me all that isn't true."

"I want to stay here with you, no matter what happens."

"You won't say that when they bring racing back. I see you better than you see yourself."

"Maybe we'll lose the war."

"Great, you and I can be POWs together."

"I shouldn't have brought up anything."

"That's what I'm trying to tell you."

"If I stay, I won't feel trapped in this town, all right?" he said. "It's a free-wheelin' casino town. I'm in love with you. You have to believe me."

"Okay. I like feeling like I once did. But I can't put everything on that."

They ate their spaghetti in the quiet for minute, and he wished the radio was playing anyway. He drank red wine and he was wary of it. The last time he'd had it was when he showed up at her restaurant with his photo of Stymie. He'd proposed to her, of all things. He'd just done it again. "I've meant everything I've said to you," he said.

"I'm going to read a book now."

"Sit with me for another minute, will ya?" He said,

"Un—. How do you say it?"

"Work the 'h.' Un-shin. Back of the throat."

"I learned a little German in the war. Commands... They were really good, ruthless soldiers...I don't know the guys we're fighting now, but I want 'em dead. Scrubbed off the earth."

She sat with her hands in her lap. "Me, too."

"It'll be over soon. Army's shot."

"I'll turn on some Christmas music." When she walked by, she didn't let a hand fall to his shoulder. She closed the door to the bedroom behind her. What he wound up thinking about was a time right near the end of the war. His battalion used German POWs for sweeping houses in abandoned villages at the French border. German soldiers sometimes booby-trapped doorways of evacuated houses with grenades and mines. The Americans would send in a POW first and the prisoner would get a sick-looking expression on his face, but then he'd shake it off, look like none of this could possibly matter to him. He'd do what he'd been commanded to do. There'd be an explosion, windows were blown out, furry-looking smoke pouring from a doorway. Nächste! The American soldiers knew how to say *Next!*

* * *

He carried the two plates to the sink counter. They might be hungry in a while. By one end of the couch, he noticed the box of ration books and on top of that was the photo of Stymie he'd brought from New York. He placed the photo on the table. Right now, the colt was getting some rest at a farm in Virginia. What would they do with him and all the other racehorses if racing never came back? Slaughterhouse, he guessed. Even Stymie? He thought that if he looked at the photo long enough, he'd feel better. He tried to think of how it had felt to be at Jamaica the afternoon of that race. Victory. Not a care otherwise.

From the bedroom he heard music, and he wanted to tell her again that he loved her. They'd done all the arguing they needed to for tonight. Ben felt now he would be in Newport until the end of this war. Ironic. The Allies were going to win. He wanted to live with Bonnie until that happened. After it happened, they would see where things were. If only she could be with him when the stands at Jamaica rocked as Stymie came barreling down the stretch…maybe she would see something in him, the way he could still feel about things. If he felt like it, he could wave his arms in the air and yell at the top of his lungs. He could, but he wouldn't have to. She alone would be able to understand what it all meant.

In the bedroom, she'd undressed down to her slip. While sitting up in bed, she had her arms crossed, held a glass of wine against her shoulder.

She said, "Remember, we said we'd walk with your dad to St. Stephen's tomorrow."

"Ten a.m.," he said. "I have to work after that. Just for a little while. What are you gonna do while I'm at work? Write a story?"

"What racetrack would run on Christmas day?"

"Gamblers need a church, too. What're we listening to?"

"Christmas concert from Pittsburgh. I brushed that suit of yours before I went to work today."

"I wore it at my mother's gravesite. I went by myself. When I stood at her grave… My father notified me with a telegram, something like, '*Your mother's dead. See ya.*' I know that words cost…anyway, I wore that suit I have to her grave. I think I still had it on when I went to see you…me in a suit. Do you remember it? Not that you should. Gimme a drink of that wine." He leaned in her direction.

She said, "I'm glad neither of us are alone tonight."

"Yeah."

"I like to listen to FDR when I'm feeling wavy about things. He talks about being strong, I crave that. It feels like he's talking to me, not some girl who's just pushing plates at a restaurant. I'm worried about him now. I know he's sick. What are we ever gonna do if we lose him?"

"I listen to him in Jamaica. I sit at the little table in the little music box I'm renting."

"He's not on tonight."

He stared at his thighs. "I bought that suit for the World's Fair, actually. Took the train up to Flushing Meadows. Saw the Trylon and Perisphere. Russian Pavilion, Hall of Electrical Living. Practically nobody around. The whole thing was built on an old ash heap. They lost a ton of money on it. Then the war started. World's Fair was abandoned, torn down. The story of the goddamned universe."

"Go to the kitchen and get some more wine for us. Maybe we'll both get lucky in a little while. Despite everything."

"Okay, sure."

"We're not going to solve anything else."

He felt that he knew what she meant. "I'll take my time, you have my word..."

6.

In the morning, while Bonnie made coffee, she reached into a cupboard, extracted a pint of whiskey and splashed some into her mug. He thought she might do the same with his, a Christmas special. She rescrewed the cap. Then, they dressed in the silence of the bedroom. He had the one suit, but it would feel better if he wore the clothes he did to the track. Those were also clean, Bonnie had seen to that. Ben pulled on a long-sleeved flannel shirt, wool trousers, boots, and his winter jacket. Bonnie wore an ankle-length black dress with red and white roses in the pattern. She offered him a shiny, parakeet-colored necktie, something she'd bought for her husband, but he'd never worn it, and because she offered he accepted. He let her tie it, too.

The sky held white with dashes of blue. Ben and Bonnie had an icy wind in their faces as they headed up Eighth Street. A block away from the Draytons' place, he put his arm around her shoulders and she didn't resist, kept her hands in the pockets of her coat. She stayed at the bottom of the steps while he walked up and knocked on the door. There stood his father, dressed for Mass, his short-brim hat in one hand.

"Miss Bonnie," his father said, as he turned and locked the door. Ben let him walk down the steps first. Bonnie held both hands in front of her and Ben's father took them.

"Merry Christmas, Mr. Held," she said.

"Merry Christmas, lovely," he said. "Shall we go?"

Bonnie and his father walked together up the sidewalk with their arms linked. Ben remained a few steps behind. He knew his father would feel better having a younger woman on his arm and Bonnie wouldn't mind at all making an old man feel that way. They turned onto Ninth Street; their arms came undone, but Bonnie and his father stayed side by side. Ben couldn't help but think they both were giving it to him. He was the one who left town. He came in from New York and couldn't keep up now. After a couple more blocks, Bonnie turned profile, said, "You still back there?"

"Keep going," he said to them.

Above the rooftops of the houses along Ninth Street

stood the cross from St. Stephen's. Dozens of Catholics in pearl-gray coats and hats were heading in the direction of the church. The church's façade was made of sand-painted bricks, and at the entrance a huge evergreen wreath hung above the mahogany doors. Bonnie and Ben followed his father into the vestibule and the bells began to chime. The Helds and Bonnie took a pew near the back, and they slid over to the middle to allow in others. She stacked the winter coats between herself and Ben. There were Christmas hymns; "O Holy Night," "Rejoice." When the congregation stood, it made a rustling sound that echoed throughout the church. The ceilings had dark mahogany beams and trusses; the stain-glassed windows held images of Mary and Jesus. Scarlet, shamrock, gold. Radiant colors in the glass. He thought of the tall windows at Grand Central, how they beamed in bright light in the afternoon.

The priest, in silver and white robes, stepped out from behind the altar and motioned with his hands for everyone to sit. He touched at his Biretta hat, and he began his sermon with, "Let us pray for victory." From the corner of his eye, Ben could see Bonnie and his father had bowed their heads.

The bright colors of the stained-glass windows brought a unique glow to the inside of the church. He wished for faith, knew it was impossible. He surmised his father didn't believe in God, though his father was the type of man who liked to keep open his options. Bonnie had said she wouldn't mind going to church on Christmas Day, not one bit. Maybe beneath her iron will, she hoped for the kind of miracle that all people did, that there was something wondrous waiting for them beyond all they had to keep enduring.

Near the end of Mass, the priest stood behind at the altar and said, "Pray for our men, every day…go in peace to love and serve the Lord." "Merry Christmas, Merry Christmas," the parishoners said to one another.

Outside, after the three of them reached the bottom of the church steps, his father extended his hand to shake with Ben and said, "I wish this goddamn war was over."

"I do, too."

The sidewalk was not wide enough for the three of them. Ben wound up next to his father and Bonnie went on a couple of strides ahead. The sidewalks were busy, but for a few blocks, all Ben could hear was the clock-clock of her shoes. His father elbowed him and said, "You ought to see what Barb Drayton has for us. A whole chicken in the oven. She made dressing for her family; their daughter and her husband picked them up this morning. She left us a lot." His father leaned closer, said, "Get up there."

Ben obeyed. He took long, quick steps, caught up to her in a matter of seconds. "Hey," he said.

"Hi, Ben."

"Nice church," he said. "Made me think of Grand Central. They got a guy who runs a newsstand there…what he does is guess what kind of magazine you're interested in. He'll say, 'You look like a man who likes a good western story.'"

"Then he tries to sell you a western magazine no one else wants."

"Sure. When's the last time you were on a train, Bon?"

"With Kenny, went down to Nashville."

"Hey, I remembered another one of those questions they had on the army test…it was 'Do ships sail on railyards?'"

"I bet somebody answered wrong, anyway."

He nudged her. "You feel like doing this today?"

"Yeah," she said. "Actually, yeah. It'll be fine."

* * *

They had the Draytons' house to themselves. Ben sat at one end of the table while his father stood at the kitchen counter and carved the chicken. Bonnie brought out bottles of beer and then the butter dish. He watched her carrying the bottles and understood that if she could get away with it, she might drink twenty-four hours a day. They sat at the table. His father said, "How does he like living in town again?"

"I'm sitting right here," Ben said.

"You're gonna hem and haw."

Bonnie said, "He's got a job. He sleeps at night."

"Good!" his father said. "They treat you all right at Pompilio's?"

"They do."

Ben said, "What did you pray for today?"

His father said, "That Barb hadn't overcooked this chicken."

"She didn't," Bonnie said. "It's good."

Ben said, "How are Barb and...Foster?" She cut her eyes in his direction.

Ben's father nodded while chewing. "Foster, he likes those casinos. So she keeps track of our ration books. He and I play poker, rummy, most every day. I'm the house now, as far as he's concerned. Good ol' boy. Later on, I thought we'd have whiskey sours and apple pie."

Ben laid down his fork, set it carefully on the edge of his plate. He folded his hands. He didn't speak until they were both looking at him. "I know y'all think I don't give a holy hell about what goes on here. Until I have nowhere else to go." The green beans on his plate looked oily. "I think about this place every day. This town...I have dreams about the flood, and I wasn't even here when it happened. By the time I got here, the waters had mostly gone back." His eyes were on his father when he said, "Bonnie, how did you find out that your mother had died?"

"I was at her side at the hospital," she said.

Ben swallowed, said, "I'm sorry, this isn't me, I don't talk like this." No one was eating now.

His father said, "Say what you're..."

"I got a telegram informing me my mother had died," he said. "It was, I think, a total of six words. I was holding a pitchfork when Hirsch Jacobs brought me the telegram. She'd already been gone a week. I came back here, visited her grave. I've never said anything about it. But I've thought about it. I've always wondered if what the telegram was really saying was 'In case you give a damn, your mother has died.'"

"I didn't want to tell you at all," his father said.

"What?"

"I thought about not telling you. We had her laid out for a couple of days. And then we buried her."

In a minute, Ben said, "I'm sorry, this isn't Christmas talk."

"Ben bought me a bookcase," Bonnie said. "For Christmas." Neither Ben nor his father spoke. She said, "Ben, we all feel useless, that's not unusual."

Ben said, "I'm gonna step outside for a minute, okay?" He forgot to take his coat. He stood on the steps, trained his eyes to the roofline of row houses down the street. The main thing was for him not to be angry about things he couldn't do anything about. He imagined that if he'd stayed, the three of them would be having Christmas together, though it would be in an apartment he and Bonnie shared...and had lived in for many years. His mother would still be gone. He thought of standing at her grave in his ridiculous suit. He tried to imagine what her last thoughts of him had been. He wondered if he'd think of her in the final moments of his own life, and if he did he hoped it would be an image of her when she was young and he was nothing but a boy and they were living down in the shotgun shack by the river.

He tossed his cigarette towards the sidewalk and went back inside. "Here he is," Bonnie said. "Tell him what you told me, Mr. Held."

His father spoke as Ben took his chair. "Last Christmas, I went with Barb and Foster to their daughter's place. I put up with that lot...I fell asleep while everybody was sitting around the living room and yapping. At one point, I heard the son-in-law saying, 'He's not moving, is he dead?' I felt like they were all worried... Without opening my eyes, I said, 'I'm here, goddamnit.' They kinda laughed, I guess. Of course, it was after dinner, and they were all as drunk as chimps by then."

Ben had his fork going. "The Draytons like having you around."

"Foster needs somebody to play cards with. Never wins. I don't owe rent again until December, 1952."

"What about you?" Ben said to Bonnie.

"What about me?"

"Christmas...last year?"

"Oh, I don't know. Listening to the radio. I took a walk down to the river. Remember when it froze over, Mr. Held? They were driving horses and buggies over it."

"That's been a few years," Ben's father said.

"Mmm," she said. "Well, what I know is one winter day I walked right across that river. It doesn't seem that long ago... Last year, I was...by myself, just listening to the radio." She reached for her bottle. "Here's to Christmas with the Helds."

"Here, here."

* * *

When it was time for Ben and Bonnie to go, his father accompanied them to the door, and she kissed his father on the cheek. Ben walked her to the apartment they were sharing, and then at work he went to the bar and asked for coffee and waved off the barkeep when he brought over a bottle of whiskey. The horse-betting area had a handful of players while the casino rooms were wall to wall. Folks clamoring to play slots, table games. On the way home, the streetlights lit the sidewalks for him. Between Third and Fourth, a fight broke out, a couple of young guys who'd stepped outside without their jackets. One of them fell to the street and then other men came running in his direction, helping him to his knees.

At the apartment, Bonnie sat up in bed, in her slip, reading. He undressed down to his undershirt, shorts, and socks. He sat with his head bowed. In the corner of his eye, he noticed she'd placed the book facedown on her stomach. "Tell me you're not praying," she said.

"Nope."

"I put your present on the kitchen table."

"You did?" He stepped right out to see about it. At first, he thought she'd bought a frame for the Stymie photo; he saw the framed photo was of Rushaway, who'd taken the 1936 Latonia Derby. Ben wondered about the tiny-as-dots faces in the grandstand. He carried it into the bedroom. "Are you in here?"

"Un-uh."

He brought the photo closer to his face. "In '36, let's see, I was in Michigan for the summer, at Detroit."

"I wanted to get you one of the Latonia Derby we went to way back. I had people looking for it, this is the closest we could get."

"It's great. Rushaway was underrated."

"Come over here, sit by me," she said. "I want you to stay with me through the first of the year. Nobody will be renting out apartments this week. I don't want you to move out during the holidays. We are going too fast, trying to make up…I'm not going back with you, okay?"

"Don't say anything until we know for sure."

"After the first of the year, okay?"

The light in the room was all right for reading but he couldn't recognize anyone in the stands. "I think Be Frank won it the year we went together. What a name…Maybe you'll change your mind."

"Maybe."

"Suppose it's the middle of January in the middle of the night and I knock on your door?"

"It's not a question of whether I'll answer. It's a question of what you'll expect."

"Suppose you appear at the door to my place in New York? Can I give you a kiss?" When she didn't say anything to that, he leaned in and kissed her.

"Come to bed. Bring your book."

"I finished reading it a few days ago. I know how it goes. Hell, I'd already read it, didn't want to be rude." Still, he laid up in bed with her and opened the book. He fanned pages, found a section.

> For half an hour after Joel Cairo had gone, Spade sat alone, still and frowning, at his desk. Then he said aloud in the tone of someone dismissing a problem, "Well, they're paying for it," and took a bottle of Manhattan cocktail and a paper drinking-cup from a desk-drawer. He filled the cup two-thirds full, drank, returned the bottle to the drawer, tossed the cup into

the wastebasket, put on his hat and overcoat, turned off the lights, and went down to the night-lit street.

7.

She helped him find a furnished one-bedroom a block from The Blue Derby. The morning he moved out, it took him a few minutes to get everything into his suitcase, and without her coat she walked with him to the corner of Seventh and Indiana Alley. It was too cold for her to go any further and she jogged back with her arms swinging at her sides. The day he moved into his new flat, horse racing was officially suspended all across America. Card tables took over the racing parlor, and he was reassigned to the roulette wheel. He worked the felt, handled payouts, sticked away the losing bets. His shift started at six every evening; they fed him before that and stood him mugs of draft beer when the shift was done. He'd get back to his apartment before five in the morning. He'd stay up until dawn and sleep until mid-afternoon. The days passed, and when he went to see his father he'd walk past Pompilio's. Twice during January, he spotted Bonnie on the street. Once, she called to him from across York and they waved to one another. The other time, they were both on Washington, heading in the same direction; he spotted her a half-block ahead. Then it was as if she'd just disappeared. He followed her for a couple of blocks. Something told him to bide his time.

When Bonnie wanted him back, he'd agree to it. He might grumble about this and that, but just for a few days, and then they would be happy together. He tried to appreciate Bonnie's position and felt he could best do this by imagining her showing up in the track kitchen at Jamaica, unannounced and then proclaiming she was in love with him on the walk back to his flat. Of course, what he'd done hadn't been exactly that. If she'd surfaced at Jamaica, just out of nowhere, and had told him she knew now they belonged together, he'd have listened. Of course, she could stay with him in his flat while they tried to figure out what was happening. When would she tire of the life he'd chosen? She might like the motel room he kept all winter at the Green Wave in Miami. When he thought of the work she might have if she stayed with him, he imagined a job at a track kitchen or a restaurant. Women were doing men's work now, in steel mills, auto plants. They were pages at Old Main. Military clerks. Airplane mechanics. Bonnie stayed in Newport, doing what she'd be doing if there wasn't a war on. She saw herself a certain way. Anytime that happened it was difficult to try and convince someone they belonged elsewhere. It was too late for him as well, though he couldn't give up on the idea it was not too late for them.

When he'd moved out, he kept *The Maltese Falcon*. He thought about bringing it to Bonnie with the excuse he didn't want her to have to pay a fine. Instead, he decided to return the book himself. That morning offered a reddish sky and freezing wind. He took the trolley down to Second Street, shuffled along the sidewalks of the L & N, then caught another trolley on the Cincinnati side. Inside the library, he went up the marble staircase and introduced himself to Kiley at the information desk. Said he knew Bonnie. Kiley didn't like him, he could tell that right off, perhaps because when he asked what he needed to do to get a library card it sounded like a come-on. Kiley explained he had to have a Hamilton County residence for one of those. Ben picked out another Hammett novel, *The Glass Key,* and sat for more than an hour reading it in the room where he and Bonnie had been before Christmas.

Bonnie lived a few blocks away from him and he was

going over to Cincinnati, to Old Main, in order to run into her. He did this once a week. He made a point of chatting with Kiley. She looked younger than he and Bonnie, in her thirties, a pale woman with blue eyes who favored wool sweaters. She looked poor, but her job gave her a place and she seemed to savor it.

Once, while he stood at the information desk, chatting with her, Kiley said, "Would you like to see the Rare Books room? Bonnie said she promised you."

"Yeah…of course," he said.

"Remain here." Kiley strode across marble floor with its checkerboard pattern toward one of the huge archways and when she returned, she had a woman at her side. Ben thought this woman would be the one taking him to Rare Books, but the woman went behind the information desk and Kiley said to Ben, "This way." They traveled through a room of occupied tables, older men mostly, staring at newspapers.

She used a key to open a door, then closed it behind them. On the shelves were leather-bound folios, books laid on their sides, the bindings two feet in length. He ran his hand along one. "Double elephants, we call them," she said. She told him the *Birds of America* volumes were purchased near the end of the last century for a thousand dollars each. They were infrequently opened now, that's how fragile they were. She pointed out the binding for a Bible published in 1535. Next to it, a 1687 copy of *Newton's Principia Mathematica.* Ben focused on a folio edition of *The Raven,* and she noticed, said he could take that one down from the shelf because it already had water damage. He sleeved away a layer of dust from a table. There'd been a teacher in elementary school who read from Poe at the end of classes on Fridays. Mr. Dwayne Hrbek, a short man who wore tweed suits and had a habit of dabbing a kerchief at the corners of his mouth. The pages of the folio were like tissue and Ben remembered "nothing more," "never more." There were water stains along the binding. On one page, he found a single line:

> Doubting, dreaming dreams no mortal had dared to dream before

"Look," he said to Kiley. She moved closer, held her hands together. "I'm glad I got the chance to see something like this." He wondered then what Bonnie had told her about him.

"Poe invented the detective story, you know."

"I didn't..."

"Lived in poverty."

Ben straightened himself; he didn't feel like closing the book, though.

"You like working here, I guess."

"Best place in the city," Kiley said.

8.

Ben visited his father. They had coffee with the Draytons if everyone was already in the kitchen. If his father felt like it, they'd take a walk. Or they'd sit in his father's room, one taking the chair, the other sitting up on the made bed. Ben made a point of stepping over to the bureau, feigning interest in the paperbacks. He'd say, "Can I borrow this?" Tuck some bills under a wood-block bookend.

"I want it back," his father would say. He wouldn't mention the money, even if it was obvious enough what Ben was doing.

Early one afternoon in March, Ben and his father were together, and his father didn't feel like lying down, so Ben took the bed and his father had the chair. Though Ben was propped up in bed, he wasn't sleepy. He'd glance to the window that looked out to the alley, then check to see if his father was dozing. When his father worked at the brewery, he wore a vest and a jacket every day; he was handsome and trim, and women smiled when they were around him. But the Depression came, then the flood, finally the death of Ben's mother. In a way, his father had always been the same man.

"How you feeling, Pop?" Ben said.

"All right."

"I got up a couple of hours ago. I felt good when I did. I feel like I'm missing something." Ben felt himself smile and he said, "Don't you have any advice for me?"

"I tell you everything I know." His father rested his arms on the arms of the chair.

"What was the flood like?" Ben said, in a quieter voice.

"The water came in fast. By morning, the house was swallowed up."

Ben stared at the bureau. "Nothing to save?"

"Your mother was never as strong after that."

"Not a lot of good has happened in this goddamned place."

"What's wrong?"

"Nothing. I'm sorry. You're gonna think all I do is complain. What's gonna happen next?" His father didn't say anything. Ben said, "If I'd lived here, how would I have turned out? I keep thinking about that. This town tells the government to go screw itself on a regular basis. Ignored Volstead, casinos everywhere now. Do you feel free, old man?"

"Lie back there," his father said. "Go to sleep for a little bit."

"Maybe I will." Ben scooted forward, bunched the pillow under his head. "Don't let me sleep too much. I gotta go in a while." He lay in bed with his eyes closed, fully awake.

* * *

One afternoon a week later, Ben stepped into The Blue Derby knocking wet snow from the sleeves of his coat. His father sat at the end of the bar, holding out a honey-colored piece of paper.

APRIL ONE JAMAICA OPENS FOR
TRAINING
HJ

"You read it?" Ben said.

"Sure."

"What day is it today, Pop?" His father's finger tapped beneath the Western Union logo: *March 18*. "Want a beer?" His father shook his head. "I gotta start work here in a…you didn't have to walk this all the way down here."

"I did, actually."

"Right." Ben had the telegram in his hands.

"Gonna head back," his father said.

"Want me to walk with you?"

He father pushed at the edge of the bar counter. "No," he said, with a chuckle.

"Everybody okay?" the barkeep said in his direction, a minute after his father had gone.

Ben tucked the folded telegram into the pocket of his shirt. "Good," he said. "Thank you." He went to work, needed to focus. The club provided Kelly green vests for the casino workers. These were kept on a rack that stood in the hallway outside the bookmaker's office. He buttoned a vest, gave it a tug and walked out to the roulette table to spell Harry Hewes, who had the shift before his. He stood at the felt, said, "All place your bets, place your bets, please." The silver pill spun inside the rim of the wheel. "No more bets. All done." At his break, he went straight to the bar, ordered a double whiskey with no ice. He wanted to ask for another, but the barkeep might say something to Denny. He returned to his post in the casino.

He handled his shift, had another whiskey when it was done, then walked the block to his apartment. Inside his apartment building, he went to the door of Joanna Messier's efficiency, to see if any light peeked out at the bottom. They'd become acquaintances; she had a son in the Marines, and, like the nuns, she wore a crucifix outside her blouse. Her apartment was nicely kept, more so than his, and when they slept together, they did so in her bed. She didn't want to be thought of as a prostitute. There were so many of those around now. She was steely and sometimes he couldn't warm her up. When this happened, she'd say, *You don't have to stay.*

There didn't seem to be any light coming from under her door. On the whole, she didn't like to be bothered. He returned to his own room. Fully dressed, he lay in bed. He felt relieved that Bonnie hadn't seen him earlier today, right after he'd read the telegram. Ben thought about how he'd felt when he'd seen Bonnie at Pompilio's, when he'd looked up and there she was, at his table. He tried to understand what these two moments had in common. The telegram meant he'd be leaving Newport behind again. He wound up thinking about the time when he'd first come home from the war. He had a little money, he didn't have to work, not right away. He'd had his whole life in front of him then. But it hadn't felt that way.

He slept for a long time. When he awakened it was well past noon, and he reached for the telegram on his nightstand and lit a cigarette while staring at it. He wanted to show it to

Bonnie. She would've just started her shift at Pompilio's. He tried to predict her reaction. The thing was, she already knew so much about him. He pictured himself showing her the telegram, like he had the photo of Stymie. He considered the brown and canary pattern of the wallpaper in this bedroom. It would be easy to move from here.

He dressed and took a walk, heading north at first. Supposedly, after the flood, the corps of engineers were supposed to design and construct a levee. The war halted that. He tried to imagine the river as frozen, huge chunks of white ice formed together, solid enough to hold a horse carriage. People could run across the surface, they could strap on their ice skates. Underneath, the river kept flowing, and it would continue to do so long after he and Bonnie were gone.

At Pompilio's, he stood outside the Washington Avenue window. It was between lunch and dinner hours, but the restaurant looked busy. He spotted Bonnie in her apron, carrying plates to a table of three women and an older man, and began to wave. One of the customers pointed. Ben went around the side of the building to the entrance and waited. She emerged a few minutes later, her hands jammed in the pockets of the coat. "Hi, Ben."

"I got the call to go back. Well, a telegram."

"Okay."

He tapped at his coat pockets, then he stopped. "What've you been up to? Can you believe it's March? I think the war's going to be over real soon, don't you? I want you to come with me. You can always come back here if it doesn't work out." He tried to grin.

Bonnie sniffed and said, "When're you leaving?"

"Soon. I'll wait a week if you need to get your things in order. Tell me you've thought about this at least."

"I have." Her eyes went to the street; a Plymouth raced

by, then a mud-streaked Ford.

"Want me to come by tonight? After your shift?"

"No."

"You seeing somebody else, Bonnie?"

"That's not your business. I'll stand out here with you for a few minutes if you want."

He found it not as easy to look at her then. Things had been going pretty well. He understood he'd been carrying around the possibility of being with Bonnie for a long time now. "You know where I live, right?"

"I helped you find it."

"Well, Bonnie, I'm leaving soon. I want you to come with me. You know where to find me."

"Hug." She held out her arms, he hesitated but then he went ahead. He didn't say anything else as he walked away, and she didn't call after him. He went up the sidewalk, for his apartment.

* * *

Later that night, and at The Blue Derby he went to the rail of vests outside Denny the bookmaker's office, selected one, buttoned it up. After his first break, he tapped on the door of the office. Ben told Denny that tonight would have to be his last night, that he'd be heading back to New York soon, day after tomorrow. From behind his desk, the bookmaker kept nodding his head. "When will it start up again?" he said to Ben.

"Soon. Very soon."

"We make more on the tables than the racing," Denny said. "But I'm glad for you. Write down your address up there and I'll send you your pay." He took a pad from his drawer, guided it across his desk. Denny grinned when he read what

Ben had written. "All right, that's you. Always have a job here. You know your way around." He stood and they shook hands.

Ben worked his shift; he had a drink at the bar after that. Then another. He returned to his apartment. When he awakened, it was close to noon and his first thought was about Bonnie. He dressed, went outside, found out he didn't need a coat. A beautiful day, a spotless blue canopy above. He walked all the way over to Isabella Street, went up the steps to the Draytons', and though he had a key to the house, he knocked on the door. In a minute, Foster Drayton opened it. Ben said, "Is Pop in there?"

"Lemme get him."

"Here, take your key back."

Ben went down two steps. He faced the door, cleared his throat when his father stepped out. "I'm leaving tomorrow. I'm still waitin' for Bonnie to change her mind. I could stay for a week, but I don't want Jacobs to give my spot away…what would change in a week, anyway?"

His father remained at the top step. "Nothin'."

"What are you gonna do today?"

"I was upstairs, reading. Probably go back to that."

"Well, Pop, I'm going to New York. I don't know when I'll be here again. Maybe I'll get up there and it'll all seem wrong."

"I'll hold down the fort."

"Thanks for bringing me the telegram."

"See ya, son." His father went back inside.

He didn't have to go by Pompilio's on the way back to his apartment, but he did. He promised himself not to hesitate when in front of the window that looked out to Washington Street. He didn't. Back at his apartment, he placed his suitcase on the bed. He thought about knocking on

Joanna Messier's door, to tell her he was leaving, then understood it wasn't necessary. He waited to hear knocking at his door and could imagine his heart jumping when that happened. There Bonnie would be, in the dress with roses in the pattern, suitcase in her hand. Even if he felt unhappy that she'd made him wait like this, he wouldn't complain. He tried to picture the green dress Bonnie had worn all those years ago. She'd shown up wearing that dress because she'd waited long enough. It was summertime, he remembered that, and he'd been sitting on the steps of his parents' home.

When she arrived now, he'd say, Come in, sweetheart. We have all the time in the world. Our train doesn't leave until the morning.

He didn't have to leave tomorrow. Jacobs wanted him, he'd sent Ben a telegram like he said he would. Ben knew that Jacobs would be there a week from now and so would Jamaica Racetrack. Neither Bonnie nor his father had asked what all the hurry was all about. Stymie didn't mean anything to them, but they knew. He thought of the ration books Bonnie used for her stories. He wished he could stay, but he couldn't.

9.

He stepped off the train at Grand Central a little after four in the afternoon. In the main terminal, he peered up to the mural painted on the ceiling, the constellations. He waited for the Long Island Railroad train. At twilight, he arrived in Jamaica, exited the Locust Manor platform suitcase in hand. The darkening sky was lit up with streaks of purple and gold, and he felt the cold air as he walked along the sidewalks of 137th. He could see over the wooden fence, and in the distance the silhouette of the grandstand. The stalls at the Jacobs barn had the webbings up. A new Caddy, turquoise with a roll-top black roof, was parked close to the shedrow. He could hardly believe he was here. Ben wanted to yell out and wave. He needed to find a bed and he knew of apartment buildings that offered rooms to racetrackers by the month. At Meyerhoff Arms on 122nd, he knocked on the door of the super, a man named Peter Barkley, who remembered him from the year before. Barkley had something furnished but it hadn't been cleaned, and Ben said he didn't care. The room reeked of rotting tomatoes and the bedsheets and blankets were all piled at the center of the mattress. Ben removed his shoes, left on his clothes, pulled a pillow under his head.

He didn't have to get to New York so soon, he knew that. He thought, what if her first night with me in New York were in this bed, in this room? She might have a very clear understanding of what she'd gotten herself into. This kind of place didn't bother him, but her apartment in Newport was a lot better. He felt himself sinking further into the mattress. He thought about the last time he'd seen Bonnie, tried to convince himself he'd said things the right way. But he knew he hadn't. She hadn't left with him twenty-five years ago, either. He thought of how young they'd once been. They could have been together through the Depression and the flood and the death of his mother and then hers, then the war and the banning of horse racing. Now, the Allies were on the brink of victory in Europe. He imagined embracing her when they heard the news of the Nazi surrender. She might cry into his shoulder. He'd murmur, We won. It's all over.

He awakened in the middle of the night, and pulled on his shoes. He didn't trust the lock on the door so carried his suitcase with him, started in the direction of Jamaica Racetrack. At the stable gate, he showed the guard his horsemen's license from the previous year, and the guard let him through. The stable area wasn't fully populated; he passed empty, dark barns. But up ahead at the Jacobs stable, he could see the illuminated tack room lights.

Jacobs leaned up against the driver's door of the turquoise Caddy, sifting through a newspaper in the gleam of a streetlight. Negroes, grooms, were setting out the feed. Ben didn't recognize any of them, they seemed to be younger guys than the ones who'd been here last fall.

"Hirsch," he said.

Jacobs squinted in Ben's direction. "Who is that?"

"Me. Ben, Ben Held."

"I know who it is, Ben. I saw you make the turn." He folded the paper. "Enjoy your vacation?"

"Great, yeah. I'm gonna set my case in the feed room, change into my boots."

"I'll introduce you to the boys you'll be working with."

Ben paused after taking a step in the direction of the shedrow. "Stymie here?"

"First stall."

"How's he look?"

"Wait till you see him in the sunlight."

At dawn, a groom, Tony T, led a tacked-up Stymie from the stall and out onto the asphalt. Stymie had grown, his shoulders were as smooth and solid as marble. His chestnut coat carried the blue of the sky. Jacobs gave a leg up to the exercise rider, a kid he called Acey, and Stymie made his way for the racetrack. Ben caught Jacobs looking his way. He said, weakly, in the trainer's direction, "Needed the time off, didn't he?" Jacobs didn't hear him or acted like he didn't. Jacobs started off in the same direction as the horse. Ben helped Tony T pitch out the stall.

* * *

He'd been back in New York for three weeks when he heard on the radio that FDR had died. He heard the news while sitting at the small kitchen table in his flat. His shoulders hunched forward. Truman had already been already sworn in as president. FDR's funeral train route would carry the body from Warm Springs, Georgia, up to New York. Ben gathered himself by neatening up his apartment. He had paper and envelopes for when he sent something to his father. He thought of Bonnie sitting at the kitchen table in her apartment, thumbing away tears.

He wrote,

> Dear Bonnie,
>
> Everything will work out. In your heart, I know you have your doubts. We find something, and we hang on to that. I don't know if it matters how things turn out. But I know you counted on FDR. I wished I was with you when I heard the news, but I was in my apartment by myself.
>
> I'm glad I came home because you were there and because you are there I will never feel like I know everything about it. I used to think I did. We'll be racing again soon here.
>
> Yours forever, Ben

Not long afterward, Jacobs brought a letter to Ben, one that had been handed to Jacobs by the racing secretary. The envelope said *Ben Held, H. Jacobs Stable, Jamaica Racetrack, Jamaica, New York.* It wasn't Bonnie's handwriting, and when he opened it he found three five-dollar bills and a one. The pay from his last days at The Blue Derby. Back at his apartment—he'd found a better place, Empire Lodge, just blocks from the Locust Manor Station—cleared out his pockets. Denny the bookmaker always paid what he owed, that was his rep. Ben thought of the bookmaker at his desk, leaned forward, going over his numbers. His thoughts changed: Bonnie's hands turning the pages of a book of poems.

A week after the Germans surrendered to the Allies, Jamaica Racetrack reopened. A week later, Stymie finished second in a race he should've won. He missed the break, came rolling down the stretch, failed only by a short neck. The following Saturday, in front of a crowd estimated at sixty thousand, Stymie roared to a big victory in the Summer Days Handicap at even money. No official at Jamaica could've anticipated a crowd of this size, and there was talk mid-afternoon that the fire marshal might have to shut the place down. It wasn't because of the riot that would've followed.

Ben didn't worry about joining Jacobs and Stymie for the winner's circle photo. Instead, he lingered on the track, near the finish wire. From where he stood, he took in the immense crowd. If Bonnie were here, she would have seen he was right about something at least. But she wasn't here, and she didn't feel what he did. If only Stymie didn't matter. They'd been young once, him and Bonnie, and even though the memories of those times would hurt, he'd rather be dead than forget them.

The race was over, and the horses were being led for the clubhouse turn. Stymie and the groom had gone on ahead of Ben. He lingered. Then it was time to go in that direction.

The Newsstand

He stood at a newsstand inside Grand Central Station. There was a long train ride ahead. He picked up several magazines and newspapers, including a Daily Racing Form *and* Plain Clothes Detective. *The small, somewhat tattered-looking fellow who ran the newsstand called himself Sammy C. "Where're you headed, buddy?" he said.*

The man buying magazines had a cardboard suitcase at his side.

Sammy C said, "Leaving New York for good? Think you got something better waiting for you? Come on, forget about this other stuff. I got this one paper in today. New publication. It's good, everything you need, I promise." He held over a folded newspaper. "Twenty bucks."

"Forget it."

"For you, ten."

"Ten bucks for a paper? That doesn't make any sense."

"You don't know what cheap is. You just got to trust me." He lowered his voice. "Because I'm here to help."

The man already had periodicals under his arm. He believed in chances, and that would always be his dilemma. "All right, here," the man said. He took the last ten-dollar bill from his pocket. "Take this other stuff back. I'm not from here but I've lived in this city for a while now. Just don't think you're conning me."

"Never." Sammy C took the ten and gave him the newspaper. The man walked away a few steps, then could see Sammy C returning the detective magazine back to the rack.

The man shuffled a few more steps, and when he again looked, Sammy C was chatting with another customer, a woman who might've been Josephine Baker.

The man opened the newspaper, which was called Racing Times. *Its motto said, "We Bring You Every Race, Right on Schedule."*

He scanned headlines, stories about races that had been run last week or even two weeks before. One preview was of a race that had been run two years ago! He started to turn the pages; they were as brittle as November leaves, the edges already flaking. He found the entries were from races run last spring. But then when he got to the results page, his eyes began to blink. The results were from races being run this afternoon! He looked in the direction of the newsstand, where Sammy C was laughing with, yes, Josephine Baker.

Outside, the man with the Racing Times *waved for a yellow cab and one immediately screeched to the curb. "Take me to Jamaica!" When the taxi was heading up Park Avenue, the man remembered he had no money left. He said to the driver, "You play the horses, right?"*

"Who doesn't?"

"I can give you a tip today...instead of a fare."

"Hey!"

"Listen, I work...I know horses! Smoke Ring's going to win the first race. You have to believe me. I'm skipping my train to play this horse! We need to hurry because we're gonna miss the double." The cabbie's eyes went to the rear view, then to the street, then returned to the rear view. The man swallowed and said, "When we get to Jamaica, take me to the stable gate."

The taxi shot through all the caution lights. The driver, under a spell of his own now, said, "Of all the godforsaken things."

The man realized he needed money in order to bet. He could borrow something from the grooms he knew. To start, they'd probably laugh at him. The King of the Sure Thing. But they'd scrape together two bucks for him. He'd be able to pay them back before sundown. He'd treat them to a case of whiskey.

The cabbie was already thinking of where he could buy a dozen red roses for his girl. They'd stay up all night.

The taxi sped through the sunlight-filled streets.

Jamaica, Queens

On July 4, 1945, before fifty-six thousand fans, Stymie stormed home on top in the Brooklyn Handicap. He also swept to victory in the Saratoga Cup. He placed in the Suburban Handicap, Yonkers Handicap, Queens County Handicap, and Whitney Stakes. In the fall, he triumphed in the Continental and Westchester handicaps. This set up a November meeting down in Baltimore with Calumet Farm's ace Armed in the Pimlico Special.

Armed, a burly, mud-colored gelding, had been rowdy, nearly unmanageable early in his career. He, too, had been raced hard and finally made the transition from devil to prophet, at least as far as his many backers were concerned. The *Telegraph* and *Form* highlighted the triumphs of Armed throughout the season and the Special was billed as the race of the year.

It turned out one-sided. After the starting gates opened, Stymie fell far behind, and finally, when he began to lengthen stride on the last turn, Armed pinned his ears, pulled further away. Ben felt the powdery track surface had something to do with the race result; Stymie simply hadn't gotten the traction he needed. Armed was given the rest of the year off while Stymie returned to Pimlico for first the Riggs Handicap and then the Pimlico Cup, races he'd been defeated in the year before. In '45, however, he won them both, including the Pimlico Cup by open lengths.

As he had the previous season, Jacobs sent Stymie to a farm in Virginia for the winter. A couple of other hard-campaigned, promising Jacobs runners, Bold Sailing and Fantastic Sport, went along. The remainder of the horses, and the stable workers, were shipped to Miami for racing at Hialeah. The Green Wave Motel again had a room for Ben, though this time, his window faced an empty lot marked off by a chain-link fence. The signs on the fence said *Development Property, call 782-Dade.* The one painting in his room was of a vase that held an ivory rose. At the races in the afternoons, he wondered if he would run into his onetime girlfriend, Kelly Brighton. Once, he spotted her in a clubhouse box with a couple of young men dressed in white. She wore a deep purple dress with black stripes, and a teardrop hat. She seemed not to recognize him, but then he caught a subtle shake of her head, knowing she meant her brother, understanding he would've asked.

He didn't bother with the clubhouse.

The horses raced six days a week at Hialeah, with Tuesday the lone dark day. On those afternoons, instead of returning to the barn, he'd linger in his room, drink, listen to the radio. He liked to take the bus to Miami Beach. He was out of place there, but the bars would accept the coins in his pocket. When it rained, he went to the movies. That winter, it was *Detour*, *I Know Where I'm Going*, *The Bells of St. Mary's*, *The Lost Weekend*, *A Walk in the Sun*, *The Woman in Green.* Newsreels came before the films and many of the stories had to do with the war. The stories showed London, what was left of it. Berlin, Hiroshima. Auschwitz, Sobibor, Treblinka. The war was over. The world was over.

People had come to the movies to be entertained, to get away, and the war pieces closed with images of impeccably uniformed American generals looking over plans for a new Europe. Right after New Year's, before a matinee showing of *Our Vines Have Tender Grapes*, a newsreel story announced that the brilliant filly Busher had been named horse of the year. The apex of her season came in the Arlington Handicap when she held off the late charge of Armed to win by a length in track record time. The footage showed Busher standing in the winner's circle following the race, stands crammed full beyond her. She was raced by Louis B. Mayer, based in California. She seemed smallish but also rugged; like Stymie she was chestnut. Ben imagined sitting in a theater one day and watching newsreel footage of Stymie and then there he would be too, up on the screen, with all the other champions.

When he'd gone barnstorming, he hadn't done so to find cleaner, clearer images of victory. He wasn't worried about leading a remarkable life. He wanted the races to wonder about and that would be enough. It seemed like a good, clear path. And now here he was, forty-five years old, unmarried, still working at the stables and it felt like he hadn't given up.

He knew he was not alone. Horse racing's popularity had soared during the war, and once the war was done, the public simply couldn't get enough of their heroes. Winston Churchill, visiting Miami with his wife Clementine, attended the Hialeah. Ben caught a glimpse of Churchill waving to the fans from his box in the clubhouse. When Churchill raised his arm, made the V-sign, Ben felt as if he were experiencing a vision. But then, at the stables, grooms bragged about having seen the same thing.

There was money around, everywhere, people didn't feel like being cautious. Stories from the war had come back to America, so many stories. Images from the killing centers. Burned Japanese cities. A world in ruin, despite the light America had shining down upon it.

A horse was an object, a representation of speed, brilliance, beauty, power, determination. A great horse was something people could count on; it wouldn't carry so many contradictions, or nightmares. Such a horse clarified the glory and simplicity of victory.

* * *

In the spring of '46, Stymie rejoined Jacobs's barn at Jamaica, the big colt completely sound and in superb condition. Jacobs wanted to try him against Armed again and the results were victories by Armed in the Dixie and Suburban handicaps. Nonetheless, Stymie had an incredible season, taking the Grey Lag, Whitney, Saratoga Cup, Edgemere, Manhattan, and New York handicaps. Those dominating wins at rowdy, blue-collar Jamaica earned him the nickname "The People's Horse." Fans in New York knew him by sight; when he was led over from the stable area to the stands for a race, the crowds at the railing were fifty deep just to get a look at him. His grooms called him "The Ice Cream Man."

Stymie developed an intense rivalry with the filly Gallorette. She was bigger than any colt in New York; she ran against them frequently because the purse money was better than in all-female races. Stymie finished behind her in the Sussex Handicap, the Brooklyn, the Butler, and the Wilson. He ran well, but something always happened. He'd get into traffic trouble, have to swing wide, the early pace wasn't fast enough. Gallorette had a smooth, easy stride and was hard to wear down. If she got hooked early in a race, that helped. When that happened, Stymie had a chance to catch her. Otherwise, she was too much.

His battles with Gallorette, Armed, and the lightning-fast Greentree runner Pavot helped to catapult Jamaica, the plainest of New York tracks, into a horse-racing wonderland. The crowds had Stymie to root for, they had Gallorette. They also had Assault, "The Magnificent Cripple," the Triple

Crown winner of '46. Like Stymie, Assault had been born and raised at the King Ranch. He moved with a limp, the result of a deformed hoof. It was doubtful he could train, let alone race. In part because he'd had given up too early on Stymie, Max Hirsch tried to see if they could make a racehorse out of Assault. The little colt walked with a hitch but at full speed he burned like a missile. Assault obliterated the competition in the Kentucky Derby, Preakness and Belmont. By the fall of '46 he was thought of as the very best horse in a generation of exceptional racers.

Stymie faced Assault for the first time in mid-October in the Gallant Fox Handicap at Jamaica. Assault was heavily favored and his jock Mehrtens must've believed they were invincible. He confidently moved his colt to the lead early in the one mile and five-eighths race—too early as things turned out. Just inside the homestretch, Stymie blew past them and went on to an easy victory. For the next meeting, the Pimlico Special, King Ranch replaced Mehrtens with Arcaro, the best rider in New York and someone who'd ridden against Stymie dozens of times already. In the Special, Arcaro didn't ask Assault for his best until he felt Stymie flying up on his outside; this time it was Assault leaving Stymie high and dry. The split decisions left racing fans debating about which of the two was the superior animal. Stymie was named champion handicap horse in America; Assault, horse of the year.

In the winter of '46, Stymie freshened on the farm in Virginia while Jacobs raced his growing stable at Hialeah. The owner of the Green Wave had Ben's room waiting for him; the window faced out to the highway, the painting in his room was of a flamingo. He went to work and, on his days off, took the bus to Miami Beach or just remained in his room, listening to the radio. He didn't think about Kelly Brighton much, and when he did he hoped she remembered all he'd told her about Stymie.

As tough as Stymie was, he couldn't race forever. When Ben was working at the barn or watching races in the grandstand, he had enough to think about, focus on. At other times, he wondered what would change in his life when Stymie retired. At Jamaica, on his days off, he occasionally liked to take the Long Island train to Grand Central and from there walk the few blocks to the New York Public Library. He looked up articles on the King Ranch, with a particular focus on the abundant wildlife: antelope, rabbits, coyotes, snakes, javelina, bobcats, deer, iguanas, turkeys, boars, cougars, hawks, owls, doves, vultures, ducks, bluebirds. Ben thought of Stymie's early days as a racehorse, what a vicious, fiery animal he'd been. Ben had barnstormed out to Nebraska, and he felt he'd learned something about the plains; the hard, vast, and vacant prairie. You could feel thunder rolling under your feet, even though there was nothing but blue sky all around. You could feel a storm coming before you could see it, and when you could feel it you were reminded that life would always be about what was to happen next.

* * *

Stymie returned to the races in late spring of '47. He lost to Assault in the Grey Lag Handicap, then took the Metropolitan, a race Assault skipped. Assault beat him decisively in the Suburban and Gallorette edged him in a stretch-long duel in the Queens County. Assault defeated him again in the Brooklyn, and following that Jacobs got Stymie a race at Jamaica, the Questionnaire, where he didn't have to face Assault or Gallorette and Stymie won in a canter. Stymie was sent to Delaware Park for the Sussex Handicap. The Delaware track had a deep cushion that he relished, and he broke the record for the mile and a quarter distance.

Stymie piled up hundreds of thousands of dollars in earnings for Jacobs, and the trainer became nationally famous. Jacobs had more money with which to buy better horses, and soon his outfit might be able to match Calumet or Greentree, runner for runner. Reporters came by the barn, articles and interviews were published in the racing periodicals. Jacobs, a Brooklyner, was chatty and friendly and likable and didn't seem to mind the attention. He worked hard. Ben tried to imagine if he were Jacobs, that is, in charge of Stymie, what he might do differently. Jacobs had proved his point that Stymie responded well to hard racing, but it was also clear those winters in Virginia were important; Stymie got his rest there. And easier races right now meant Stymie's season might last longer. Those tussles with Armed, those had been a waste of time. Ben believed in Stymie, heart and soul, but there was also reality and Stymie couldn't beat Armed, not unless Armed put in a subpar effort, which Armed never did.

The races against Assault and Gallorette were better propositions. These horses could be defeated, but the circumstances had to be just right. In the summer of '47, Armed had been sent to California to compete in the rich handicap races while Assault and Gallorette remained in New York. Ben felt that the wiser move might be to detour around those two until the fall, let them brawl while Stymie took on lesser foes. In the fall, when the Jockey Club Gold Cup and the Manhattan came around, Assault and Gallorette would've worn each other down, and a fresh, strong Stymie could clean up.

A few days after Stymie broke the track record at Delaware, he was entered in the Butler Handicap against both Gallorette and Assault. Stymie had won the Butler in '45 but dropped a narrow decision to Gallorette in the race the following summer, having moved at her too soon. He had to rely on another horse sticking with her early, keep Gallorette working through the opening mile. Arcaro, aboard Assault, would be too smart for that. And unlike Stymie, who always lingered at the back of the pack early in a race, Assault was nimble and could be placed anywhere. He raced without fear in traffic. Last year, he'd proven to be an unusually gifted runner, and so far this year he seemed even better. Arcaro, who rode with complete disregard for losing, had been a perfect partner for him.

On the morning of the race, Stymie had already finished a light training session by the time the sunlight found the neighborhoods of Jamaica. Adjacent to Jacobs's barn stood a small pasture. Ben liked to lead the horses out there, get them some green grass. Early afternoon on Butler Handicap day, he'd brought out to the pasture a two-year-old filly, Lady Rocket, and let her nibble at the blades. He stood in the shade of the red maple, and the branches of the tree held bright green leaves. He smoked a Lucky, kept checking in the direction of Stymie's stall. Stymie stood at the back of it, in the shadows, facing in the direction of the opening. Alongside the stall opening, the horse's groom, Jumbo, sat on an upside-down steel bucket, cleaning a horse halter with a rag. He was a massive, pear-shaped man who'd grown up on a farm in Ohio. He was gentle with horses, that's also what Ben knew about him.

Ben had the flutters, the not-unpleasant onset of nervousness and excitement. If it were his choice, he'd have bypassed the Butler with Stymie, let Assault and Gallorette have it out. Jamaica was Stymie's best track, of course it was, and Jacobs wanted it to be known that any horse wanting to find the winner's circle in a big race there would have to go through Stymie to find it. Now they were in the Butler, and

Ben contemplated how the race might play out, how Stymie's rider Permane ought to handle things. In a way, riding Stymie was the simplest proposition in the world: Stymie always took himself out of the race early, got a feel for how it was going, and when it was the right moment, his head would raise and he'd take off after the leaders. If Ben could get Permane off to one side, he'd say, *Look, catch 'em by surprise, hug the rail around the first turn and man, as soon as there's an opening on that rail on the backstretch, go for it. Save ground, make the others have to go wide for once. They won't be looking for you to do that...*

Standing outside the shedrow now was the reporter from WKRC, Nicky Berryman, a white-haired man in shirtsleeves, canvas bag slung over his shoulder. Lady Rocket, a big bay filly with hooves like pie plates, probably would've been happy to spend the entire afternoon out there grazing, but Ben felt she'd had enough. She walked demurely at his side, a young filly with beautiful manners. Jumbo disappeared, he simply didn't trust strangers. Lady Rocket's stall was down at the far end of the shedrow from Stymie's, and after Ben had refastened the webbing across the opening, he draped the shank over his shoulder, found himself walking in Berryman's direction. He wasn't ten yards from the reporter when Jacobs appeared from around the corner of the barn. Ben halted, heard Jacobs say, "You been waiting?"

Berryman said, "Not long."

"I'm ready." Over the reporter's shoulder, Jacobs spotted Ben.

Berryman held a microphone. They stood just outside the shade provided by the roof of the barn; everything beyond them sparkled in the sunlight. Into the microphone, Berryman said, "Here we are with Hirsch Jacobs, the trainer of Stymie. Hirsch, what can you tell the racing fans out there about Stymie?"

"Am I live?"

"We record this and then we edit it before the broadcast."

"Oh, very good. You asked me…"

"About Stymie. How's he doing?" He tipped the microphone.

"Stymie's good. He feels good."

"Looking in on him, he just doesn't seem to have a worry in the world. Is he a quiet horse, Hirsch?"

"Quiet? Horses are quiet."

"Well, sure. Can you tell us what makes Stymie such a terrific racer? He has a strange way of running, Hirsch. When he's starting to make a rally, his head goes higher. People in the stands get excited, it's a peculiar thing."

Jacobs was holding an unlit cigarette. "Honestly, I can't," he said. "We can ask Stym—"

"Hirsch, you bought Stymie in a claiming race back in forty-three, when he was just a two-year-old, a racing record nothing to speak about…what exactly were you looking for?"

Jacobs flipped opened his lighter, got a cigarette going. Smoke floated from his face, and he said, "I saw him in the saddling ring, liked the way he walked. Once I had him for a while, I started to see there was something special. Mainly, I got lucky."

"Just like the star horses here, Jamaica Racetrack has unique nicknames: 'The Factory,' 'The Meat Grinder.' Can you explain those?"

"This is Queens."

"You've got Bobby Permane riding Stymie today…you switch jockeys regularly with Stymie, why is that?"

"Not any one guy owns the mount on this horse. Permane's not afraid of Arcaro, that's for sure."

"You think other riders have been?"

"What's the next question you have for me?"

"Racing's popularity has taken off since the end of the war, can you explain that?" Jacobs frowned at the reporter, who said, "People want to celebrate, they want to have a good time, don't they?"

"We won, didn't we?"

"Sure, Hirsch. Great. Well, tell us, do you expect to win today?"

"Yeah, of course. You can tell your listeners I said so." And then, Jacobs was motioning. "Hey, I want you and the listeners to meet somebody…come over here, Ben." The reporter swiveled his shoulders. Ben stopped a couple of steps away. "Nicky, this is Ben Held, shake hands there, Ben… Ben's been with me since, what, I think forty?"

"Spring of forty, that's right," Ben said.

"Ben's my barn foreman here, he's been with Stymie all the way."

"Well, that's just great," Berryman said. "Tell us who you think will win the big race today."

After a pause, Ben said, "Stymie will, of course."

"That's great, thank you so much. Hirsch, thank you again for your time." He lowered the microphone. "Now, lemme turn this shit off." He worked his hand inside the flap of the bag. "There it is…good luck today. The interview will play prior to the broadcast of the race. I'm pulling for you."

After the reporter left, Jacobs shook out a Chesterfield for Ben. "He probably says that to everybody. How'd I come off? I sound like an asshole when I do these things. Interviews."

"It happens."

"Thanks."

"I didn't mean…"

"Forget it. When you get to be somebody, you got to do this. Hey, you're gonna be on the radio today. Tell your buddies to listen. Your girl."

"I will."

"I'm gonna go back to the office, take the phone off the hook."

"I'll keep an eye on everything."

"I know you will."

* * *

Later that afternoon, from a seat high up in the grandstand, Ben watched the pre-race warm-ups for the Butler. In the row right in front of him were three college-aged kids, too young to have been in the war. Had a pint bottle to pass around. They agreed all their money would go on Assault; the steadiest one went to get the tickets. Permane had given Stymie some rein and they broke from the parade line, jogged for the clubhouse turn. Ben had already made his bet: twenty-five dollars on Stymie's nose. Not all of his savings.

The crowd detonated at the start; a booming cheer could've been heard in outer space. Stymie's stride looked choppy during the first few seconds of the race. There were two pace horses in the small field, Risolater and Rico Monte, both tough colts in their own right, and they were allowed to set moderate fractions. Gallorette and her rider Guerin spied the leaders from third, a few lengths ahead of Assault. Stymie tracked them all, the colt's stride leveling out as the field slung around the first turn. Arcaro stayed as patient as an undertaker; Stymie stuck behind Assault's bobbing tail for one furlong, then another. On the last turn, Assault darted into contention, but Arcaro had to check his mount as Gallorette swerved before him. Stymie made a slingshot move, came wide around the others, and inside the stretch there were five runners in full flight, like right at the start. Stymie had clear sailing, while Assault got caught between a drifting Rico Monte and a weaving Gallorette and his momentum stalled again. With a sixteenth to go, Stymie had the lead and was going the best of them all. Somehow Assault found daylight and scampered to the flank of Stymie. Once they'd drawn even, Permane panicked and struck Assault's head with his whip. Arcaro implored Assault onward, and the lion-hearted colt responded. At the finish, inches separated Stymie and Assault, and Arcaro stood first in the saddle, telling the crowd he'd won. The thunder of the crowd lingered in Ben's ears. He'd felt the strides of Stymie in the beating of his heart.

On the gallop-back, the horses trampled over the hats that had been tossed onto the track. Even the Jamaica flock couldn't jeer Gallorette or Stymie, though a few railbirds hollered at Guerin and Permane for not putting Arcaro over the fence. Assault was the last to return to the homestretch and his still-buzzing hoard of backers.

Stymie had given everything, and back at the barn cooling him out took two hours. At twilight, work was done, the horse returned to the back of his stall. The adrenaline from the race had dissipated in Ben. He and Jumbo had lost their bets, but Ben hadn't wagered everything this time, something told him to keep a few bucks back. Assault was so goddamn tough. "Here," he said, holding out a five-dollar bill to Jumbo. "Pay me back whenever."

He hit the sidewalk, thought about having a tap pull at Rinksy's, but everybody in there would be talking about the race. Maybe if Stymie had won. In a few days would be the second Graziano-Zale fight, and he'd probably watch it on the set there. Graziano was a Brooklyn boy, so Ben could get odds on Zale, "The Man of Steel."

Only later the night of that terrific Butler Handicap, when Ben was in his own bed trying to get some sleep, did he start thinking about the fact he'd been on the radio today. Of course, he'd been working at the time of the broadcast. Thousands, hundreds of thousands, must've been listening.

What had he said? *Stymie will.* He could've spoken his mind about giving Stymie easier races until the big fall stakes came around. People didn't want to hear that anyway, some no-name racetracker running his mouth. *Stymie will*, he kept thinking about the words he'd said. They'd probably put that on Ben's headstone, if he even wound up with one. He wished Permane had tried to save more ground on the turns, especially the final one. When a horse raced wide, it had to run further than the others. It probably didn't matter because Stymie had given everything. That's what Stymie did. He wished he'd said something like that on the radio—even if that, too, hardly mattered. Ben's restlessness began to fade, and he felt closer to sleep. The next time he was on the radio, he would say, *It's incredible how far he's already come if you really think about it.*

He imagined a microphone in front of him, reporters standing in a semicircle. Their pens would be scribbling on their notepads, and he would make sure to speak in a deliberate way so they wouldn't miss a word.

The Hard-of-Hearing Priest

The girls of the eighth grade at St. Joe's cleaned the parsonage every Friday. One of the nuns would line them up at the bottom of the steps. The girls held buckets and brooms and mops. They walked up the steps in single file.

They cleaned the parsonage while the priest presided over confessions in the church. While still a relatively young man, the priest became hard of hearing, and in the confessional he had to ask a confessor to speak up. As a result, anyone kneeling in the pews outside was likely to hear. It didn't matter. The verdict was always guilty, the penance always light. Say the "Our Father" three times and be on your way.

After lunch period on Fridays, the priest visited the classroom the seventh and eighth graders shared. He sat at Sister Alice's desk and asked questions related to the Bible. The students stood when answering. They knew to speak clearly and amplify their voices. Sister Alice lingered in a corner of the room with a peaceful expression, hands folded at her waist.

Though the priest was hard of hearing, he did not speak loudly himself. He delivered his short sermons in a soft-spoken way. Some of the older members of the parish were hard of hearing, yet they appreciated his brevity.

One night, a Friday night in fact, the parsonage was robbed; the priest happened to be at the house when the thieves arrived. He didn't hear them wedging open a window. They tied him up. They decided to give him a beating. The priest had a small safe in his closet and the thieves took it away with them.

The priest was discovered the next morning when two altar

boys went to his front door because he was late to say Mass. The police interviewed the priest in his hospital room, and he said he didn't get a good look at the thieves. The theory from the police was that the priest knew their identities, but they were also members of his parish. A further theory was that at least one of the thieves had a sister who'd cleaned the priest's house and knew about the safe.

The parishioners, when talking amongst themselves, could list any number of potential suspects. This parish being what it was.

Because the priest could not, would not, name his attackers, a case was never pursued.

During his stay at the hospital, the doctors investigated his hearing loss. They discovered the priest had brain cancer. The priest died soon afterward. The doctors said the cancer had been growing in the priest's brain for quite a while and this might've explained his hearing condition.

The doctors wondered, too, why no one in the parish had ever encouraged the priest to have his hearing checked.

Owner for a Day

While in his stocking feet, Ben parked on a bale of straw and used a hoof pick to scrape at the cake-icing of manure that had accumulated in the creases of his boot soles. He noticed Stymie's groom, Mickey Finney, standing a few yards away, and Ben said, "The last lady I had over to my place said it smelled like cow dung."

Mickey, a Negro who wore eyeglasses and had a thin mustache, didn't smile. "He wants to see you."

"Yeah?"

"Don't think he feels good."

In his office, a pale Hirsch Jacobs sat behind his desk, his hair damp and combed back. He'd had a cold, kept insisting it was nothing. "Come over," he said. "Here." Onto Ben's palm dropped a little piece of metal, a horseshoe-shaped silver lapel pin with *Delaware Park* written in cursive around the bend. Ben brought it close to his eyeline. "I ain't gonna feel better in time by tomorrow."

"What is this, Hirsch?"

"You wear it to get into the clubhouse at Delaware. Represent us, okay? I have a box right there on the finish line. Be an owner for a day. Take a Pennsylvania Railroad train out of Grand Central. There's a spur for Stanton, stops right behind the grandstand."

"What about Stymie and Mickey? I usually…"

"Mickey can handle it. Stymie doesn't need two men with him anymore. See the other side for once. Here, take my binoculars."

"My eyes are fine."

Jacobs had already gone into a lower, deeper desk drawer. He came up with a leather case. "Well, I thought you'd be happy about this."

"Didn't expect it."

"We were talking about it last night, me and Ethel. She's mad as hell I came into work today."

"I wear this pin and they let me into the owners' boxes?"

"That's the size of it. You'll want a suit though. Can I front you? You can get one off the rack at…"

"I have a suit."

"Check the train schedules, head for Wilmington in the morning."

"Hope you feel better."

"Get the money."

Ben slipped the pin into his trouser pocket. With the binocular case in his right hand, he began his stroll through the stable area. He already knew that Jacobs felt sorry for him in a way Jacobs didn't feel sorry for the Negroes. As a white man, he was missing out. It was a pretty nice gesture, though. Sitting in an owner's box, soaking it up.

In his flat, Ben placed the lapel pin next to the electric radio on the pinewood kitchen table. He glanced out the window that looked down to a section of 138th Avenue. Doors open to Jack Neagle's Barber Shop, Mann's Hot Dogs & Sundaes. From the closet, he extracted the one suit he owned, a light-wool gray number he'd bought on special from Carbey Bros. in the summer of '39. A half-back jacket with six buttons, and matching trousers with the wide waist and cuffs. He hadn't been in New York long, a few months. Luck would have it that the World's Fair had opened. He'd used his afternoon off, caught a train and then two buses to get out to Flushing Meadows. He'd imagined the crowds would be massive, like for the Belmont Stakes. His train car was half-empty, people dressed in clean-looking, bright summer clothes.

The fairgrounds had once been an ash heap and the air smelled of heated plastic. He'd paid his one-dollar admission to see the future and have access to five concession stands, and past the gates, he began sweating as he approached a clean, sterile-looking world. He'd seen magazine photos of the Tryon and Perisphere and he followed the ramps to enter the Perisphere, a round, white, miniature planet. Inside were moving walkways, and on the ceiling of the dome played a film called *Democracity*, something about a future Utopian city. He walked the length of Constitution Mall, with its rectangular pools of water, and stood before the bright white statue of George Washington. He found the Russian exposition and studied the faces of Marx and Stalin in the façade over the entrance. He investigated the exhibition called *The World of the Future*—which turned out to be all cars and highways. There were pamphlets, free cotton candy. Also, a button he kept that said *I Have Seen the Future.* What he remembered about the train ride back to Jamaica were all the young couples getting into arguments.

He tried on the trousers and the jacket; he bet he hadn't gained a pound since the World's Fair. A plate-sized mirror hung over the bathroom sink, and as he lingered in front of it he sniffed at the jacket's sleeves. He realized he'd never worn the suit to the racetrack. He pictured himself sitting in an owner's box at Saratoga or Hialeah. The Greentree people would have their box, so would Admiral and Mrs. Markey of Calumet Farm. And the great industrialist Ben Held. The inventor, the explorer. A man who loved the sport. At night, he went home to a mermaid who never aged. None of these things were true and they never would be. Nonetheless, he'd be taking the train down to Stanton to see Stymie run in the Sussex Handicap.

Ben needed to get back into his work clothes and return to the stable. Any time Stymie raced out of town, the horse shipped out the day before. The trailer arrived late afternoon, and as they loaded bales of hay and straw, Ben and Mickey talked about the latest Graziano-Zale fight. They agreed Zale was the better boxer and this time he'd proved it. The van driver, perhaps a Graziano man, stood with his arms crossed. Mickey brought Stymie from the stall and, as usual, allowed the horse to stand before the ramp. Nostrils widening, Stymie craned his neck in the direction of the Jamaica stands. Mickey spoke quietly, "Come on, it's time now, it's time..." Up the ramp they stepped. Last year, Ben had ridden down to Delaware on the van; he and Mickey had arranged the bales so they could play cards. Today, he watched the horse van pull away.

* * *

On the morning of the Sussex, he arose at going-to-work time, four a.m. He took a seat at his kitchen table, in the chair by the window that looked down to the street, which was illuminated in places by the gray glow of streetlights. He flipped on the radio, listened to music, to Sonny Burke, Duke Ellington, Charlie Spivak, Billie Holliday. "Can't Take That Away from Me." His new favorite was "Do You Know What It Means to Miss New Orleans?" *Do you know what it means, to miss New Orleans? I miss it each night and day.* Was Billie Holliday the best? He couldn't think of anyone better. Famous Negroes had to be wholly fantastic. He thought of Mickey waking up in a tack room this morning, maybe he shared it with other grooms who'd shipped down with their horses for the Sussex. His thoughts moved to the race today; Stymie was seven years old, perhaps past his prime. He had opened the season with four straight losses, including two at Jamaica. Once spring turned into summer, the horse had found his form, taking three of five starts, including the Met Handicap at Belmont.

At sunrise, Ben dressed in his World's Fair suit. While standing in the humid air of the Locust Manor platform, he shed his coat. At Grand Central, he picked up a copy of the *Telegraph* and *Form* but didn't dig into the races until he had his window seat on the train for Wilmington. The seats next to him were occupied by a pair of fair-skinned, red-haired women about his age. The analysts from both newspapers picked Stymie to win; a write-up on the race mentioned that the year before, Stymie had broken the Delaware track record for a mile and a quarter. There were six other runners facing him in the Sussex today, but only the filly Rampart could be counted in Stymie's class. A terror in the Mid-Atlantic region, she'd won seven stakes races, clobbering males on several occasions. The purse this year was thirty grand, the winner's share sixty percent. Eighteen thousand. He did the math: eight and a half years' salary.

A conductor started down the aisle, asking for tickets. He wore a short-brimmed hat, a dark jacket, and his vest pockets bulged with schedules and receipts. "Next stop is Cherry Hill, Cherry Hill, New Jersey." The conductor's voice was like a whisper; the passengers seated behind Ben might've been sleeping.

Ben wore a suit, but he couldn't pretend he owned Stymie, not even for a minute. He had nothing to do with industry, nor business, nor Cadillacs. Had he simply lost his ability to fantasize? Lie to himself? Reflexively, he thought of Stymie. Years ago, he'd felt that Stymie would turn out to be special; he could envision that because he'd learned something about the horse, and he knew racing. Was that more arithmetic than imagination? Maybe that wasn't the question. What could he imagine for himself now? He thought back to when he was younger, or tried to, and immediately felt the futility of this. He'd tried to be a trainer himself, but he didn't have the right personality and certainly didn't get the breaks. As a result, he had the life he did. A Negro's job. He examined the cuffs of his suit jacket. He had the *Delaware Park* pin fastened to his lapel. Didn't Jacobs say he was to enjoy this day? He leaned back in his seat, closed his eyes. The scent of lilac perfume had him thinking about the last woman who'd been to his apartment, Bernadette Vosburgh was her name, somebody from the neighborhood who liked the races. Bern, she wanted to be called. She was the one who said the apartment smelled of cow shit. She'd stayed the night after Ben agreed to put his boots out on the fire escape. Then, she wanted to dance in the nude, so he turned on the radio. She loved Lena Horne, "Little Girl Blue." She placed a hand on his shoulder, told him he needed to be in the buff, too.

* * *

The spur platform for Delaware Park turned out to be fifty yards from the grandstand entrance. A small facility like Jamaica, but with a green infield and a lake. He'd been here when Stymie won the Sussex last season, spent the whole afternoon in the stable area. He didn't have to check on Stymie today, but he wanted to, so he walked along the outer rail of the far turn, for the stable gate. Twenty-foot-tall hedges lined the stable area beyond the clubhouse turn and he caught the heavy wintergreen scent of liniment in the air. From his wallet, he picked his horseman's license, showed it to the guard at the stable entrance. The guard said, "Receiving barn's there, first barn on the right."

"Was there last year, too," Ben said when he was a few yards past him.

Ben found Mickey sitting on a bale of straw with another groom. The bale they shared was set between stall openings and the other groom's name was Otis. He'd shipped up with a horse from Kentucky, a runner on one of the undercard races. Ben looked in on Stymie. "Any problems on the ride?"

Mickey didn't move from the bale. "A little snortin' and pawin'. Usual. I told him it was gonna be all right."

"Need me to walk over with you?"

"He's good now. He'll be even better on the ride back...tired."

"We'll be better when he wins."

"No doubt."

Stymie stood in the shadows of the stall. The horse would never walk to the front of the stall to see if Ben had a peppermint or carrot for him. Stymie had not grown to like people, though some horses did. If Ben were swept away by a flood tomorrow, Stymie wouldn't blink. Or if Stymie noticed, he certainly wouldn't be concerned. This was how it was with Stymie.

He turned to the grooms and said, "I'll leave you the *Form* or the *Telegraph*. Which one?"

"*Telly*," Mickey said. He reached in his shirt pocket for his glasses.

"Here," Ben said. "We're in the seventh."

Nothing left to do but head for the stands. Atop the roof of the Delaware grandstand were four American flags, and the flags stirred in a breeze that hadn't found him. Ben couldn't help but wonder what would happen when Stymie was finally retired from racing. Ben might finally get back to barnstorming. If he did, he'd more than likely have to start off as a groom, just like he had at every other place. He wondered if he'd be up to it. There'd always be more to life than barnstorming, racing horses, caring for them, placing a wager when the time was right. Ben thought, *Even though there isn't.* He liked the smell of the wintergreen. He had his jacket folded over one arm, the folded *Racing Form* in one hand, binoculars in the other. At one point, he brought the jacket close to his face. Perhaps it could smell like wintergreen, too.

As Jacobs promised, the lapel pin allowed Ben access to the owners' boxes. He located the one that had *Hirsch Jacobs* on a small, engraved plaque near the opening. The row of box seats was just outside the shade provided by the edge of the grandstand roof, and a program had been placed on each seat. Not all the boxes were filled, and no one wore a suit in the style of the one he did. *How'd that guy get here?* Maybe people didn't want to be that way, but they were. He fixed his eyes on the line of evergreens that ran along the backstretch; it felt different, sitting at the finish line in the midst of all the owners who'd made it big. Men in summer suits, women in light-colored dresses. At the top of the homestretch a couple dozen men in uniforms had gathered. The public address came on, the Delaware race caller said, "And now we turn your attention to our Fourth of July ceremonies."

Decorated soldiers from both world wars walked in single file in a procession down the length of the homestretch. Applause grew while a recorded version of "Glory, Halleluiah" played repeatedly over the public-address system. From the paddock tunnel came stocky Arabian horses ridden by women in satin blue outfits and white cowboy hats, each of them carrying an American flag. The Arabians stood in a line inside the outer rail; past them, the soldiers faced the stands as well and waved their hats. The public address played "This Land

Is Your Land," then "The Star-Spangled Banner." Ben stood, though he might've been the final one in his section to do so.

He noticed someone in a sergeant's field uniform and overseas cap from the First World War. He'd worn something like it. He removed the binoculars from the case, brought them to his eyes, adjusted the focus. There were tens of thousands of infantrymen in that war. But he wondered if he knew this man, if he'd fought with him or been stationed with him. There were so many faces from that time.

He said, "Clyde?" He kept the binoculars on the man until he was nearly sure of it. He went up the aisle, then stepped around people sitting on the steps that led to the asphalt apron. The soldiers left on the track were milling about, shaking hands with one another. Ben saw that the man he thought was Clyde Strawbridge had slipped away from the others and walked with his head down, along the outer rail past the finish line. From the patrons' side of the rail, into the soft breeze, Ben said, "Clyde. Clyde Strawbridge...Clyde!" The man swung his head in the direction of the stands. "Back here! Hey," Ben said. "Goddamnit, I'm sorry." He felt himself smiling. "Are you Clyde Strawbridge?"

The man considered Ben's face, his expression. When he tilted his head back his eyes went to slivers. "Benny," he said.

"That's right. Ben Held."

As they shook hands, Clyde Strawbridge said, "Benny Held. From..."

"Kentucky. Newport, Kentucky."

"Kentucky, right. Well, lord, good lord." Clyde had a faint mustache, deep creases down each cheek. He had a long face with deep-set eyes. A section of the railing ran between them.

Ben said, "I saw you from the stands. Of all the guys in the infantry..."

"How about a beer, Benny? I've had enough of this sun. How do I get to the other side?"

"Go back there, near the finish, there's a section of portable rail, ask the security guy to take it down for you. You'll see a path that'll take you back into the saddling ring."

Ben made his way under the stands and then back out into the sunlight as he aimed for the paddock. Clyde Strawbridge stood by himself in the middle of the modest, oblong-shaped lawn. Ben showed his horseman's license to the guard standing at the entrance to the ring, then he strode in Clyde's direction. They shook again; Clyde's hand was rough, his grip pretty darn firm. The railbirds probably wondered who they were, if somehow these two men were notable. Ben didn't normally feel out of place at a racetrack. Clyde rocked back and forth on his heels. He said, "Where is this?"

Ben felt he understood. "Where the horses are walked before a race. The jockeys come out of that building right there. How 'bout if we go for that beer? I've got a box, right at the finish line." He thought about correcting what he'd said. They moved for the exit of the ring, and then they were in the shadows again, under the grandstand. Ben went to a concession stand, bought two cone-topped cans of Gibbons Ale, waited for the cashier to open them, held out a dollar, collected the cans and said, "Keep it." The cans had been sitting in a metal trough filled with ice and Clyde moved his can from one hand to the other. "The box is up here. Come on." He felt strange, like a child. They walked up the flight to the second floor; Ben turned his shoulder so the usher could see his pin and said, "Come on," to Clyde. Nobody in the clubhouse would raise a stink about letting in a man in a uniform.

Their seats in the box looked out to the racetrack. By

now, the horses for the first were being led over from the barns. "Here's to you, Clyde," Ben said.

Clyde removed his cap to reveal a bald head. He took a couple of gulps from his can of Gibbons. Then, he looked around, down the homestretch; beyond it, an acre-wide lot, rows of parked cars. "So, what're you, some kinda top dog?" When he turned back to Ben, Clyde was grinning.

"This is the owner's box. See his name right there. Hirsch Jacobs. I work for Jacobs."

Clyde reached up to loosen his top button. He placed his hat on the empty seat between them. "Must be important… man, look at you."

"Do you come here a lot?" Ben said.

"Not really. Not at all." Clyde leaned back, crossed his legs at the knees. "I live in New Freedom, Pennsylvania. They found me, you know, asked me to be in this parade or whatever you call it, last year. I declined, but then I thought maybe I shoulda. I think they do it every year for this kinda stuff, ask the guys who live around here. You don't live around here?"

Ben finished another drink from the can. "I live in New York," he said.

"New York City?"

"Jamaica, Queens. There's a track there. It's not like this…the plant's all concrete…no amenities." He motioned in the direction of the infield. He tried to think of the last time he'd seen Clyde Strawbridge; maybe at a commissary after they'd been sent stateside. Clyde had been a good soldier. In battle, whenever he was firing his rifle, he yelled and grinned crazy, a clown's smile. *Yah! Hah, hah, hah, hah!* Otherwise, he was mild-mannered. "We brought a horse down here for a race today…Stymie."

Clyde turned his head. "You own Stymie?"

"Hirsch Jacobs owns him. This is Hirsch's box. I just work at the barn. Do you follow racing?"

"Not really, no. But I know who Stymie is."

"He's in the Sussex."

"Gonna win?"

"Absolutely."

"Yeah?"

"Getting up there in age, but he's in good form."

"Man, you gotta be making a killing. Look at you."

Ben guessed it might be pointless to convince him otherwise.

Clyde said, "What race?"

"Sussex."

"What number race?"

"Seventh."

"I'm not planning to be here that long. In fact." He turned the can he held so he could check his watch, and nothing spilled.

Ben said, "Stay for the double, anyway." Clyde was looking out to the infield odds board. "What do you do?"

"Mid-Atlantic Hardware. Clerk. Own a little farm. Goats, sheep." He leaned back in his chair. "This thing smell moldy to you?"

"No."

He seemed to be considering Ben's suit. "I've been to New York a couple of times. Coney Island…they had a little circus there. This ringleader guy in a top hat, he danced with a tiger. The tiger walked on two legs. The guy held up one tiger's paw, like this, see? They were *waltzing*. Damnedest thing." By this time, Clyde was on his feet. He waltzed with an invisible partner, his knees knocking into chairs.

Clyde returned to his seat and Ben said, "I like the dogs, the hot dogs with the cooked buns the way they do it. I try to make 'em in my apartment like that, with mustard, but they don't taste the same."

"You married, Benny? How many kids?"

"No. None. Right after the war there was a girl…but no. What about you?"

"Yeah, sure. We live out in York County. Have two daughters…they're grown, married. You know, you don't have to put on for me, if you made it big, you made it big. That's what we fought for."

He felt like taking the program from his pocket, showing Clyde the name of Stymie's owner, right there in print. "My old man's got my uniform. I left it with them, long time ago. Nobody's ever asked me to march in anything." Couldn't find me, he thought. But Clyde didn't need to know about all that. Clyde held his cap in his hands. "You a gamblin' man?" Ben said.

"No."

"Well, come on, the first is coming up. Let's pick something. Here, you're sitting on your program…the horses will be coming out of the tunnel right there." Ben turned the pages of his program to the first race, hoped for a familiar name, some runner that had also shipped from New York: Ideal Gift, Watercolor, Cessation, Son Forever, Pretty Nymph, Silver Skirt, Liberty Babe, Glory Be. Nothing clicked. From the corner of his eye, he could see all the owners' boxes were now occupied. Here he was in his World's Fair suit with Clyde Strawbridge in his uniform from two wars ago.

"What am I looking for?" Clyde said.

"I know the horses in New York. We're probably better off just picking a number. Want another beer?"

"In a second." Clyde stared out to the oddsboard again. When he was out in the Midwest, Ben had run into plenty of soldiers from the first war, especially in the years immediately following it. But never anyone from his outfit. The soldiers he met didn't seem like complete strangers to him, and in their presence he always had a vague notion about bringing up something only another soldier would understand. He wasn't going to do that now, but he would've bet Clyde felt the same way. You were happy to run into an old soldier and then you weren't, that's how Ben felt about it. Ben wasn't as self-conscious with Clyde here.

He said, "I used to gamble quite a bit. I played cards in the outfit. You didn't play, I don't remember you playing."

"No, I promised my mother when I went away. No foreign women, no gambling." He reached up and wiped his forehead with the palm of his hand. "My wife and I took our daughters to Coney Island…ten years ago, maybe longer than that. My youngest, Charlotte, she got sick on the Whip ride, you know where the discs are turning. That looked dangerous to me. Threw up in the backseat of the Ford."

"We can skip this race," Ben said.

In another minute, the field for the first race threaded their way forward from the tunnel. The horses, in post position order, walked down the homestretch, in front of the stands. There were bays and chestnuts and a smoke-colored gray, the seven horse. "I like Gibbons," Clyde said.

"How about we watch this race, then go down and get another one."

"After that, I gotta get going."

Ben kept his eyes on the horses as they went into their pre-race gallops. The starting gate was positioned along the backstretch for the five-furlong sprint. The field began to load. Then, the gates opened, and the horses flung forward. The dust rose behind the field of runners as they sped down the backstretch. For a horse to keep track of, Ben followed the gray. Into the homestretch, it slipped through an opening along the inside and finished well. The winner, the four horse, Forever Sun, put together a strong rally down the crown of the track. Clyde watched the horses gallop around the turn and Ben supposed he was trying to appreciate something about the race. He said, "Pretty good. What's the least amount you can place on something?"

Ben passed the program over to Clyde. "Two bucks. Write your name and address on the bottom of that page for me. I'll make a bet on Stymie for you, send you the winnings."

"Is it gonna win?"

"No problem. Here's a pen."

Over an ad for a realty company, Clyde wrote,

Mr. C. Strawbridge
12 Glenstone Meeting Road
New Freedom, Pennsylvania

"Yeah, a Sunday drive from Gettysburg. Of all goddamn places." Clyde was reaching into his trouser pocket. "I think I brought a five. Here. Can you make change?" He gave a quick nod to an older man in a gray suit who seemed to be watching them. "Yeah, howdy," Clyde said. "Hell, let's live...bet the whole five."

Ben slipped the currency into his coat pocket. "Ready for that beer?"

"Suppose your horse gets beat?"

"He won't." Ben never felt so sure of anything. "I'll buy the Gibbons."

They walked down a flight, made for the concessions. They sipped from their open beers and walked out to the apron between the stands and the outer rail of the track. Clyde said, "So, you were sitting up there and you saw it was me."

"Not bad," Ben said.

Clyde patted at his belly. "Only been thirty years." His uniform fit him. Clyde took another long drink from his can. "I guess I gotta head out."

"You ever get to New York, you gotta let me know. Like I said, Jamaica is up in Queens..." He tried to think of other ways Clyde could find him. "Go to the stable gate at the track." Somehow, he couldn't imagine Clyde bothering with all this. "That's where I am."

Clyde put out his hand. "They'll be waiting for me. Don't want 'em to worry. 'Cause that's what they'll sit around and do. You know what I mean."

"I'll send you the winnings," Ben said. Clyde shook with him and then he frowned. He didn't say anything, but it was something about Ben's hand. Anyone could tell it was a working man's hand. Maybe Clyde understood then he was on the level, that Ben Held wasn't any big timer. After Stymie won today, Ben would make sure to send Clyde his winnings. Of all the things that could've happened, he'd seen old Clyde Strawbridge. He removed his jacket because it was a very warm day.

* * *

For the mile-and-a-quarter Sussex, the gate was positioned in the chute at the top of the homestretch, where the soldiers had been earlier. Ben watched from a row high up in the grandstand. After Clyde left, the owner's box didn't feel like the right place. No one had been asking him to pretend, but he worried it might bring bad luck. He felt the dancing of his nerves, which always happened. Dark-coated Rampart drew cheers when she stepped onto the track, but it was nothing like how the crowd hollered for Stymie.

When the runners broke from the gate, Ben let out a yell. The field of seven rolled down the stretch for the first time with Stymie trailing. Rampart was up close to the lead. The pace wasn't demanding. Not a great scenario. The horses streamed down the backstretch, and somebody a row in front of Ben yelled, "His head's up!" The runners began to bunch around the turn and the crowd noise around Ben drowned out the call of the race. At the top of the stretch, the runners fanned out; dark-colored Rampart darted to the front. Out in the middle of the track, Stymie came rolling. He built momentum, but there didn't seem any way he'd get there in time. With just a hundred yards left, he pushed up to Rampart's flank, then, in a flash, he went by her. Stymie hit the finish line a length in front. At Ben's side stood a young couple jumping up and down, holding on to one another. The roar from the big crowd finally subsided, but when Stymie jogged back, the stands turned noisy once more. The grooms stepped onto the track to collect their horse.

Mickey escorted Stymie in the direction of the clubhouse turn. The defeated runners had gone on ahead. Ben could've hustled down to get in the win photo or at least joined Mickey and Stymie for the walk back. They didn't need him. He could've stayed for the nightcap, the final race of the card, but what he decided to do was see about catching the next train for Grand Central. The horse trailer would arrive at the Jamaica barn past dark, but he could be there to meet it.

He also needed to cash the tickets he'd bought on Stymie. The big colt had gone off at odds of 3-5; Clyde Strawbridge's five-dollar ticket was now worth eight bucks. He imagined Clyde receiving an envelope in the mail, then taking out the money. He'd know who it was from. They'd been in the infantry together.

Literacy

Are we sure what events will happen next year?

Do the land and sea look just alike?

Are exalted positions held by distinguished men?
Is a civil answer contrary to law?
Are scythes always swung by swarthy men?
Does confusion favor the establishment of order?
May meat be cut with a knife?
Are amicable relationships disrupted by increased
congeniality?
Are milksops likely to perpetrate violent offenses?

Is irony connected with blast furnaces?
Is misuse of money an evil?
Is an avocational activity ordinarily pleasurable?
Are many nocturnal raids surreptitiously planned?
Is special information usually a disadvantage?
Do stones float in the air?
Are ledges common in mountain districts?
Does success tend to bring pleasure?
Is a dilapidated garment nevertheless clothing?
Does close inspection handicap accurate report?

Do 100 cents make a dollar?

Are diamonds mined in mid-ocean?

Does water run up hill?
Are stamps used on letters?
Do ships sail on railroads?
Are attempted suicides always fatal?
Do transparent goggles transmit light?
Do illiterate men read romances?
Do avalanches ever descend mountains?
Is one more than seven?
Are "precipitancy" and "procrastination" synonymous?
Are intervals of repose appreciated?

Are textile manufacturers valueless?
Do thieves commit depredations?
Are intermittent sounds discontinuous?
Does a baby cry?
Can a hat speak?
Should criminals forfeit liberty?
Do hens lay eggs?
Is a stone soft?
Are pernicious pedestrians translucent?
Do pirates accumulate booty?
Are some books black?

Do dogs bark?
Is coal white?

Again:
Does confusion favor the establishment of order?

Manhattan

Near the end of summer, in what looked to be his last year in New York, Ben spent his Tuesday afternoons at the public library in Manhattan. He'd take the Long Island train down to Grand Central and, from there, walk the remaining blocks. He had a library card and could check out books, but what he liked more than anything was taking a book to the Rose Reading Room. He'd forget that he might be leaving New York soon. He could forget he even worked at all.

Sometimes a woman named Marla Faust stood behind the counter of the information desk and Ben liked to speak with her about the latest in war literature. When Marla asked him if he liked poetry, even though he wasn't sure, right away he answered yes. She told him that the poetry section that might be of interest to him was on the second floor. She wrote down the call numbers for a shelf that specialized in war poets. He discovered *Poetry* journal and found previous issues that featured war poems. He liked "Poem for a Soldier's Girl" and "Reflections While Oiling a Machine-Gun" by John Ciardi. He read the journals in the Rose Reading Room, would finish a poem, look up to the ceiling, the chandeliers that hung from it. He read a poem by Karl Shapiro, "Troop Train," decided he'd like to copy a stanza, so he asked a man seated at his table for a sheet of paper. The man, who wore a beard and eyeglasses with half-dollar-shaped lenses, stared at him and Ben said, "We're not allowed to check out magazines." Without smiling, the man removed a sheet of white paper from a folder and slid it over.

Here is a deck of cards; out of this hand
Dealer, deal me my luck, a pair of bulls,
The right draw to a flush, the one-eyed jack.
Diamonds and hearts are red but spades are black,
And spades are spades and clubs are clovers—black.
But deal me winners, souvenirs of peace.
This stands to reason and arithmetic,
Luck also travels and not all come back.

On the other side of the paper, Ben copied a partial from E E Cummings:

what if a much of a which of a wind
gives the truth to summer's lie,
bloodies with dizzying leaves the sun
and yanks immortal stars awry?
Blow king to beggar and queen to seam
(blow friend to fiend: blow space to time)
—when skies are hanged and oceans drowned
the single secret will still be man.

He folded the paper and fit it into his shirt pocket. A little while later, he sat outside in the little courtyard, on one of the wrought-iron benches, and considered *Truth*, the marble fountain on one side of the entrance steps. The figure was of a burly, aging man, seated, with a toga draped loosely over his shoulders. The man's palm was turned upward, to Ben it seemed to be a gesture of someone trying to reason. Above it was an inscription that read,

BUT ABOVE ALL THINGS TRUTH BEARETH AWAY THE VICTORY

Finally, he spotted Marla descending the steps of the entrance. It was September now, a cloudy afternoon but warm enough to feel the air. When she reached the lowest one, he was waiting. "My name's Ben," he said.

"You told me your name," she said. "Inside."

"I knew you had to get lunch sometime." Ben was almost fifty and he felt he looked his age. At least. Marla was younger, maybe by a decade. She had brown eyes and full dark eyebrows.

"Ask me some other time," she said. She held his gaze and then she strolled out past the two stone lions that faced the sidewalks of Fifth Avenue. He knew enough not to go after her, he didn't know her. He thought she might change her mind and turn around. But she didn't.

When he thought of her, he felt that his age might be an issue, but also if someone looked him over for a second, he felt their impression might not be favorable. He looked, he dressed, like a ditch digger. When he thought of her, he felt that a wealthy woman didn't have to work at any public library, so perhaps she wouldn't see him as someone beneath her.

He returned to the library the following Tuesday in a newly purchased navy-blue shirt with plastic, light-blue buttons and he spent a couple of hours in the Rose Reading Room. Then, he went outside to wait for Marla's lunch break. This time, he sat on the side of the courtyard that held the sculpture *Beauty* and listened to the sound of flowing fountain water. The sculpture there was of the nude female figure looking up to the heavens. She held her right hand near her shoulder. She could use an explanation. Above the sculpture was the inscription,

BEAUTY
OLD YET EVER NEW
ETERNAL VOICE
AND INWARD WORD

Marla walked out and started down the steps. Halfway down, she spotted him. "Are you waiting for me…Ben?"

"Ben, right." He put out his hand to shake with her. She had on an olive-colored dress, black heels. He'd previously noted she didn't wear a wedding band. "Feel like taking a walk?"

"Let's find a bench…right here, for a few minutes."

"Great." Over in the *Truth* courtyard, some guy sat cross-legged in the shade of a tree and picked at a banjo, the case open in front of him. On the bench they chose, Marla perched forward, her legs crossed at the knees. He said, "That's a sycamore, right?"

"They call them London planetrees," she said. "They're like the sycamore, can tolerate city life."

He said, "I work at the racetrack. At Jamaica, in Queens."

"Don't they have a library in Queens?"

"Been there. That's where I got my card, actually. I like to come down to Manhattan though. You ever heard of that racehorse Stymie?"

"Hmm?"

"Stymie?"

"I don't read the sports page."

"He's about the best horse in New York. Used to be." He

tried to smile. "He was great for a while, a long while, actually. The guy who owns him wants him to be the first horse ever to make a million dollars."

"The horse doesn't get the money though, right? When you say the horse makes a million dollars, the man gets the money."

"Of course."

"I see."

"Maybe you'd like to see him run sometime. He doesn't have many races left."

"I have to say I'm not all that interested, Ben. Were you a soldier? How're you doing with that poetry?"

He wished he'd brought along that piece of paper where he'd copied the stanzas, but that was back in his apartment. He said, "I'm trying to understand bits and pieces. Cummings is one of the guys I've been reading. He's anti-war, I guess they all are."

"Yes."

"I know I can't put out of my mind what I've seen."

"When I started to see the photos from the death camps, I'm surprised my heart kept beating. Industrial murder."

"Where I grew up, there were a lot of Germans, Northern Kentucky. My name is German. Held. I cannot believe this world, anymore."

"You could?"

"When I was a kid."

"Faust is German. From the Latin, it means fortunate. I, however, come from a generation of Emporia, Kansas, dirt farmers."

"I've been to Kansas. Back when I was barnstorming."

"And?"

"Very flat," he said. Palm flat and facing down, he motioned horizontally with his hand.

"You were there. I never dreamed of a world like this. But here we are."

"Consulting the poets." He nodded in the direction of *Beauty*.

"Very good, Ben. You should know that women write war poetry, too."

"Ever heard of Christina Rossetti?"

"Christina Rossetti wasn't a war poet."

"I know, but I know women write poetry, that's my point."

She had her hands folded in her lap. "I'm meeting someone for lunch," she said.

"I'll walk you."

"No. So, you live in Jamaica Queens, and you take the Long Island train to Manhattan on your days off. You come to the library, you read, and you go back to Jamaica."

"There's more to it than that."

She turned her wrist, checked her watch. "I have three minutes."

"This is my last season in New York. I want to come down to the city and take in more…I walk around, I like Central Park. I've lived in New York for almost ten years now. I keep winding up in the library. It's my favorite place in the city. I'm gonna go to a farm in Kentucky with Stymie, once he's retired. The boss offered me the chance. I have the idea I'm gonna miss New York. Maybe I'm just trying to understand how much."

"Next week, after work, you can wait for me on this bench. If it's raining you can wait for me at Sandy's on Forty-first. That way."

"Sandy's, yeah, all right."

"They have pastries, sandwiches, whatever you like."

"You goin' there now?"

After she stood, she whisked her fingers at some imperfection near her hipbone. The dress seemed a bit loose, the olive color brought out something in her eyes. "No. See you here next week, Ben."

"Unless it rains."

"That's right."

The following Tuesday it rained. When he stepped off the train at Grand Central, he carried an umbrella. He'd already decided not to go to the library; he wanted her to think he had plenty of things to do. He went to the Criterion Theatre, caught a showing of *Pinky*. With the rain, the theatre was crowded, and he wound up in the second row from the front. The film was about a Negro woman from the South who'd moved to the North, where she passed as white. When she returned home, she was treated like a Negro again. Jeanne Crain played Pinky and he'd read something about that; it was controversial to have a white woman portraying a black woman. Why hadn't it been the other way? After all, that's exactly what was going on. The best scenes were with her mother, Dicey. The men seemed rather dense, but to be fair it wasn't a film about horse racing.

Outside, Ben popped open his umbrella and walked through the rain for Sandy's on Forty-first. On Fifth Avenue, he went past the entrance of the library where the empty courtyards held pools of water. At Sandy's, he took a table for two by the window that looked out to the street. He ordered a coffee and a whole pickle. He thought about the movie. He thought of a line Pinky had said, "You can't live without pride." By then, it had turned to twilight.

A few minutes after six, Marla stepped into the deli. She carried her closed umbrella at her side. She eased into the seat across from him. He noticed her examining his empty plate. "I had a kosher pickle. Good. Feel like something?" She appeared quite dry.

"Coffee," Marla said. "You wore the same shirt as last week."

"You agreed to meet me here last time I wore it." She looked pretty. "I went to a movie this afternoon. *Pinky.* I liked it."

"At the Criterion? I want to see that. It just came out...don't tell me what happens."

"You like movies? Everybody likes movies, I guess...I'm looking for the waitress here."

She leaned back in her chair and said, "My train's at seven-oh-nine."

Ben had started to raise his arm, then brought it down. "Got it."

"Tell me about this horse. Because I looked it up, this is a well-known horse."

"He is."

"So, what do you do, what's your, I guess, role in all this?"

"I help to take care of him. I'm the stable foreman. I keep the grooms organized." He wanted it to sound like nothing and something all at once.

"This horse has won a lot of races"

"Thirty-five," he said. "He's running Saturday in the Manhattan Handicap. Won it in forty-six, second in it in forty-seven."

"As I read, I kept thinking, 'How did I not know about this?' That's the thing about New York. You can't keep up."

"When'd you get here?"

"Nineteen thirty-six. I wanted to work in the theatre. That did not pan out. I thought I might write a book after that. I will, I know I will."

A young waitress wearing light gray slacks and a tucked-in, collarless white shirt stood at their table. "Coffee, please," Marla said. "Do you have any pie?"

"Blueberry, cheesecake, strawberry."

"Which one's the best?" Ben said.

"Blueberry," she said.

"I'll have blueberry," he said. "And one more coffee, thank you."

Marla said, "Strawberry." The waitress moved away. She hadn't been carrying a pad. "Blueberry pie and a pickle," Marla said.

"Yeah. That's me. Well, do you want to go? Saturday? I can meet you at Grand Central and we can take the Belmont train together. You know who else will be in there? Assault. He's making a comeback. He won the Triple Crown, spring of forty-six."

"I think I have heard of that one. Maybe."

"There are trains running out to Belmont all day. There's a twelve thirty-five."

"Did you come here to work with Stymie?"

"I got here in thirty-nine, caught on with an outfit in Jamaica. Just kinda barnstorming around before that. Nebraska, Michigan, Maryland. The guy I work for took a shot when he bought Stymie. We knew something, but nobody had an idea, really…"

She was beaming and it was the first time he'd seen her like that. "But see that's New York," she said.

"I guess so."

He was glad when the waitress brought their coffee and pie slices. This was usually about time he had dinner. He pictured himself seated at the kitchen table in his apartment. "Yeah, this is good," he said, after swallowing the first forkful.

She watched the rain, he thought, not the people.

"So, what do you think about Saturday?" he said.

"I already said I'd go," she said. "Didn't I?"

He said, "Just making sure."

"Main terminal. You know, where the stars are up on the ceiling?"

"The constellations," he said.

"That's right, the constellations."

* * *

The morning of the Manhattan Handicap, in the feed room at the barn, Ben changed into his city clothes. He didn't wear the blue shirt again, that would've been ridiculous. He pulled a brown jacket over a black-and-white-checked shirt. The street shoes he wore, he'd shined the night before. Once he was dressed, he stored his barn clothes in a shipping trunk and left for the Locust Manor Station. He stood on the platform, smoked two cigarettes and looked over the sheet of paper where he'd written down some poetry stanzas.

When his train arrived at Grand Central, it was still minutes before noon and he went to the newsstand to purchase his horse racing-literature. He had the papers stuck under his arm when Marla appeared at his side. "Hello, hello," he said, and gave a little bow. She wore a shin-length dress, close to the color of the sky holding the constellations. Her outfit included a black sweater and a black, turban-style hat with a starfish-shaped brooch on the side. He said, "We'll have time to go back to the receiving barn and see the horse before the race."

"Aw, I'd like that," she said.

"Need a ticket or do you have a pass?" he said.

"I have a pass."

The car they boarded for Belmont was stuffed with racegoers, but improbably she spotted two seats side by side and they laughed like people in an advertisement after grabbing them. "Look, I got two racing papers," he said. "The *Telegraph* also has articles about movies and what have you. The headline is about the Manhattan..." While she read, he opened the *Form* and studied the field for the sixth. The Manhattan was at a mile and a half, purse twenty-five grand. Stymie had post seven and Assault post eight, they'd be leaving the gate right next to one another. To fire up Assault, Max Hirsch had sent him through a demanding mile-and-a-half workout three days ago. "Oh," he said. "I brought along something..."

"I'm not finished reading," she said.

Most everybody knew that the racing careers of Assault and Stymie should've been done already. Assault had been retired the year before, had been sent home to the King Ranch to begin a career as a stallion. He proved infertile. They'd experimented on him with hormone injections, mated him with mares of European pedigrees. Nothing worked, Assault wouldn't have sons and daughters. It was decided to bring him back to the races. This season, he'd won the Brooklyn in his second start, then failed badly as the heavy favorite in MassCap in Boston. He'd finished third in the Aqueduct Handicap, ahead of Stymie, who was making his first start of the campaign.

Ben unfolded the paper with the poetry; he now was sheepish about it, he felt pretentious and wanted to put it away.

"Let me see," Marla said.

"I copied it down in the library. 'Member when I asked you about that?"

"Mmm-hmm."

The passenger at the window seat was an older woman with white hair who wore a half-veil over her eyes. "I like reading about the war. Or maybe the way to say it is I feel the need to do it." He liked Marla, and he liked it that she worked at the library. "I guess these guys are trying to explain what it means." She sighed. What he said he felt was true but maybe he was coming on too fast. Then he figured it out. Ben said, "There aren't just men poets. So, what do you think of these?"

"Well, they aren't the entire poems, so I can't say. The language is quite beautiful. Maybe that's the thing you're really interested in." Their eyes met and he felt like kissing her. It seemed obvious. Her expression, he thought, turned cautionary. "The war in a different language," she said.

"I knew what you meant," he said.

She sniffed and looked down to the *Telegraph,* which she had folded back to quarter size. "This article said your Stymie is making a comeback. Or trying to."

"That's a fair assessment," Ben said, he felt himself frowning. The article related correctly that Stymie had been injured the previous summer in the Monmouth Handicap, which kept him away from the races for more than a year. In his return, Stymie had finished dead last in the Aqueduct Handicap and followed that with a pair of third-place finishes in allowance races, beaten by rivals he would've obliterated had he been anywhere close to top form. All Ben could think to say was, "Today's another day."

The train platform of Belmont Park lay adjacent to the grandstand parking lot. Ben whisked Marla away from the flow of passengers streaming for the turnstiles. At the security gate to the stable area, he opened his wallet and showed his horseman's license. "She's with me," he said, pointing his thumb.

The guard looked her over, then said, "Go ahead."

At the receiving barn, Stymie's groom Mickey sat on a

bale of straw, his back leaned against a section of cinder-block wall just outside the stall. He wore his eyeglasses, held open an *Ellery Queen's Mystery Magazine* with a cover that had a white guy in a white suit falling forward with four bullet holes in his back. He lifted his straw hat when Ben introduced Marla. "No problems on the trip over?" Ben said.

"Not a one."

Ben moved for the stall webbing, made room for her. The cool air carried aromas of straw, horsehair, manure, rubbing alcohol.

"He's a big one." Her eyes were pinned on Stymie. "What happens if he charges right at us?"

"We'd duck out of the way. Finish his oats, Mick?"

"Each and every one." Mickey stood a few feet off to the side.

"Hear anything about Assault?" Slowly, Mickey shook his head.

Marla had turned and now she could view both men. "You wouldn't know this horse is famous. Not by looking at him… I rather like his aloofness. Does he know he's famous?"

"Yes ma'am, he does," Mickey said.

"How can you tell?"

Mickey's eyes went to Ben. Ben said, "He knows the crowd is cheering for him."

"And how does he know that?"

When Ben didn't say anything, Mickey said, "He wins."

It seemed bound to be an incomplete discussion. Yet Marla appeared satisfied by something. Ben said, "Mickey saw Joe Louis in Williamsburg last week."

"That was my cousin who saw him," Mickey said. "Joe Louis on the sidewalk with his lady. He said they were getting along."

"She sang with Kay Kyser," Ben said.

She said, "What's her name?"

Ben said, "Marva."

"Marva, what a marva-lous name." She waited for them to smile, and so they did. "I think I've seen pictures of her."

Ben said, "Joe Louis isn't done. He's Joe Louis."

"He's fat now," Mickey said. "Walcott's still fighting. He'll beat Ezzard Charles next time."

"Louis is still great," Ben said.

"He's fat," Mickey said.

Ben said to Marla, "Seen enough?"

"I have," she said. "Bye, Mickey."

"Good day."

Ben and Marla moved up the packed dirt path for the security gate. The trees beyond the far turn were full of autumn colors, pumpkin, cherry, saffron. The path they were on brought them close to an entrance to the tremendous Belmont grandstand; Ben would be able to get them in for free using his horseman's license. "When I leave, Mickey's taking over my job."

"When's that going to be?"

"December, I guess. See, Stymie's kind of a particular horse and the boss feels like he should have a familiar face with him at his new place. Honestly, I think they wanted to send Mickey with him…but Mickey doesn't want to go to Kentucky." Ben showed his badge to the guard at the entrance to the paddock, then stepped aside to let Marla go first.

"Where's hers?" the guard said.

"She's with me."

"You can go in," the guard said. "She has to have her own pass."

The guard stood a head taller than Marla. Ben thought she might give him a smile, coax him along, but she didn't try that. "Is there another way in?" she said.

"Around the stands there, see where? Thank you, ma'am," the guard said.

"We catch the one security guy doing his job," Ben said as they headed away.

"I have to ask you something," she said. "It sounds to me like you don't want to leave New York."

She hadn't asked him a question, but he understood. "After I accepted the new job, I started to think about it. I wouldn't say I want to leave. Here…" He reached for his wallet as they approached the grandstand entrance. He handed her a dollar and said, "There's another horseman's entrance at the far end down there. I'll use that. I'll meet you inside. There'll be a program booth. Get us a couple, will ya? With the change?"

Inside the admission gate, he found her near the back of a line at the program stand. At his side, she said, "Stymie didn't even react when you were standing there."

"What we are to him isn't what he is to us. What he's capable of, that's all that matters." Maybe she was interested. When it was their turn, he said, "Two please." He pointed with his thumb to Marla. "She's got it."

They were each holding a program and she looked up to him, smiling. "What now?"

"We find a place to sit."

They discovered empty seats in a row in the general admission section of the grandstand. It was as perfect as fall could ever be, the cloudless sky shining like a gem. He wondered about asking what Marla thought of him so far, but that would make them both self-conscious. He hadn't done a lot of this type of dating while in New York and felt like admitting as much. The hum of the immense crowd was pleasing to him. "Tell me about yourself," he said. "If you want."

"I did, didn't I?"

"You said were from Emporia, Kansas. You wanted to be in the theatre. You're gonna write a book." She turned the pages of the program. "Third race we're on now," he said. "Stymie's in the sixth."

"What did that mean when you asked Mickey about Assault? That's the top pick in the race, number eight."

"Mickey knows people, grooms at other barns. There's always, what's the word, scuttlebutt. Going by what Mick said, Assault's not a hundred percent."

"He didn't say anything."

"Trust me, that's what he said."

Ben wanted to not mind the questions. He wanted to enjoy the afternoon as best he could. It wasn't lost on him that the number of afternoons to enjoy Stymie at the races were dwindling. If Stymie ran poorly today, maybe this would be it. He wondered if Marla could get him a job at the library, filing books…anything to start. He pictured himself in a sweater with elbow patches like some of the men wore. It was a fantasy. He wanted to appear interested in something happening on the track, though he wasn't, not right this second. For the moment, his existence felt like a fantasy. New York, Stymie, Marla…the sweater with patches. She was saying, "…so we can bet everything we own on Stymie today."

"My boss wants Stymie to become the first millionaire and King Ranch wants Assault to be the first millionaire. But it's not going to happen."

"So, we bet against them."

"I'm not betting against Stymie."

"That's sentimental," she said.

"No, it's not. It's bad luck."

"That's superstitious."

"Which one is worse?"

She said, "Theoretically, we have a big advantage. If we know the two top horses aren't going to win. Betting wise."

"I didn't think you'd care about betting."

"I don't. But if I did, I'd be betting against men who are sentimental and superstitious."

He liked her bright expression but also felt she meant what she'd said. "We have to be somethin', I guess."

"Actually," Marla said. "I'm kind of flattered. This clearly is a pretty big day in your life, and you asked me to be a part of it."

"It's just a day," he said, but his voice was on the quiet side. She leaned closer, circled her arms around his bicep.

"I know, I know," she said. The horses were out on the track for the third row; he was glad to have the post parade to focus on. "You okay?"

"I'm fine," he said. She'd pressed him and now he felt exposed. "If you left New York, where would you go?"

"To live?"

"Yeah."

He thought she might take a shot at him, say *Not Kentucky*. Marla said, "That's the question, I guess. It's hard for me to imagine living somewhere else at this point. But it's as if I'm not really getting anywhere right now. I've been working at the library for a decade."

"Seems pretty nice…"

"It is. But that's not the point. I didn't move to New York to work in a library."

The horses for the third were going into the gate and when the runners broke in a line, the clamorous crowd united in a cheer. The Belmont oval was huge, a mile and a half around. Ben pointed, "They come around and right there, down the stretch is the finish line." He could barely hear the race caller's words over the growing din. Ben didn't say anything else, not while the race was taking place. Her eyes were wide open. "Your first horse race?"

She said, "Everybody's just sitting here and then, boom, they go crazy."

"That's kind of the way it goes."

"It was over pretty fast though."

"Well, that was five furlongs, five-eighths of a mile. Stymie's race is a mile and a half. More than twice as long." He opened the *Racing Form*. He pointed out some things about how to read the past performance lines.

From their spot in the stands, they watched the fourth race, and the fifth. Then, the grooms led the horses over for the Manhattan. "There's Mickey and Stymie. See 'em? I used to walk over with them, but that's when Stymie was acting up a lot. He was fighting with what it was all about." He looked to Marla to see if she was paying attention. "You see him?"

"Yes."

"Assault's there, walking in front. He's a chestnut, too, see? He and Stymie were both born on the King Ranch in Texas. King Ranch thought Stymie was a tramp, so they gave up on him. Hirsch Jacobs, that's my boss, paid fifteen hundred bucks for him. Made over nine hundred thousand. I've seen him run over a hundred times. Well more than a hundred. I can't believe it."

"What can't you believe?"

"Everything, I guess." It wasn't as if he felt emotional, but he didn't feel like talking right after that. He supposed she understood that much; from the corner of his eye, he could see she'd busied herself with the *Form*.

"The horses are coming onto the track," said the race caller. The infield odds-board showed Stymie at 4-1. Assault stood at 5-2, the favorite. During the post parade, Ben felt that Stymie received the louder ovation. The runners broke the post parade line, took to their pre-race warm-ups. Assault's gallops were never fluid. How had that colt raced for so long on that deformed hoof?

The starting gate was parked at the finish line and when the gates opened, the field escaped together. The speedy colt My Request took an early lead, and Arcaro, always dangerous on a frontrunner, immediately began to back down the pace. Stymie and Assault both raced at the rear of the field, lapped on one another for the first half mile. The field of horses breezed down the backstretch; Permane wanted Stymie to get closer, kept throwing the reins. The only horse behind them was Assault. Inside the top of the stretch, Donor, a smallish but hard-running roan, made a run at My Request and they pulled away from the others. Donor caught him fifty yards from the line. Stymie put together a modest rally, passed a few faders to wind up a well-beaten fourth. Assault came home last.

The crowd buzzed at the results, and there were jeers as Stymie and Assault jogged back in front of the stands. Marla said, "That's unkind."

"They're booing the guys who ran them. Stymie looks okay…he's just…I don't know."

"What do we do now?" The sky had turned cerulean, and Ben could then feel the chilly air.

He said, "I guess we go home. Take the train back to Grand Central. Unless you want to stay for the last race."

"Not really. I mean, it's, you know, it's okay." She closed the *Racing Form*, folded it twice.

Past the admission gates, the train platform had no room for them and they didn't attempt to wade their way through. She said, "Where do you live, Ben? Queens?"

"Jamaica. 140th and 173rd. Get off at Locust Manor."

"What do you do usually after a horse…Stymie, races?"

"Depends."

"On?"

"How he does. Go back to my apartment. Maybe a bar in the neighborhood or something. We can do something different."

"I feel like doing something other than sitting in a bar," she said.

He'd been thinking the whole thing had been blown, though not necessarily because of Stymie's finish. To her, he was merely a curiosity. He said, "Whatever you want."

She didn't respond. When the train pulled up to the platform, people waiting behind them edged closer; Ben and Marla worked their way forward in half-steps. Somehow, they fit onto a stuffed car. They didn't get seats and she wound up standing close to him. He studied the starfish broach pinned to her hat while her hip rubbed against him. They arrived at Grand Central in time to dash for the Long Island train, and they made it. The car had plenty of empty seats and she wanted one by the window. Once the train pulled ahead, she tipped her head to his shoulder. He hadn't expected this, and he wondered what he'd done right. It probably was the racetrack; women enjoyed the races, though in his experience, no one except a racetracker was as interested in the work it took to get a horse ready for a race. He wondered if Marla liked him a lot more than she let on. Did she want in on his life? If she showed enough interest, would he change his mind about leaving New York? Did she want to marry him? A train hurtled by in the opposite direction, the chrome of the speeding cars caught by the moonlight. Then came the lighted windows of apartment buildings. When he started out barnstorming all those years ago, he'd imagined living out his days on the Nebraska prairie in a hay loft at some racetrack where a winning purse turned out to be a sawbuck and a free lunch in town at a diner named for somebody's grandmother.

"Hey, we're here, we made it," he said. She had dozed and he guessed she liked him after all. Outside, the air felt warmer than it had earlier in the afternoon. Even though there was nothing he could do about it now, on their walk to his apartment Ben pictured the way he'd left it this morning. The place had a light switch just inside the door and when he flipped it up, he was glad for the dimness. Kitchenette, small table by the window, bed against the wall. "The bathroom's there," he said, gesturing to the door just beyond the foot of the bed. "Does it smell like crap in here?" he said.

"No, just horses!"

He said, "Want a beer?"

"Yes."

"I also have whiskey."

"Beer," she said.

"In the winter, the stable goes to Florida, I stay in a little motel room down a piece from Hialeah racetrack."

"The room is little, or the motel is little?"

"Here," he said. "Schaefer, hope you like it."

He'd made openings in the cans with a church key. "Thank you." By now she was sitting on the bed. She tossed her hat in the direction of the pillow.

Ben remained on his feet, raised his Schaefer. "Both," he said.

"Cheers." She took a drink. Marla said, "My place is like this. But not exactly this. I also have a cat whose name is Hector. I left him with plenty of food and water. Under the heading of you just never know. Are you going to work in the morning?"

"Yeah, oh yeah. I get the one day off...and that's when I take the train to Manhattan."

"That's funny. The race today was named 'Manhattan.'"

"They do that here, name big races after parts of the city. There's the Brooklyn, the Stuyvesant, the Metropolitan."

"'Metropolitan' is not a place...but I do understand."

"I think we've run in every damn one of 'em."

"You think it's over for Stymie?"

She was quite matter of fact, he'd picked up that much about her. "In so many words. He put in a little lick down the stretch. So they won't give up on him yet. Assault's done. They oughta leave these great horses be. But they keep squeezing 'em, you know?" He hoped he didn't sound too serious. It had been a dreamlike afternoon in New York, and he'd heard the crowd cheer for Stymie before the race started.

She patted the space next to her on the bed. He sat, felt the springs press against his thighs. She said, "Let me lay it out for you. Do not shoot your stuff in me, okay? I'm not kidding. Do you have any rubbers or anything?"

"I don't think so. I know what you're saying."

"You can kiss me now." He did it right; in a moment, she had her hand on the back of his head, pressing his mouth down into hers.

In another minute, he said, "What do you want to do about the light?"

"Oh, is the light on?" she said. "Hey, how about a glass of that whiskey first?"

* * *

After her whiskey, Marla stripped down. Her armpits were hairy, her skin smooth. She threw back her shoulders and said, "Ever seen a tumbleweed like this, cowboy?" She was gifted with energy and kept him up till midnight. When they lay down in the bed for rest, they shared the pillow. They could fit on the mattress if they both lay on their sides. His arm stretched all the way past her knees. Next week was the New York Handicap; Stymie had won it in '46. If Stymie wasn't at the end now, the end was close at hand. Ben thought about the kind of place he'd have in Kentucky. He told himself, *New York will always be here. Always.*

If he had one wish, it wouldn't be that he would marry Marla or that they could become a couple or just that she'd get on top of him again, though he would've liked all of these things. If the marriage didn't work, they could always break it off. Marla clearly enjoyed fucking. Ben thought vaguely about his neighbors complaining about the noise, though they'd made plenty of their own that summer with their beer parties, their proclamations about the Dodgers. If he had a wish, it would be that Stymie would race for another season. He wasn't what he used to be, but for the winter the horse could go back to the farm in Virginia, kick off his racing plates, perhaps rediscover his youth. Ben would go to Florida and work with Jacobs's stable, with another season of racing Stymie in New York to look forward to. He would get another spring, summer, and fall here. Above all else, that's what he wanted, though he knew that wishing it would continue was another sign that it was almost over.

He had a few Tuesdays left to take the train into the city and the thought of that made him feel a little better. If Stymie ran in the New York Handicap next Saturday, he could invite Marla, but he wasn't sure about that. Stymie would lose again. He might just want to go back to the barn after the race, see that Stymie had cooled out all right. Tonight with Marla likely would be a onetime thing. She'd wanted to see something, and she'd seen it. The city was a momentous place, and he didn't have a whole lot else to offer. She hadn't even mentioned where she lived; she had a cat, and for all he knew she might have a boyfriend, some guy who was deeply in love with her.

Ben slept on and off that night and by four, he was wide awake. He stood from the bed, went to the toilet. He turned on the light in the kitchenette so he could see what he was doing with the electric coffee maker. From the bed, Marla said, "You going to work?"

"I tried not to wake you."

"You did when you got out of bed." While on her back, she shook out the blanket. Remaining under the covers, she turned and lay on one side. "I want to sleep for a while, okay?"

"Sure."

"Lock the door after me when I go?"

"Just close it, that'll be fine." He thought about making a joke, What do I have to take? but in time thought better of it. "Or stay until I get back. I'll walk you to the train..."

"When will you get back?"

"Eleven, noon at the latest."

"I'll be gone by then. You work in the stables with those shoes?"

"Boots are at the barn. Got your train pass?"

"I do."

Ben said, "I need to get going." He switched off the light. He carried the mug over to the bed, leaned in to give her a kiss; he caught her cheek. He stood back. "I guess I'll see you at the library."

"Yep." Her voice sounded as if she were ready for more sleep.

"I wished we'd started up in the spring," he said.

In a groggy voice, she said, "That's really pretty. Actually."

That was good. It was time for him to go.

Outside, the streetlights beamed their fuzzy gray cones down onto the streets. The sky beyond them was purple...as purple as what? he thought. Grape soda, an eggplant? He stood at the corner of 134th and Rockaway, and from where he stood he could hear a train heading away, in the direction of the skyline. Newspapers were scattered up and down the sidewalks, on the street. The shabbiness of the Jamaica neighborhoods could be tiresome, especially if someone was on a losing streak. He thought of how a grandstand looked after all the races had been run, all the tickets had been ripped up and discarded. He tilted his head towards the sky, to see the stars. When he looked down to his shoes, he appreciated the shine they still had to them.

The River

book i

It had rained for nine days and there was talk the whole town would be washed away. He owned two suitcases. I was thirty-five years old, never been anywhere other than here. We sat up in bed that night. I must admit I was excited.

We heard shouting from the street below. Get out! It's rising! When my husband and I stood at the window, we could see black water rushing down Third.

We ran into shin-deep, cold water, turned up Washington while holding hands. The streetlights weren't working, and we could hear the water rolling and people calling out. My parents lived on higher ground, of course, and I thought of the look on my mother's face when she'd open the door and there would be me and my husband, a man from Indiana she told me not to marry who I'd been married to for six months so far. But the problem was my husband didn't know anyone that he didn't owe money to. So we went to my parents' house, up on that hillside past Ninth. They weren't surprised. The water came all the way to the stoop of their steps. They'd wondered about us.

That night, they let us stay in the attic. I'd played up there as a child, but I didn't want to feel like a child, so after my folks had gone to bed, I told him to make love to me. We laid out the blanket my parents had given us. I hoped they would hear. Later, he and I lay side by side. My husband started talking about money, which was something he always did after we made love. Then, he talked about the flood and what might be waiting for us in the morning.

I still have plans, you know, he said. There was always a little of that after making love to me. He'd never say it directly, but it was as if me and my glorious vagina kept getting in his way.

I didn't feel like listening. Maybe it was because we were in my parents' attic. I said, Let me tell you about this river. When I was eighteen, it froze. 'Bout this time of year, late January, the war was going on, the big war. Steam had been rising from it for days. I was working at my folks' grocery store. One morning, we heard customers saying the river had frozen solid. My mother and I pulled on our coats and walked out to the street to get a look.

I said, I want go down there, Ma. She called after me, We have soup cans that have to be stocked! She went back inside, to her register.

I could see a horse and buggy out on the middle of the river, making its way to the Ohio side. Men in coats and hats. There was a ramp the ferry used, and I started out onto the ice. There's nothing harder in this world than ice. The river was craggy and then it was slick. I held my arms out to my sides for balance. I heard someone shouting at me, I didn't see any women walking out on the river. I kept going. My mind sped, I thought, what if I fall in, what would the newspaper say? 'Local Girl Swallowed by Ice.'

I was terribly excited and a little afraid. It took a while to get all the way over. I was moving so carefully. I told myself not to look back. I made it to the ferry ramp on the Ohio side. That horse and buggy took people back and forth, charging ten cents a ride! I did it on my own. I stood on the ramp, waved over to Newport as if I were saying so long forever.

All I'd done was walk across a river.

book ii

I said, Sweetheart?

Yeah, he said.

You feel okay?

He pulled me closer. I have big ideas for us, he said.

The windows of the attic were curtainless. In the morning, when he and I were standing outside, down on the sidewalk, I looked up to those windows and saw myself, fucking my husband in my parents' attic.

I took his hand and we walked down to see about the flood.

We could get as far as Sixth. Down on Second, there were the spines of roofs sticking up from the surface of the water. There were rowboats and somebody yelled out to us. Did we need to be taken somewhere? I waved them off. The sounds were of things cracking, like a giant going through a forest. I felt as if I were in a dream and in the dream, someone had dreamed up the city and dreamed up the river but then had gotten carried away with the river.

My husband and I would have nothing left and we knew it. He liked to dream big in his own way and who was I to say he shouldn't. I wanted to stay in town, just find another place. Perhaps because my husband and I hadn't anything to lose at all, we stood at the edge of the floodwaters and talked about the things we'd discovered up in my parents' attic. My father collected tobacco cards of boxers. There was a silky magician's cape folded up in a trunk that otherwise held old shoes and boots. Crates of canned beans and bean soup, which they'd hoarded because of the Depression.

Maybe they'll give us a box of soup cans for our first anniversary, I said. My husband, well, he looked concerned about something. He was from the heart of Indiana, that's the way he described his little town. He was not from here.

Don't worry, I said. I took his hand. We'll make it a whole year, I said.

Sporting America

In the stallion barn at Galileo Farm, Ben Held napped in his office. The radio on his desk across the room was tuned into WKOG from Louisville and he'd fallen asleep on the leatherette couch listening to Pat Boone. Like the stalls in the barn, the walls of the office were unpainted cinderblock. When he awakened, the sunlight from the window above the couch reached all the way to the base of the wall across the room.

The Platters, The Five Satins. The news. Recently re-elected Ike laying out his plans for a second term. A report about how CO2 gases were affecting the radiation balance; a dangerous, potentially catastrophic warming trend on the earth had begun. At this, war images filled Ben's mind. Nazi killing camps. In the war he'd fought, he felt he had seen all the horror life had to offer. At the Nuremburg trials, men said they were only following orders. Evil was in the heart, that was the only explanation. He waited for different thoughts to find him. Music returned: "The Twelfth of Never" by Johnny Mathis.

Next to his radio, the office phone rang.

"Hey, hey," Hayley Padgett, the farm secretary, said. "Happy Thanksgiving. Belatedly."

"Happy late Thanksgiving."

"Company's coming. Reporter and photographer from *Sporting America*. They want to do something on Stymie. Should be there directly. Ask them to stop by my office again on their way out, please."

After hanging up, he reflexively opened a lower drawer of the desk, extracted the binder with the articles about Stymie, placed it near the phone. Ben left the office, walked from the shadows in the barn hall out into the late autumn sunlight. Galileo Farm stretched out across a rolling countryside of brown fields. He could see a silver Chevrolet heading his way on the narrow farm road. The paddock fences that ran along the road were dingy, boards were missing.

The driveway was as wide as the road leading to it and the visitors pulled in. Ben stood as far inside the barn as the sunlight reached. "How do," the driver of the car said, striding in his direction. "I'm Dusty Lynch, *Sporting America*. That there is Lyle Entwhistle. In case you can't tell from what he's carrying, he's a photographer."

"Ben Held."

"Hi, Ben." Dusty shook hands with Ben, so did the photographer. "You know what we're here for?"

"I guess to do something on Stymie."

"Right. That's right. 'Where-Are-They-Now' feature. We're traveling across the country, me and Lyle, doing short pieces on boxers and ballplayers and all that. Blackjack Billy Fox, Glenn Davis...we just came from Georgia, talked to Alice Coachman. Editor wanted to do a couple of horses, something from right after the rah-rah of the war, you know." Dusty had a pink face, reddish hair, touch of gray at the sides.

"Billy Fox, great puncher," Ben said.

The photographer, Lyle, had a high forehead and blank-like Buster Keaton expression. "Bad shape. Don't ask."

"Alice is a schoolteacher now. You can read about it," Dusty said.

Ben said, "What other horses..."

"Assault. We were down in Texas, too...that King Ranch is wide open, man. Lyle here thought he saw a rattlesnake."

"How did Assault look?" Ben said.

Dusty grinned in an easy way. "Like a tired old horse. I usually cover baseball, but it's off-season…so what we'd like to do is talk with you, I can do that, and Lyle can find the light he needs." He frowned at the empty fields. "Where's Stymie?"

"In here."

"Can you bring him out, give him a walk? We can photograph that."

"I have an office back here, a scrapbook," Ben said.

"Lead the way."

Ben returned to the shadows of the barn hall. He pointed to one of the two occupied stalls. "That's Tim the Tiger, son of Blenheim…here's Stymie." Stymie stood by the window at the back of the stall. The horse knew they were there, though Stymie didn't turn in their direction. Ben walked to his office.

Following, Dusty said, "Assault was out in a huge pasture. The ranch hands didn't even try to catch him."

Ben placed his hand atop the scrapbook. "They couldn't if they tried. There's a place…" Dusty reached for his back pocket, extracted a slender pad of paper, started flipping pages. He took the pen clipped to his shirt pocket and jotted something. Then, he sat.

"What's your title here, Ben?"

"Stallion barn manager."

"The lady at the front office…"

"Hayley Padgett."

"She said you came down from New York."

"Stymie was stabled at Jamaica Racetrack for most of the time. That's in Queens. I have this scrap…"

"Already interviewed Hirsch Jacobs, he mentioned they're tearing that place down…maybe next year. Going to modernize Aqueduct, have glassed-in stands for winter racing. Jamaica's a dump, right? What was the nickname for it?"

"The Factory."

"...The Meat Grinder, yeah. That was it. So where you from originally?"

"Newport. Kentucky. 'Bout a hundred and fifty miles north of here. You oughta do somethin' on Gallorette. Armed."

"Mmm-hmm."

Ben said, "At one time, this office was a stall. Converted it for me...what's King Ranch like? See any of those...javelinas? Supposedly they growl like dogs."

Dusty could not help but appear preoccupied, though he allowed for a moment of quiet. "So, you look after Stymie. How long you been doing this now?"

"I'll be here seven years in December. Before that, I was with Stymie at Jamaica...throughout his whole career."

"Nice job, huh?"

"How do you mean?"

Dusty held his smile. "Well, this is a retired horse. There can't be much to do."

"He breeds."

Dusty shrugged.

"He's still a bear."

"Right...that's right. Actually, Max Hirsch said something..." He read from the pad, "Max Hirsch, the trainer for King Ranch, said Stymie was the meanest horse he'd ever been around."

"I heard Max Hirsch wouldn't talk about Stymie."

"Well, he was the trainer of Assault. It was a phone interview. I got in one question on Stymie, anyway. Can you walk it out to that road there and then lead it back, even if it's still rough as a bear?" Ben placed his hands on the arms of his desk chair. Dusty remained seated. "I guess Jacobs wanted you with the horse."

Ben said, “It was his idea.”

“Right…you live on the farm?”

“Have a place in the town. Stokes. On Decker, that’s the main street. You guys go see Gallorette?”

“Who?”

“A horse…Assault get visitors?”

“Not many…that ranch is so far out of the way.”

“This ain’t exactly Union Station,” Ben said. He noticed Lyle standing outside the screen door.

“Losing my light,” he said.

Dusty said, “Oh, shit. Okay.”

Ben reached for a rope shank hanging outside the screen door. He extracted a soft brush from the tack box near Stymie’s stall. Stymie didn’t turn when Ben slid the door. Stymie’s winter hair had started to grow in, and it was as soft as the brush bristles. Ben swiped lightly at the horse’s neck and chest, then guided the brush along the withers.

Stymie walked in a solemn way at Ben’s side as they moved in the direction of the large rectangle of sunlight at the open entrance of the barn. Lyle kept his camera at his hip until they were outside. Ben guided Stymie out to the edge of the single-lane road. Further away stood the breeding shed, a maroon-painted barn with a bonnet roof. For Stymie this past spring, there had been fewer trips over there than ever. Ben steered the horse in the direction of the other men. The clicking of the camera was mixed with the sound of soft hoof steps. Stymie had not worn racing plates in years and the muscles in his shoulders were buttery. They paused a few feet from the *Sporting America* men.

“Move over, please,” Lyle said, motioning to Ben.

Ben gave Stymie more of the shank and shifted a step and a half. “Don’t want him to make a break for it.”

“Stymie’s what now?” Dusty said. “Is he fifteen?”

"Sixteen," Ben said. "Turns seventeen January one."

"Would he?" Lyle said, the camera at his side again.

"You can never be sure. You notice how he likes to hold his head up," Ben said. "He did that when he was running."

As Dusty scribbled in the notebook, he said, "We saw that newsreel footage, Lyle...did you get it? That's fine, Ben. Thank you." Ben and Stymie crossed back into the shadows. Inside the stall, Ben removed the halter, which was one of the last things he did every day at the barn. Lyle and Dusty had chatted by the Chevy; Ben ambled in their direction, carrying the shank like a lasso.

"Give me your address and I'll make sure you get a copy of the article," Dusty said. He seemed hesitant about handing over the pad. Ben put his hands out. He wrote:

Ben Held
Box 247 Decker Street
Stokes, Kentucky

He passed the pad over to Dusty. "Make sure to stop by and see Hayley." He stood inside the barn; the Chevy turned onto the farm road. In his office, Ben sat behind his desk and considered the plastic cover of the binder. The scrapbook was something Hayley had put together years ago, not long after Stymie had arrived at Galileo. Ben could show it to the people who came by the farm to get a look at Stymie. The horse was here, of course, the real thing. But the racehorse in Stymie was gone. To her, Ben might've seemed on the quiet side with visitors, people he didn't know at all.

Pasted on one page of the scrapbook was the cover of *Turf and Sport Digest* from February 1949. A color painting of Stymie, in full flight, heading for the finish line. Ben liked the fiction stories they published in *Turf and Sport.* He kept copies in the closet of his bedroom. The stories would begin with lines like, "He was struggling desperately for an occasional mount when he ran into Geraldine Carrol."

On the next page, a *Blood-Horse* cover from November 19, 1949. A photo of Stymie, untacked, standing in the middle of the homestretch at Jamaica, right past the finish line. Mickey Finney, Stymie's groom at the time, posed by the horse's head, his hands on the reins. Mickey wore a hunting jacket and a necktie. Beyond them were the packed stands of Jamaica Racetrack. The photo caption said, "Stymie, A Last Look Around."

The scrapbook had an article by the *New York Trib*'s Joe Palmer:

> Racetrackers, I think, save most of their affection for the horses who do it the hard way, pounding out mile after bitter mile, giving weight and taking their tracks wet or dry, running for any jockey, and trying with what they've got even when they haven't got enough. That's why Stymie fitted a farewell better at Jamaica than a welcome in Kentucky…
>
> This tourist will long remember the way Stymie came around the turn in the Pimlico Cup Handicap, making pretty good horses look as if they had just remembered a pressing engagement with the quarter pole.
>
> He was not a great horse in the sense that Man o' War or Equipoise were great. He isn't versatile…but give him a field with enough speed in it, at a mile and a half or more, and horses better get out of his way, even Whirlaway…
>
> Anyway, another fine and ardent and satisfactory story of the turf was brought to a close at Jamaica.

> And it was happy to note, for all the long campaign, it was not a battered and limping warrior which left it. Stymie never looked better with his bronze coat in great bloom, and the high head carried as proudly as ever.
>
> As he stood for the last time, before the stands, people around the winner's circle enclosure were shouting, "Bring him over here, for just one more time."
>
> The groom didn't obey, and probably was right. Stymie never got in a winner's circle without working for it. It was not time to begin.

Near four, Ben fed the two stallions in his barn. He returned to his office, where he sat in the quiet. Then, his workday was over, and he slung his windbreaker over his shoulder. He drove the pickup the farm leased for him in the direction of the farm entrance. Up ahead was the main office, a two-story stone building built in the 1800s. He spotted Hayley's Falcon parked out front. She had a seventeen-year-old son named Ernie who took the car out on weekends. Dried mud went up to the door handles.

The office had a storm door and he tapped on the frame before opening it. From behind her desk, Hayley had a *Life* magazine, a lit cigarette in her left hand. "All done?" she said.

"It's been a while since we had reporters."

"You didn't cuss too much in front of them, did ya?" Ben felt himself stammer. "Kidding," she said.

"What's that on the cover there?"

"Egyptian soldier. War in the Middle East." She displayed it so he could see: A perspiring man lay in profile. A canteen of water held to his lips. "Take a cigarette, rest your dogs for a minute." On one corner of the desk sat a typewriter with a vinyl covering. Portraits of legendary nineteenth-century racehorses Hindoo and Kingston hung on the wood-paneled walls. Past her desk was a hallway that led to the office of David Beagles, the owner of Galileo Farm, who was hardly ever here. "How was your Thanksgiving? Go up to see your dad?" Hayley's face was oval-shaped, her faint, hazel eyebrows almost matching the color of her eyes. He took one of the leather armchairs across from her desk.

"Stayed here. Listened to the football game. I'll get up there before Christmas to see him. What about you?"

"We had over Hardin's family. Sweet potatoes, greens, and ham. They brought a jug. Shine. Kinda surprised I'm here today." Hardin, her husband, was a nearly-always-busted gambler who worked at odd jobs, never at one thing for long.

"Maybe that article will stir some interest…'Where Are They Now?' If I wrote it, it would be the shortest article of all time."

"Here?" she said. She beamed, the reaction he was seeking.

"You got it."

"You sound like my husband," she said. "Speaking of."

"Yeah," he said. Hardin was built like a cast-iron safe. Hayley liked to keep him happy. As Ben walked for the door, she said after him, "I'll bring some of the leftover ham on Monday."

***

He drove a few miles to town. He lived in a shotgun-style, wood-frame house, which came with a porch and bedsheet-sized front yard. Leased for him by the farm. He had a little driveway for his pickup, a push mower he kept under a tarp around back. He could walk to the town square, where there was a grocery store, a butcher, and two restaurants, neither of which served alcohol. When he drove up to Newport to see his father, he stocked up on whiskey, beer and wine. That evening, Ben sat on the porch with his jacket on, a highball glass of wine in his hand. How might Dusty characterize the work he did? A fifty-seven-year-old man caring for a retired horse. That's what it was. For the thousandth time since he'd moved here, he wondered if he should've stayed with Jacobs's stable, or perhaps gotten on with a different outfit heading west. The plan for his life had been to barnstorm, ride the rails, keep up his spirits. There were no races in this county, nothing of that kind to get lost in. He was, however, glad to be with Stymie. Jacobs, who stopped by the farm on his way to Florida each winter, had once said to Ben, *You've earned this*. He always tried to feel appreciative.

In the living room area, he had a television set, a fritzy Meck that had come with the house. Still an hour before *The Life of Riley* and *Blondie.* He'd listened to *The Life of Riley* while he'd been living in New York, had laughed at it. Then it would be Walter Winchell. "Good evening Mr. and Mrs. North and South America, and all the ships at sea." He said it right after Winchell. On Saturdays he had off half a day and when they were running races in Louisville or Lexington, he might take a drive. At the races, he would once in a great while run into a horseman he knew from New York or his earlier barnstorming days. If the conversation went on for a few minutes, he'd say what he was doing now, running a stallion barn with just two horses, but his main assignment was caring for Stymie. *You got it made, Ben…wow, look at you.*

He thought of calling his father, who he hadn't phoned on Thanksgiving day, not that his father would've expected it. A call happened when one of them felt like it, even if he didn't have a ton to say. Neither Ben nor his father had a bad life—his father hadn't worked since the Depression and people, including Ben, had always provided for him—and he felt that he and his father had different, yet predictable, regrets. His father disliked it when he asked for advice and Ben couldn't remember the last time he'd done that, anyway.

When he went inside, there was still time before *The Life of Riley.* He dialed the house on Isabella Street. Foster Drayton answered on the fifth ring, and Ben said, "Hey, it's me."

"Hold on, I'll get him."

It took another minute, and then he heard his father say, "Son."

"Hey. What're you doing?"

"Watching television, I guess."

"Good. Yeah, we had a couple…easy day, today. Like yesterday, the day before."

"Good."

"Yeah, I'm gonna drive up there and see you in a little bit. 'Bout out of wine."

"Those dry counties are rough."

"I had a TV dinner for Thanksgiving."

"How was it?"

"Everything was in its own little space."

"I wanna try one of those."

It would be close to impossible to explain, especially over the phone, how Ben felt at this moment. He envied his father because his father knew the people around him wouldn't let him starve. Ben had always worked. He didn't feel cheated, however. "I wanna…I don't know, do something."

"Take it easy." Of course, his father would say this.

"I know."

"What was in the TV dinner anyways?"

"Piece of fried chicken, peas, some kind of melted apple pie."

"Goddamn. When you comin' up?"

"Sometime. Want me to bring some of these dinners or whatever?" His father didn't answer. "How you feelin', old man?"

"When you come up, we'll take a walk, if the weather's good. You don't need to call, just show up."

"I know."

"All right, son."

"See ya."

Ben returned the receiver to its cradle. He understood that he wanted to tell his father he was thinking of going back to the racetrack and he wanted his father to talk him out of it. To give up this cupcake job on the farm? His father was nearly eighty now. Ben sent him a check every month. Their conversation on the phone had only taken a couple of minutes, which was typical. But he'd been glad to hear the sound of his father's voice. He understood that was why he'd called in the first place.

* * *

In mid-January, he discovered a copy of *Sporting America* in the slot assigned to him at the Stokes post office. He checked his box once a week; *Sporting America* was the lone piece of mail. At his kitchen table, he flattened the magazine at the edges. In the "Where Are They Now" series, there were sections on Assault, Alice Coachman, Glenn Davis, Doc Blanchard. At the very end:

Stymie: "The People's Horse" Content at Kentucky Retreat

by Darrell Lynch

The 1950s have featured some of the greatest horses in this still-young century: Native Dancer, Tom Fool, Turn-to, Nashua, Swaps. The start of the decade saw the first millionaire ever in Citation. Stymie perhaps couldn't beat any of these horses, though it's unlikely any of them could ever be as popular as he once was. The beloved clay-toned colt who became a champion for the working-class horseplayer can be found these days at Galileo Farm, in lower-central Kentucky. The quiet of the bluegrass countryside marks a considerable contrast to the noisy, rambunctious crowds Stymie raced in front of in New York. Stymie, now stocky and docile, seems to have put his infamous roguish behavior behind him.

"That happens," said Hirsch Jacobs, who owned and for a half-dozen years trained Stymie. "They become more like us." Jacobs, who claimed Stymie for $1500 from the powerful King Ranch operation, is stabled for much of the year at Jamaica, a small racetrack in Queens. He's raced a number of Stymie's sons and daughters, a few of which have turned into class racehorses, including the multiple stakes-winning mare Affectionately. "None will be as good as he was," Jacobs added.

Famous farms like Calumet, Claiborne, and Greentree passed on the opportunity to stand the colt at stud, perhaps in part because of Stymie's unusual pedigree. The horse is a product of the King Ranch's "line-breeding," which is the practice of in-breeding in order to produce the best traits from previous generations. Stymie's infamous temperament might've produced hesitation among breeders as well. King Ranch's great trainer Max Hirsch called Stymie "the meanest horse" he'd ever been around.

David Beagles, the owner of Galileo Farm, said, "Stymie has been a very popular horse on the farm. I brought him here, in part, because of his many fans." Beagles, a land developer, world traveler, and big game hunter, believes Stymie will eventually become a great sire. "There's been a drop in the number of mares he gets each year, that's true," Beagles said. "But one day he'll come up with a son or daughter that'll make him a household name again."

Though Stymie might be past his peak in any number of ways, his future is seen to. "He's set for life," Jacobs said. "We owe him that."

The photo accompanying the article was of Stymie standing outside the barn at Galileo in the late fall sunlight, his coat clean and bright. In the corner of the photo, at the end of the shank, was Ben's right hand. He thought of drawing a circle around the hand holding the shank and mailing the magazine to his father. He'd write *guess who*.

He couldn't find anything in the section on Blackjack Billy Fox.

The following morning, before dawn as always, and with the magazine on the passenger seat, he drove for Galileo. The weak headlights of his pickup pushed into the purple darkness. He turned onto the farm road, went past the *Welcome to Galileo Farm* sign, the crooked post it was mounted to. Hayley had asked Ben, when there was time, to reset that. In his office, he made coffee and then set the feed for the two stallions. He returned to his desk and took a pair of scissors to the article. He cut out the piece on Stymie and placed it after the page of the *Blood-Horse* cover. He began to leaf through the binder pages again. He tried to imagine what kind of article would follow the "Where Are They Now" piece. He dropped the binder into the drawer, closed it. He plugged in the electric heater he kept by his desk in the winter months.

A couple of weeks later, Ben was just outside his office, sweeping out the barn hallway when the phone rang. "Ben," Hayley said, "I'd like you to get up to the office right away."

He drove by one empty pasture, then another. The morning sunlight was bright; at dawn, there'd been a frost covering the dormant grass but that had melted. Hayley's Falcon was parked at the farm office; nearby, he spotted a hardtop Mercury Eight without hubcaps. He pulled in next to the Falcon; two men were leaned up against the Mercury on the driver's side, facing away from him. Negroes. Ben shut the door of his pickup, and one of the Negroes turned his head partway. Ben pulled open the storm door, then knocked twice because the main door to the office was locked. Hayley opened it a sliver, then she closed it after him. "I'm 'bout to call the sheriff. These spades want to see Stymie. I don't want trouble, okay? I saw 'em pull up outside. I opened the door, told 'em I'd need to check to see… One of them said to me, 'We just want to see a horse.' I just don't appreciate that. I don't need to be questioned like…that. They're lucky somebody hasn't pulled a shotgun…I said, 'I think y'all better wait. I'm about the call the sheriff.' You know Wayne Wray, he hates attitude."

Ben said, "Who are they, Hayley? Did they say?" The blinds were open partway and he used the tip of his index finger to create a better view.

"The one boy said he worked with Stymie. But that

doesn't give him any right to…"

"Do not call the sheriff. I'll handle it. Do you understand?" She held one hand to the base of her throat. "I know…"

Outside, Ben went in the direction of the Mercury, to the driver's side. Both Negroes watched him; to the older of the two, Ben said, "EJ? It's Ben Held, EJ."

The older man said, "Goddamn."

"You remember me?" Ben said.

"Don't believe it," EJ said. Ben embraced EJ, gave him a pat on the back. They all seemed startled by it. Ben made a quick turn in the direction of the office window.

"Who's this?" Ben said, returning to them.

"My nephew, Franklin," EJ said. The nephew wore a wool jacket, a white shirt buttoned to the top. He had on glasses with black frames. "Shake hands with him, son." Franklin had a big clammy hand, a tentative grip.

"Hayley doesn't know racetrackers. I guess you know what I mean. Where you comin' from, EJ?"

"Arkansas, Prairie Bayou. Came this far to see Stymie."

"Come on." Ben waved to the window as he spoke. "Ride with me."

EJ sat in the middle. Both of Ben's passengers smelled of gasoline. On the drive, Ben checked and rechecked the rear view. At the barn, he switched off the truck's engine; EJ got out after Franklin on the passenger side. They walked to the fender. Ben said, "All the way from Arkansas? How long is that?"

"Eight hours," EJ said.

"That's my barn, I run it," Ben said. "Stymie's inside. Come on, this way." The three of them went into the shadows at the barn entrance. "The hall's a little dusty, I was sweepin' it when Hayley called. You got enough coat on there?"

"Oh," Franklin. "It's good. It's wool." He whisked his hand at the button line.

"It's all right," EJ murmured.

Ben noticed that Franklin swallowed. "Stymie's right here." He neared the stall, then stepped off to one side. EJ and Franklin moved up to the vertical bars that made up the top half of the stall door. Stymie stood at the back of the stall, in profile to the men. "Stymie," EJ said. The horse turned his head. "See."

In a moment, Franklin said, "You could've said 'cornmeal' and it would have looked."

"He knows," EJ said. In a moment, Stymie returned to standing profile. "Tell him, Ben."

"Stymie doesn't like people, but he knows people..." Ben said. "Want me to bring him out for you?" When neither of them spoke, he went to get a lead rope. He said, "Let me get around you here, guys." He slid open the door just enough, walked through the straw to Stymie, clipped the lead to the ring on the underside of the horse's halter. Stymie didn't move. Ben heard the stall door slide. Steps. EJ's hand reached for Stymie's neck, patted it. "This son of a gun tried to kill me a hundred times," EJ said.

"He's not kidding," Ben said. He turned partway to see Franklin behind the bars of the closed stall door.

"Man, I never thought I'd see you here," EJ said.

"He knows you," Ben said.

"Probably wonderin' why I ain't carrying brushes. You don't have to bring him out. Get on in here, Franklin."

Franklin took one step inside the stall but came no further.

EJ said, "I followed him, listened to his races on the radio." He reached forward, waved his hand through Stymie's mane. “He’s thick now, ain’t he?”

“You musta really wanted to see him,” Ben said. “Hey, I got an office. Used to be a stall. Back there.”

“It wasn’t that long ago,” EJ said.

Ben waited for him to say more. “There’s a track in Arkansas, right? Oaklawn Park? What’s it like?” Slowly, EJ shook his head. Ben considered Franklin’s expression, then he said, “Man, he really ran his heart out, didn’t he?”

“Felt like we ought to see him,” EJ said.

“Does he really know?” Franklin said.

In the next moment, EJ said, “Yeah, he does. Got any coffee or anything, Ben? If I know you.”

“Office,” Ben said.

In the office, Ben plugged in the electric coffee maker. “Sit, please,” he said. Both EJ and Franklin wound up on the couch. “I don’t have any sugar or cream.” He stood near the desk with a hand on his hip. “You guys drove all night?”

“I let him have the wheel a little this mornin’. He needs to learn. See, there was this magazine and somebody showed me a picture of Stymie. I tell some people I worked with Stymie, but these boys…they aren’t too worried about some horse.” His head bobbed as he spoke. “We got to be back in Prairie Bayou tonight, can’t miss too much work. Brought our own gas. Cans in the trunk.” He accepted the mug of coffee Ben brought to him. “Article didn’t say anything about you.”

“Why would it?”

Franklin said, “You have any cream soda?”

“Just coffee.”

EJ said, “Got sorghum cake in the car, cream butter, fried chicken. What’s left of it.”

“I’m okay,” Ben said.

“I was there at the start,” EJ said. From the pocket of his jacket, he brought out a pack of Pall Malls. He offered one to

Franklin and then one to Ben. A moment later, all three were smoking. Ben brought over a tin ashtray, and Franklin reached for it.

"Stymie knows you," Ben said.

"I knew he would."

"What do you grow on your farm, EJ?"

"Sorghum, soybeans. Lotta work."

"Sorghum. When I stabled in Nebraska, we mixed that in the feed. Making money with that farm, I guess?"

"Hell no."

"Pretty nice ride you got."

"Borrowed it, best-runnin' car from all the people we know. I got a pickup."

"We ain't stopping at any gas station," Franklin said.

EJ said. "He's gonna start at Tougaloo in the fall…college. In Jackson, Mississippi. Skipped a grade in high school." He rubbed a hand over his face. "Do you run this whole place?"

"I do not. I'm in charge of these horses. Breeding season starts pretty soon, but they ain't booking many mares. Owner's got a lot of money, but this place loses…one day we'll get a phone call saying he's shutting us down. Stymie'll be pensioned after they squeeze the last few bucks out of him."

Franklin said, "Will the woman call the police?"

Ben had made himself a coffee. He was now seated at the desk. "Her problem is the sun rises and sets in this county." He flicked his ash into the tray on his desk. "I'm sorry about that."

"This looks like a good set-up," EJ said.

"When I lose it, I'll appreciate it more. That article you saw…" He thought about the way he'd been with Dusty, the way he'd answered the questions. He hadn't seen EJ in a dozen years at least. Ben said, "I have a title, but I'm a fucking groom. That's all. How's the coffee?"

"Good," EJ said. "I usually take a little sugar in mine."

"No sugar today, buddy. So, you got a farm in Arkansas."

"It's leased," EJ said. "But it's mine. My work."

"You marry Liza?"

Frowning, he said, "You know Liza?"

"One time at the barn. No way she'd remember me. But yeah. She like Arkansas?"

"She likes our land. We live where we please, sir."

"I gotta say something," Franklin said. "If y'all don't allow Negroes, there should be a sign. If y'all are friends, I can speak. Sorry…it ain't right. I don't know what you want me to do here. A sign is at least honest."

"We're having coffee with this man," EJ said.

"You don't have to apologize," Ben said.

EJ said, "I wasn't going to." He leaned back on the couch.

"How's Stymie look to you?"

He said, "He looks okay, Ben. Looks like you're takin' good care of him. I got it in my head I had to see him." EJ stared in the direction of the door. "She said it was foolish. Franklin's gonna be a writer. When he's an old man, he can tell everyone he saw Stymie…we won't stay here too much longer. This is what we came here to do."

"You're safe on the farm. We don't allow any nonsense. Nobody's firing any guns. Agitate the horses. Y'all can spend the night at my place if you want to."

"If we stay here too long that lady will call the sheriff."

"It's my barn, fellas," Ben said.

"No trouble," EJ said. "Slip in, slip out."

"The offer is good," Ben said. "Maybe when I'm in Arkansas, I can look you up. Prairie Bayou. You can put me to work. You followed his career."

"If it was on the radio. Not much for readin.' But Franklin here."

In Franklin's direction, Ben said, "My last name is spelled just like it sounds."

"We don't need to stay too long, Ben," EJ said.

"Finish your coffee, anyway. Get one more look at him."

***

EJ and Franklin were outside the door of Stymie's stall. Ben went to the entrance of the barn and surveyed the surrounding countryside. In the quiet of the barn, he could hear their voices, the two of them. Hayley's Falcon was parked where it had been, and from where he stood he could see the post of the crooked *Welcome* sign. He would go to the farm office and perhaps try to explain all of this to her. He and EJ had worked together when Stymie was only a rogue…he caught EJ and Franklin in the corner of his eye, approaching. EJ had his hand out to shake. "Thank you, Ben," he said. Franklin's hands were in the pockets of his jacket. EJ said, "I'm glad you were here."

"That Eight run okay? When did they stop makin' those, anyway?"

"Got us here."

"If I'm ever through Prairie Bayou," he said.

"That's right."

"I'll drive you back."

From the office lot, Ben observed the Mercury turn from the farm road onto the main road. Hayley might've been inside the storm door, doing the same. In another minute, he'd return to the shadows of the barn, his office; when he felt less futile about things, he'd call Hayley, tell her the visit went fine. He'd say, *That guy who left, he was a great groom. He drove hundreds of miles just to see Stymie.*

The Mercury was gone from his view.

Arkansas, there was a place he hadn't been. He'd ridden through Kansas in the back of a pickup on a summer afternoon, and they'd passed endless fields of sorghum. Destination, Michigan, the Detroit Fair Grounds. By the time they'd reached the Missouri line, night had fallen, and he laid out, used his duffel to rest his head. That farm work looked like hard work, but EJ must be doing all right. Of all the people.

He'd seen pictures of Oaklawn Park in the *Telegraph,* they had the Arkansas Derby. The track was also known for its apple blossom trees in the infield. He knew that was not all there was to it. Those old Mercurys were pretty sturdy models and he wished EJ and Franklin a good ride back to their farm. EJ had to see Stymie. Ben felt it was good that an old racetracker like himself was here to make sure that EJ could.

Correspondence

Ben had seen an ad in *Noir City* for a Magnavox television, and when he walked down to the hardware store on Simpson Street he brought the magazine with him. He pointed out the ad to Owen Edgar, who ran the store, and Owen nodded solemnly. Yes, that could be ordered. He would call Ben when it arrived.

The Magnavox set had a stand with four stout, mahogany legs. He set it up in one corner of his living room. Ben liked the big dial for changing the channels. The V-shaped antenna made him think of a Martian's headgear. While he watched television, he drank. He bought beer and whiskey and red wine, for which he had an ever-growing fondness. Because he liked red wine, he finally had to go out and buy himself an alarm clock. He bought this, too, at the hardware store. Every afternoon, one of the first things he did after getting back from work was wind up his alarm clock, return it to the nightstand by his bed. Then, he would make his dinner.

One Sunday evening, right after he'd finished a meal of spaghetti and meatballs from a can, his phone rang. He carried a highball glass of red wine with him and then sat down to answer it. He said hello and his father said, "Ben?"

"Pop?"

"Ben, are you there?"

"I'm here."

"Got something to tell you. Bonnie Dennert died last week. In the hospital."

"Pop. Say it again now."

"You heard me." Ben didn't speak, and his father said, "I thought you'd want to know."

"Where was she?"

"What's this?"

"When she died, Pop, where was she?"

"Son, she was in the hospital. She fell on the street, middle of the afternoon. Hit her head on the sidewalk. Somebody said she'd been drinking…she drank… Had the funeral already. It's over. She's in the ground. I didn't go."

"Are you sure it was Bonnie?" Ben said.

"Are you all right? Is this Ben?"

"Pop, it's me."

"Why're you asking me all these questions?"

"I…I don't know."

"Well, Ben, I'm sorry I had to be the one to tell you. I thought about whether to call you."

"I'm glad you did."

"You're glad?"

"Just an expression. I needed to know."

"I didn't think it mattered when. I guess that's it."

"I'll drive up soon."

"How's that?"

He knew his father heard him. He said, "You had to tell me."

"I did."

"I'll see you soon."

Ben had been drinking but it didn't feel that way. He didn't know what else to do, so he went out to the kitchen and filled his glass again. *Maverick* was coming on; it was one of his best new shows and he decided there was nothing else to do but try and watch it. At some point he turned off the TV and went for the shoebox in his closet. While on the edge of his bed, he sifted through the things Bonnie had written, sent to him. He came across a poem in his own handwriting, though it was something he'd copied.

I. Italian Child's Ditty
One, two,
I've got the flu.
Three four, we sleep on the floor.
Five, six,
We're good Catholics.
Seven, eight,
Who should I hate?
Nine, ten,
Mama's fat again.

II.
When I returned from mare-steaming Europe,
Remembering the slow and the dead,
I sat and cried in my pantry,
And ate every dry piece of bread.

But now that I've firmly established,
That it was all a meaningless dream,
I laugh at the pregnant children,
And cigarettes float in my cream.

He went to bed without removing his shoes. Next thing he knew, the alarm. He reached for it, fell to the floor, and when he stood, he picked up the clock from the stand and hurled it across the room. Even after it hit and the wall and landed, it kept ringing. Still, he wound up just a few minutes late for work. He checked on Stymie and Tim the Tiger, went to set their feed. The horses were fine, and in a while he'd turn them out in the fields. At sunrise, he sat in the quiet of his office. In the window, he noticed the lightening of the sky. Soon, he'd drive up and tell Hayley he wouldn't be able to work a full day today.

He'd created his own policy about bringing books to the barn office; if he had a bunch of them lying around there it might seem like all he had was free time. Maybe someone would decide his job wasn't necessary after all. Also, he did tend to get lost in whatever he was reading. He was being paid to do a job here. But he decided that morning it was a ridiculous thing to worry about and he would've liked to have something to read. There was only the scrapbook about Stymie in the lower right-hand corner of his desk. He had books back at the house, and after he left here, he might spend the rest of the day reading and sleeping. Hayley got to her office around eight, so he wouldn't have to wait too much longer.

He remembered finding "Children and War" by Robert Lasson in an edition of *Poetry* magazine; he'd been in the Rose Reading Room at the New York Public Library. He copied it for himself and then wrote out another copy for Bonnie. He didn't offer a greeting or a salutation, just put a return address on the envelope. He had written her right after the death of FDR and never heard anything back. Sometime later, he'd sent her "Children and War" and the result was the same.

Each year, on his way to Florida for the winter, Hirsch Jacobs paid a visit to Galileo. He wanted to see Stymie, and then he and Ben would sit in Ben's office and chat. One December, Jacobs had brought with him a manila envelope that had been addressed to Ben at Jamaica Racetrack. There wasn't a return address on the envelope, but Ben recognized the handwriting. He told Jacobs he'd look at it later, whatever it was. He waited until he was back at the house. Inside the envelope, he found five ration books, each with its full complement of stamps, six pages worth. In four of the books Bonnie had written a little story, and in another one she'd made a poem out of the Devens Literacy Test, given to some recruits in the big war. She wrote in cursive, and she had to do this carefully in order not to tear a page of stamps. The stories were about a hopeless gambler, a priest, a flood. A woman who'd gone to see a movie.

He kept the envelope in a shoebox, along with the poems he'd copied. The box would be at home, waiting for him. He told himself not to drink today, it would make everything worse. His father said that Bonnie had been drinking when she'd fallen—had he said that? Ben thought that if he'd been there, been with her, she'd wouldn't have fallen on any sidewalk. He would've caught her. Or they would have been holding hands. He felt ready to leave the barn.

At the farm office, he pulled in next to Hayley's Falcon. He walked up the stone steps, tapped on the storm door and waved to her from behind it. From her desk, she motioned him in. Hayley had the phone to her ear; she held up an index finger and he remained by the door. He bowed his head, noticed his clothes were from the day before, the unwashed, dusty workpants. He thought he heard the phone being replaced on its cradle. "Hi, Ben," she said.

"I didn't mean to…"

"You're fine."

"Ah, actually, I'm going to go home. I'm under the weather this morning."

"Oh, all right. Something going around?"

"I don't feel like working today." He stayed near the doorway. "My father called me last night, told me that my ex-wife had passed away. Not my ex-wife, but someone I'd wanted to marry. That's all…"

"Do sit down. Come over here." From behind her desk, she stood. She led him over to a chair opposite her desk. Ben had never mentioned Bonnie before. He took a chair.

"I feel like driving up there, to Newport, but she's been dead a week already." He sat with his knees apart, his hands folded in front of him. "I'll go up there to see her grave. When I find the time."

"You should."

"He did that to me, my father, when my mother died. Didn't tell me right away. Sent me a telegram about it, though not right away. When I asked him about it, and he said, 'Son, there's nothing you can do.'"

"You always think there's something you can do."

"He hates to deliver bad news…he hates the idea of bringing me any more trouble." His shoulders hunched forward a bit. "I'm okay. Horses are fed. Can you get somebody to look after them today? I'll be back tomorrow." He supposed by now he might look quite upset. She didn't even know who Bonnie was, but she appeared on the verge of turning emotional. "Bonnie and I grew up a few blocks from one another. My father said she tripped and fell on the sidewalk. Hit her head, never woke up."

"That's a shame."

"I might spend a day or two in Newport. I haven't seen her in…I guess it's thirteen years. I go to see my father, and I wondered if I'd ever run into her again. Everything was over a while ago. But the way I feel right now."

"You never use enough of your vacation days."

"Who will you get to look after the horses?"

"That new guy, Artie. He knows plenty. We got him from Claiborne."

Ben wanted to object; Artie was supposed to be this

sharp horseman who knew everything about bloodlines. He was also brought in to help fix paddock fences. The fences had remained in bad shape. He said, "I'm going write out the routine, so he'll have it. Can I get a pen…paper?"

She slid over a sheet of farm stationery. On it, he wrote:

Turn out horses: 10am.
Clean stalls.
Sweep barn hallway.
Fill water buckets.
Fill hay racks.
Return horses to stalls.
Afternoon feed: 3pm. 2 cups of oats apiece.
Remove halters.

He thought, again, about the stanzas of poetry he'd copied, and then he thought about telling her about the ration books. All of it was so particular though, the way he and Bonnie were. When he'd opened the manila envelope and found the ration books inside, he'd felt all that was only known to them.

Hayley guided the directions he'd written so she could see. "Simple enough," she said.

"Yep." He held out the pen and she reached for it. He said, "I'll call you later and let you know about tomorrow. I might want to come in, don't know yet."

"Sure, Ben."

When he was sitting behind the wheel of his pickup, he didn't reach for the ignition right away. He made himself a promise not to start drinking, not at least until evening. He could spend the day reading.

At some point, he'd call his father and he didn't want to be drinking when he did. He didn't want to bother his father, but he wanted to know where Bonnie was buried. His father would anticipate his wretchedness. His father, knowing that he would call and that he would want to know, would've already found out for him.

Footage

She's arrived at the Majestic on Monmouth to see Harvey, *a movie about a man who has an imaginary six-foot-tall rabbit as a best friend. She had read the play years earlier, and one of the things it made her think about was an old friend who traveled with horses. Said he wanted to stay optimistic. She envied him, and when he left, she allowed part of her soul to go with him.*

She's alone and feels comforted when the lights go down; the other folks in the theater seem to disappear. From her purse, she removes a flask.

There are newsreels. Bits of General MacArthur's farewell speech to Congress. He quotes the old army ballad, "Old Soldiers Never Die." She had seen photos of him in uniform, with all the decorations. He makes his speech in uniform, without them. A sign of humility? It seems honest enough. The wars will never be over. Next is a story about Sunset Boulevard *winning the National Board of Review Award for the best film of 1950. There are images of the film's premiere from earlier in the year, a gray-suited Bill Holden walking with Gloria Swanson in her shiny tiara.*

She saw that film three times in this very theater, alone, of course. She liked it. She liked it that the story was voiced-over by the dead man in the swimming pool. The swimming pool scene was the first scene, and the story was so good she forgot about that. In the end, he was still dead in the swimming pool.

She's opened the flask, is ready for her first drink but pauses before getting it to her lips. There's footage of just-retired Citation, the first racehorse ever to earn a million dollars. The newsreel shows Citation winning one race after the next, the Kentucky

Derby, the Pimlico Special, and the Tanforan Stakes.

Wasn't that one of the places where they kept the people with Japanese blood during the war? Tanforan Racetrack? In her mind flash images of London burning. Faces of terrified Jewish children...the interminable, nightmarish war...it's been over for years, but things are never over, never completely, not if you care about fighting for your own life. In an instant, she's sniffling, wiping at her nose with the back of her hand. She continues watching. Citation is a beautiful animal. Even in her sorrow, she is touched by his glorious strides.

"And so we say good-bye, Citation!" the voice of Mel Allen says. "We'll never forget you."

The image of Citation lingers in her mind, even after Harvey *has begun. She cannot help but think of her friend, the one who left to work... She tells herself to focus, she's paid good money to see this. Jimmy Stewart is Elwood P. Dowd, the bewildered, kind-natured man who has conversations with the imaginary rabbit.*

It's wonderful. The audience never sees Harvey, and it's not hard to understand. Elwood prefers his own company. Elwood amuses himself. He alone can keep his spirits up. She knew she would like this. She finishes what's in the flask. She remains in her seat until the credits have rolled through all the way.

The house lights glow and an usher in a light blue uniform with gold buttons happens along with his broom and dustpan. He sweeps between the first and second rows of seats. He notices she is watching him.

"I guess that's it," she says. She collects her things.

"There's a showing at six," he says. "But you'll have to buy another ticket."

"I have to be at work," she says. She snaps her purse shut, gets to her feet, reaches for her coat. She walks up the aisle and without turning says, "By the way, you're missing a button on your jacket."

Galileo

He no longer had a television to watch. Not long after he received word of Bonnie's death, he took his Magnavox to the hardware store and asked Owen to see if anyone would be interested. He'd tried to watch television in order not to think about Bonnie, and trying not to think about her made him feel unstable. When the set was sold, he mailed the $220 to his father and asked that the money go for her headstone. Not long after this, his father mailed the money back and said everyone at the restaurant and her friends had chipped in to purchase one.

For a time, he could not bring himself to visit the cemetery, and when he did he wore the green tie she'd given him for Christmas during WW2. This was the tie she'd bought for her first husband. Bonnie was buried near the base of a tulip poplar tree that could have been a hundred years old. He stood before the beveled headstone with her engraved name and felt everything go out of him. His life had ended, and he understood that upon leaving the cemetery he would be a ghost of himself. His remains should go here, next to hers. He went to the office of the funeral director with the money from the sale of the television. He asked about purchasing a spot next to hers. One was available.

In his house, he opened his old books. He felt his past coming back to him because he'd been in other places when he'd first read these books. Books made him think of libraries, and he'd been to grand libraries. One morning, after feeding Stymie and Tim the Tiger, he lay on the couch in his office and turned the pages to F. Scott Fitzgerald's *The Last Tycoon*. The chores for the morning were finished and it was raining outside so the horses remained in their stalls. Horses could get wet, that wouldn't hurt anything, but the rain was cold and there would be nothing for the horses to do but stand out in it. He didn't want to be in it at all. He was stretched out on the couch in his office, and he kept thinking about the sound of the rain. He closed the book and considered the dust jacket. The author's name was in white lettering, the book title in red letters, with a black background. The subheading said, *An Unfinished Novel.*

He awakened with a start, had napped past afternoon feed time. In the feed room, he filled a bucket with oats. He coaxed open the door; Stymie remained at the window that looked out to an empty field. Stymie didn't move for his bucket even after Ben had dumped in the oats. He watched the horse for a time; Stymie seemed rigid. Ben stepped in the horse's direction. "Come on, you old shit." He reached for the halter, and with that Stymie rose, reared, and struck at Ben with his front hooves. One hoof glanced his skull, the other caught his elbow. The empty bucket clattered to the stall floor. Stymie's sides heaved, as if readying to charge. Ben crawled out of the stall on his knees and one good hand, slid the door using his shoulder. The blood dripped past his eyebrows, splashed on the pavement. Doubled over, he made for his office and the phone there.

Hayley drove him to Stillville Hospital where they put seventeen stitches in his head. His elbow was reset, then wrapped in a bandage and covered with a plaster cast. The doctor suggested the pains would continue, and Ben needed to stay quiet, get his rest. Hayley drove him to his house, said they'd bring his truck later. She asked him to call her in the morning at the Galileo office, and he said that he would.

He'd been given a bottle of pain pills. His name was typed on the label, along with directions: *take for pain every four hours.* He unscrewed the lid and dumped them onto his kitchen table.

How many times in the past decade and a half had he done this, reached for Stymie's halter? Thousands. As a young colt, Stymie had been a living, breathing minefield. In those early days, Stymie reared, propped, even fired his back hooves, though the horse never hurt him. Ben felt the two of them were accustomed to one another. Occasionally, Ben might've fooled himself into believing he and Stymie had a unique bond, and because of this, Stymie would never injure him. Stymie knew him, his manner, his ways, and perhaps even appreciated him.

An hour after he'd taken the first pill, he took another; he poured bourbon in a glass and cut that with a splash of water and he thought of the book he'd left on the couch in his office. His thoughts continued to float around, and he remembered when Jacobs had first offered him the job on the farm, about going with Stymie and that it was such a generous offer he couldn't refuse it. Though all he'd had to do was say no. He could've, should've said, No thank you. I want to stay here, near the races. Stymie will be fine without me. All true. But he'd said yes, and it wasn't all politeness.

In the morning, he awakened on the floor next to his bed, in the clothes he'd worn the day before, including his boots. In his mirror in the bathroom, he considered the stitches in his head, the dark blood on his shirt. Suddenly, he began heaving, wound up with his face stuck in the sink. Pumpkin-colored, foamy spittle. He brought his forearms to the rim of the sink, then turned on the water, let it run over his head, and once he straightened himself he felt cold shivers. He thought about calling the farm, seeing if Hayley could come over and look after him. But that wasn't her job. He felt Bonnie's presence, as if she were in the next room, sitting on the edge of the bed, waiting for him. He dried his face with the sleeve of his shirt.

Mid-afternoon, he made lunch, swallowed another pain pill. He called the farm and informed Hayley he was getting along all right. She said for him to take it easy. He decided to take a walk outside. Somewhere along the line, it had stopped raining, last night or maybe this morning. The road was dry, and the late fall sky was mint-colored and empty. Someone had brought his truck. His left arm was the one that was broken, so he could work the gearshift and when he had to shift, he placed the cast arm on the steering wheel.

Hayley left at 4:30, and it was past that now so the parking lot outside the farm office was empty. At the barn, he could see right away that the hallway hadn't been swept. The hay racks for Stymie and Tim the Tiger were half full, anyway, but their water buckets needed topping off. He used his right hand for everything, turning on the water spigot just outside the barn entrance, carrying the bucket to a stall, sliding open the door. He was irritated enough to consider sweeping out the hallway himself; his broken arm ached, and he decided against it. He stood before the stall that held Tim the Tiger; the horse noticed he was there but then turned to the hay rack. Like Stymie, he had a marvelous red coat. There was a school of thought out there that chestnuts were generally more temperamental, and sons of Blenheim had this reputation in particular. Tim the Tiger, despite the dynamic name, was rather mild-mannered. He had been purchased by the farm a few years ago; by that point, it had become clear that Stymie would not be a highly sought-after sire. Blenheim was the most accomplished stallion in the world; his progeny included Whirlaway, Jet Pilot, Ocean Wave, A Gleam—all champions.

He moved to Stymie's stall, and he stood there at the closed door; Stymie, too, was at the hay rack and Ben felt the horse was watching him from the corner of his eye—waiting for a beating, or maybe just for the chance to strike at him again.

Stymie had been a vicious young horse. At the King Ranch, he'd been broken by ranch hands, and it wasn't hard to imagine that the experience left him hating people. He was a nasty, volatile, angry animal. The King Ranch people must've been happy to see him go, and once Stymie joined his barn, Hirsch Jacobs, too, felt he was worthless. Stymie was raced hard and that could have easily ruined him, given him a one-way ride to the slaughterhouse. Stymie had learned, just enough, about what men needed him to do. He'd been durable enough to survive the demands of the life set down in front of him. But he was not and would never be the same wild horse he'd once been on the ranch. Ben had felt the truth of Stymie's impassivity, his indifference. He remembered being afraid of him, too, back in those days at Jamaica. A horse could kill a man. Lots of things could. It wasn't difficult to go back further in his past, to the war, and then even before that. Were there signs that cruelty would come so easily? He thought of his parents, their shack on the river side of Second Street. As a boy, he'd fished in that river. When he thought of this, he felt fortunate indeed because he'd known of a life before the war, too. As he'd grown into a teen, the lives around him seemed dismal indeed, but he did not feel that way now because cruelty was not all around him then. Life was cruel, he'd learned that.

The racetrack was a cruel place. A horse had to show its value, else it would be dispensed with. This could not be explained in words, it had to be shown with force. No animal was born so that it could spend much of its life in a stall. And when it was out of the stall, it was instructed on how to be and what to do. This understanding was beaten into the horse, there was no other way. Horsemen, like all men, owned a nature that included cruelty. Though he knew it was only wishful thinking, Ben wanted to believe that he'd used up a lifetime's worth of cruelty in the war. The truth was that the potential for that wouldn't be extinguished until he'd taken his final breath.

Now, here they were, Stymie in his stall and Ben with stitches in his head and his arm in a cast. What had triggered Stymie's attack? He wanted it to make sense. Had Stymie flashed backed to the days when he'd been broken on the King Ranch? Did that happen to horses? He believed that horses dreamed, that as they slept images floated through their minds. By striking at Ben, was Stymie trying to tell him something, that he was sick of seeing Ben's old, ugly mug? Or had a memory floated through Stymie's mind, had he, just for a moment, felt the anger he'd always carried inside him? Stymie had once been a free horse roaming a vast prairie. How life must have felt, everything a wonder and a mystery. Ben's thoughts went back to when he was just a boy himself, fishing in the river. From behind, could hear his father's voice, asking if he caught anything.

* * *

In the morning, he slept past dawn, and after he made coffee he called the farm office and Hayley told him not to worry, Artie would be looking after the horses. He did the dishes, made his bed, then he went back out to the kitchen to see if he still had a pack of Luckys in the odds and ends drawer. A few years ago, he'd stopped smoking just to see how it felt, and after a few days not smoking had felt all right. But then he'd gone back to it for some reason. He tried not to smoke just because he was bored, and this morning he didn't get the cigarette halfway burned down before sticking the butt under the faucet. He wrestled with the idea of driving out to the barn—but he kept thinking, Jesus Christ, is this it? I can't do anything else? I don't want to go anywhere else? A pill helped, but as soon as it started to wear off, everything bothered him. He felt like dumping down the sink the few pills he had left, and then thought better of it.

By early afternoon, he thought it would be all right to visit the barn, just to see how things were going. As he pulled into the barn driveway, he saw the hallway wasn't swept. Artie's white DeSoto sedan was nosed into the barn entrance, and when Ben stood in front of the screen door to his office, there was Artie sitting up on the couch, reading *The Last Tycoon.* He remained there until Artie looked up and said, "Hey. Jesus, look at you."

"Horses been fed?"

"Yep." He didn't close the book and Ben pulled open the screen door with his good hand. "This is yours?"

"Yeah."

"It's pretty good. I like Ray Bradbury, *Dandelion Wine*, you know that one? I read it this summer. Everything okay?"

"As long as the horses are all right."

"I just said I fed 'em."

"When?"

"A little while ago. Gonna turn 'em out here in a little bit. Do the stalls, clean the buckets, the whole thing." Artie had a narrow-looking, almond-shaped head. A lean man, pale, some cousin of Hayley's husband. Ben assumed the chair by his desk. "I like Hammett, too, you know Dashiell Hammett? Even if he's a commie, hell of a writer. I heard they had him scrubbing toilets in West Virginia. You here for any particular reason?"

Ben wasn't sure he had any authority over Artie and right then wasn't all that interested in establishing any. "There's a radio there."

"I don't listen to the radio when I read. I like that song 'Sixteen Tons,' though. If there was a record player, I'd play it."

"No record player. No television."

"I don't like television. Except for when the races are on. Or baseball. Or Groucho. Jayne Mansfield. What about you, bud? Who do you like?"

When Ben spoke, he said, "You mean women?"

"Yeah, sure, I guess so."

"Ava Gardner, Bacall—Lauren Bacall—Natalie Wood." He wanted to say Hayley, because he liked her, he thought of her. She was the only woman here.

"So, you like brunettes."

"Lauren Bacall is kinda blonde."

"Yeah. You look really beat-up." Artie traced a line at the crown of his head. "That's gonna be a huge scar. The stitches look like where you grip a football. Don't mean anything by it."

After Ben cleared his throat, he said, "He got me pretty good."

"Old Stymie, acting up like that. What's that all about?" At Claiborne, Artie had helped look after Nasrullah and Princequillo and made sure everyone at Galileo knew that. He didn't need to be told anything about horses. "I like Stymie," he said, his voice growing quieter. "I remember when he was good. Nobody can hold a candle to Native Dancer, though." He gave Ben an expectant look, waited for the argument. Then, they both heard the sound of a car engine; it quieted, then came the opening and closing of a car door. "Who will this be?" Artie said.

"Hayley," Ben said. They could hear her heels.

"What're you doing here?" she said from outside the screen door.

"Artie and I are talking about Native Dancer."

"Are you now?" He swerved in the seat; she held her arms across her middle. "I saw your truck...you really shouldn't be...Ben. My goodness, look at that black and blue."

He eased himself upward. "Just leaving." Hayley moved to the side and caught the door as he passed. She spoke to Artie.

In the barn hall, she said, "Artie'll do it. He's gonna move his car..." She went a few steps past him, in the direction of the barn entrance, and then she stopped. Ben joined her and they walked for the opening and then around the side of Artie's sedan. Hayley had her Falcon and she stood by the driver's side door; the air was cold but there was plenty of sunlight and she relaxed her arms. He guessed that she was trying not to stare at the stitched-up gash on his head.

"What does it matter if I just come by?"

"Stay at home, a week at least."

He felt himself smiling, faintly, because for a second it seemed like they were married. Like she'd ever have anything to do with him. "I promise, I'm not gonna do any work," he said.

She played along. "That's as much as I'll get out of you." She started the engine, worked down the window. "Everything's fine," she said. He felt like asking if it looked like he was worried. The Falcon traveled up the narrow road and he waved in that direction. He spotted Artie standing at the DeSoto, a car he kept as neat as a pin. Artie seemed to be squinting at him.

"Shoot me," Ben said.

***

So he stayed away from work, and without work to lose himself in he wanted to make up his mind about what he needed to do next. *I Have Seen the Future*—he spent an hour one afternoon trying to find that goddamn button he'd gotten from the World's Fair. It was just a button, but he wanted to hold it in his hand.

In his closet, he had stacks of old *Forms* and *Telegraphs*; whenever he got over to Lexington or Louisville, he'd buy that day's edition and then he'd hang on to it. He liked the routine of turning the pages of a *Racing Form* or *Morning Telegraph*, even after the races from that day had already been run. He'd reread articles. Because he'd never been out there, he liked to read articles about the tracks and racing out west. At one point, he picked up the phone and asked the operator to make a call out to Turf Paradise, in Arizona.

He drove to the barn the next morning, pulled up right at dawn, noted the sparkling frost on the grass. He'd brought some books with him and turned on the electric heater in his office. He checked on Tim the Tiger and Stymie; they were fine, the stalls were dirty, but each horse had hay and water. He made coffee, lay out on the couch in the office and started to read from a story collection by Dashiell Hammett. "The Diamond Wager" was one of his favorites ever. He'd finished reading the story and his eyes were on the window in the office, which held whitish light. By the time Artie opened the office door, Ben was sitting up on the couch, close to the same position Artie had been in when Ben stopped by the other day. "Morning," Artie said.

"There's coffee over there," Ben said.

"I don't drink coffee," Artie said.

"Of course, you don't," Ben said, in a murmur.

"You coming back to work?"

"Nope," Ben said. "Just back to the barn. I got this Hammett reader here. You can have it after I'm done."

"Okay, yeah. So, you didn't do nothin' with the horses yet?"

"No sir."

"I'll go feed then." Ben had a piercing hangover, a sore skull, and dagger-like pains in his elbow. He returned to the book. Artie got back, plopped down in the chair at the desk. His arms were limp at his sides. "I don't even like the smell of coffee."

"What'd you do last night?"

"I don't remember. You look a little better, I guess."

"Listen to the Kentucky game?"

The horses rattled their feed buckets trying to get the last of their oats. "It's cold in this fuckin' office. There should be another door besides the screen door."

"The screen door is so you can hear out in the hallway what the horses are doin'."

"I know why it's there," he said. "I'm only saying something out loud." He heaved forth a sigh. "Are you here checking up on me?" This time, Ben didn't answer. Artie began to go through the books. There were some mystery novels, but the one he selected was George Orwell's *1984.* He opened it to the middle, started leafing through pages. Artie said, "There's this scene at the cafeteria where they have their metal trays and pannikins."

The feed buckets rattled, and then those sounds ended. Artie closed his book. "You brought these for me?"

"I guess so," Ben said. "And me."

"I get it. Gonna turn 'em out now."

After Artie left the office, Ben paused inside the door. Artie and Stymie shuffled up the hall together. Stymie had the paddock to the left of the driveway; Tim the Tiger was turned out in a paddock on the opposite side. While Artie pitched out the stalls, Ben stood in the driveway and studied the condition of both horses. He would've given anything to know if because of what they'd done at the races there was a difference in how their days felt to them now. He supposed he knew the answer. Ben would've brushed the coat before turning out any horse, but yes, there was something to be said for *not* doing that, especially at the start of winter and there was no one else around. Artie might've felt that Ben watching the horses was a way of checking up on him and the work he was doing, though Ben had also brought him some books. Artie cleaned out the stalls, emptied the manure tubs outside, behind the barn. It made for good fertilizer and farmers around here took away the pile for free, Artie just needed to pick up the phone every so often.

He walked out to where Ben stood. "You ever heard of Turf Paradise?" Ben said. Artie appeared a little brighter now that he'd done some work.

"The racetrack?"

"Out in Arizona. Phoenix. Some fella bought a thousand acres of barren desert, and he built a racetrack. Opened a couple years ago, I think. I don't know much more about it, but their season starts in January. I called out there. What do you know about it?" Artie had tucked his hands in the pockets of his overalls. "When I was on the phone with the racing office, I asked what the temperature was, and you know what they said? Sixty-one degrees."

"You fed up with all this?"

"I could feel a little more optimistic."

"Get some ragtop and joyride out there."

"Catch a train," he said. A decision made, Ben felt, momentarily, as if he ought to pass down some words of wisdom. But all he could think of was what he'd just said. "Probably have to take one from Louisville. You can give me a ride to the station, right?"

"No problem, Ben."

* * *

Their Christmas Eve party at the barn would also serve as Ben's going away. Hayley was the one who had the idea and she'd shown up at the barn to talk with Artie and Ben about it. She'd make the food and Ben could bring the spirits; Artie would oversee getting a tree and decorations. They talked about inviting other people, or maybe it could be just spouses or partners. It didn't matter to Artie or Ben because they didn't have anybody, but they thought Hayley should bring whoever she wanted. She decided it would be fine if it was just the three of them. She'd said to Artie, "Oh, you need to call Braxton Feed, get a delivery, enough to carry into New Year's. Go on and do it, please. Walk me out, Ben." As Ben and Hayley emerged out into the sunlight, she told him, "Nothing stronger than beer at the party, just a few bottles, okay?"

Ben didn't need to call his father ahead of a visit, but he wanted to get the Arizona plan out of the way, and that evening when he phoned his father and told him about it, he said a man out there had read of Stymie's whereabouts in a magazine and had called, made him an offer to come out there and be the foreman for his stable. He didn't like to lie to his father, and for this reason alone what he said certainly had to sound like a lie, though his father was good enough not to call him out on it. His father asked him when he was going and Ben said right after the first of the year and then his father said, "Union Terminal?"

Ben said, "I'll catch the Hummingbird out of Louisville. Change in New Orleans."

"Yeah, all right," his father said. "You got it all figured out."

"I'll be up in a few days."

"Come whenever."

When he showed up at the Draytons' unannounced, he told his father he needed to buy some beer, and even though it was cold and the sky looked like nothing more than a dirty ashtray, his father wanted to take a walk with him and suggested they head for Columbia Street, the Wiedemann Brewery. His father had worked there when they had the shack down past Second. Along the way, Ben explained the reason for the mark on his forehead, the cast on his arm, said the cast was coming off soon. There might be a scar left on his head, but he felt good and strong.

His father was quiet, and Ben believed they would miss one another. He liked it that when they arrived at the brewery and ordered three six-packs his father didn't bother to tell the cashier that some moons ago, he'd once worked there. It was something both Ben and his father knew. He cradled the six-packs with his good arm. As they headed for Isabella Street, Ben said, "The other day, I was thinking about when I used to fish in the river. I'd stay out there so long you'd have to come and get me."

In front of the house on Isabella, he placed two of the six-packs in the bed of his truck, which he'd parked right along the curb. He brought the other six-pack over to his father. "I'll write," Ben said. "Send you my address."

His father said, "Thank you, son."

Ben stayed at the bottom of the steps until his father had closed the door to the house behind him, and on the drive back to Galileo it began to snow, flakes so tiny he didn't even have to turn on his wipers.

* * *

On the day of the party, it was cold enough to set the cans of beer outside the door of the barn office. Hayley fried up a whole chicken and made cornbread and black-eyed peas. She brought paper plates, paper napkins, plastic forks. Artie said he'd gotten a deal on the five-foot-tall blue spruce that stood in one corner of the office. Department store star, made of tin. He and Ben had talked about getting ornaments, maybe some little plastic horses or something, but the stores didn't seem to have anything like that. The Christmas music was from WLW in Cincinnati and the feast went on with Hayley seated at the desk and both Artie and Ben on the couch, plates on their knees. They wanted to know about Turf Paradise, though what Ben knew was primarily what he'd read. The horses raced from January to November and the guy at the racing office told him it did get hot in the summer. "Probably palm trees," he said, "like Hialeah. Worked at Hialeah for a few winters. Nice place to be during a war." Ben pointed his fork in the direction of the door. "He raced there one winter, but after that we learned he needed his winters off. Made all the difference in the world, not to pound on him all the time." The radio was playing "O Holy Night," the singer sounded like Dean Martin. The way Artie and Hayley looked at him made him think that because he would be leaving soon, moving on without Stymie, everything he said would be sentimental. "Turf Paradise is out in the middle of a desert, as I understand it, anyway." He felt himself nodding.

"I'll probably write you."

"You know the address," she said.

He bit into his drumstick and right after swallowing said, "What're you doing for Christmas, Artie?"

"For Christmas? This," he said. "I'm gonna be out here tomorrow. Feeding, cleaning shit."

"The horses have to eat," Hayley said. "We're having over my folks, Hardin's folks. I'm not sure what that boy of mine's gonna do…show up if he wants. When's your last day?"

"Today, I guess," Ben said. 'I mean, technically, I'm still on, right? But I got all these vacation days built up…and he's doing the job, so heck."

"I'm takin' you to Louisville on the second," Artie said.

"That's right," Ben said. "Okay, yeah, I'm gonna come to the farm between now and then. Get my books."

"See Stymie and Tim," Hayley said.

"See Stymie and Tim," he said.

"I'm gonna go check on 'em for a minute," Artie said. "Before you suggest it." He shoveled in forkfuls of black-eyed peas. He'd had a couple of beers and that was all, maybe felt they were watching him. Artie stood from his spot on the couch, balanced his plate on the arm of the couch and made for the door. Once he was gone, there was the sound of the radio, "Peace in the Valley," by Elvis Presley.

In a minute, she said, "I don't know that this counts as a Christmas song."

"I was gonna say the same thing," Ben said. "But it's Elvis Presley."

"As long as that boy loves Jesus. Goodness, this heater doesn't provide all that much heat. Cold in here." She sniffed. "Arizona?"

"Indeed."

"So, you gonna miss Stymie, Ben?" She'd already asked

him this, though Artie had been here.

"I'm used to looking at him for answers, you know what I mean. You look at something, you want it to tell you something, to make you feel like everything is all right."

While he spoke, Hayley lit a cigarette. She said, "Being down here makes me think of when Stymie first arrived. The boss, he used to say we just need one of these sires to hit. We'd have an empire here, a horse farm known all over the world. All the farm employees came down to watch him walk off the van. You remember that? We clapped and he stood there with his head up, just taking it all in, I guess. That was years ago. How many years?" He didn't say anything. "He was supposed to save our bacon," she said.

He wiped at a patch of dust above the knee of his workpants. "I think Artie's doing a pretty good job. A guy spends a lot of time around horses, he's gonna be a little screwed up…you know what I mean when I say you look at something because you want it to tell you something?"

"I think so."

He felt himself lurching forward. He wanted to say more, he wanted to tell her that it felt like Stymie had been trying to tell him something when he'd reared up and struck him in the head. He wanted to tell her that Stymie was trying to tell him to wake up. Stymie was trying to tell him to get out of here, get back on the road. Otherwise, he would remain here and sink deeper into regret about things that were done. Stymie was saying, I don't need you anymore, never needed you. One day we'll be ghosts forever. He wanted to say it, but out loud it would sound brainless, even crazy, and she wasn't the right person to say it to. "Anyway," he said, "I like the road."

"That's good. Won't be the same without you, though." He liked the factual way she said this and the way they knew one another. "Where's Artie?"

He rose and with the cigarette in the corner of her mouth, Hayley offered her hands to take his plate.

Artie stood at the gate of the paddock where Stymie was kept. Ben went over to see Tim the Tiger. He stood at the gate of that paddock and watched the chestnut picking at the ground with his chunky teeth.

Then, Ben walked over. "Everything all right?" He arrived at a section of the fence near the gate. Stymie stood at the far end of the paddock. He stared off at something in the distance, something to do with the fields stretching out to the horizon. In Ben's mind came the image of the plains, fields of sorghum, like he'd once seen in Kansas.

"He likes to run the fence line. Was doing it a minute ago." Mist appeared with the words Artie spoke. He had on a jacket, Ben did not. Artie might've wanted to give Ben and Hayley a few minutes to be alone because he knew Ben liked her. A nice gesture if, in fact, that was what he'd been doing. Artie said, "You worried about me looking after him? Anyway, Stymie looks after us, right? Without him, we'd be on the street." Ben gave another glance in the direction of Stymie, who stood near a section of the fence line across the field. "Merry Christmas, Ben."

"I won't be that far away, anyway." Ben said it so quietly Artie might not have heard. It was cold and Ben stood at the fence with his hands in his pockets. "Yes, Merry Christmas."

Together they walked for the barn entrance and the shadows there.

Author's Notes

In addition to the cited passages in the text, the following works/media also helped to shape the content of this book.

Beautiful Hialeah by Bert Clark Thayer, New York, 1938.

Before Vegas, There Was Newport, documentary directed by Brandon Faris, Zone Communications, 2012.

Champions by the editors of the *Daily Racing Form*, 2000.

"The Devens Literacy Test," *Futility Closet*, https://www.futilitycloset.com/2018/03/07/the-devens-literacy-test/.

Free & Public, 150 Years at the Public Library of Cincinnati & Hamilton County by John Fleischman, Public Library of Cincinnati, 2002.

"Good-bye Jamaica..." by Teresa, *Brooklyn Backstretch*, October 7, 2011, https://brooklynbackstretch.com/2011/10/07/good-bye-jamaica/.

The History of Thoroughbred Racing in America by William H.P. Robertson, Prentice-Hall, 1964.

In Our Time by Ernest Hemingway, 1925 (reprint, Scribner, 1996).

King Ranch, 100 Years of Ranching (1853–1953), Corpus Christi Caller-Times, 1953.

Life on the King Ranch by Frank Goodwyn, 1951 (reprint, Texas A&M University Press, 1993).

Nam: The Vietnam War in the Words of the Men and Women Who Fought There by Mark Baker, 1981 (reprint, Berkley, 1986).

New Deal Photography: USA 1935–1943 by Peter Walther, Taschen America LLC, 2016.

Newport (*Images of America*) by Judy L. Neff and Peggy Wiedemann Harris, Arcadia Publishing Library Editions, 2004.

Newport in Vintage Postcards (KY) by Robert Yoder, Arcadia Publishing, 2005.

1939 New York's World's Fair Newsreel "World of Tomorrow," documentary, 2015, PeriscopeFilm, https://www.youtube.com/watch?v=HcfgvzwaDHc&list=PLIp8e66RJrrIilNfxOKjxXvodN0WUfe4G&index=1.

No Man's Land: Fiction from a World at War, edited by Pete Ayrton, Pegasus Books, 2014.

"Ohio Impromptu," playlet by Samuel Beckett, 1980.

Old Latonia: America's Most Beautiful Race Course, documentary, 2016, Cam Miller Films, https://www.youtube.com/watch?v=grpNmO9-xbA.

Racing through the Century: The Story of Thoroughbred Racing in America by Mary Simon, Lumina Media, 2002.

"Sergeant's Field Uniform," National Museum of the United States Air Force, https://www.nationalmuseum.af.mil.

Spuds, Spam and Eating for Victory: Rationing in the Second World War by Katherine Knight, The History Press, 2011.

The Stranger by Albert Camus, Gallimard Publishing, 1942.

"The Tide" by Don Smith, *Turf and Sport Digest*, February

1949.

Wartime Recipes: A Collection of Recipes from the War Years, Jarrold Publishing, 2000.

"Winston Churchill's South Florida Visit in 1946–Part 1 of 2" by Casey Piket, *Miami History*, April 17, 2024, https://www.miami-history.com/p/winston-churchills-south-florida-visit-in-1946-part-1-of-2.

My father, who spent his childhood in Northern Kentucky, provided invaluable background to this manuscript. On a fall morning in 2015, after an all-you-can-eat breakfast at a Big Boy restaurant, he and I walked along the streets of Newport, including Isabella, where his mother's family had lived for decades. He provided tales of family-style cookouts and banquets. He pointed out the one-time homes of bootleggers and bookmakers. He explained how the chalkboards looked in the first casino he'd visited on Monmouth Street. It was a chilly morning, and I felt he was ready to get out of the cold. However, the more he talked, the less we seemed concerned about the weather. He became quite animated, and his memories brought him happiness.

Then, he and I drove over to Western Avenue in Cincinnati. We strolled through Union Terminal. In one of the exhibition rooms is a model of downtown Cincinnati, circa 1940s. The model is offered in meticulous detail, and my father pointed out things he remembered as a boy, places his mother had taken him. At one point, he noticed that I was not scribbling down notes, and he asked me about it because he understood all of this could be for a writing project. I said not to worry, I'd remember.

While writing the various drafts of *Stymie,* I listened to Sirius/XM radio's *Tuxedo Junction,* which is dedicated to music from the 1940s. The opening lyrics of "Jingle, Jangle, Jingle" helped to provide the invention of the character Kelly Brighton, featured in "Dade Taxi."

Twice, I visited the King Ranch in Kingsville, Texas. The first time, I went there following a job interview (unsuccessful) at a nearby university. Then, years later, I happened to be in San Antonio and decided to make the drive to see the ranch again. I signed up for the wildlife tour. The brochure suggested visitors bring binoculars, so I brought along the pair I always carried to the racetrack. The guide said he could lend me something more high-powered. On the four-hour-plus tour, these borrowed binoculars allowed me to better appreciate dozens of bird species, as well as the bobcats, wild turkeys, and, from an agreeable distance, American alligators. Herds of javelinas—perhaps the most famous of all local wildlife inhabitants associated with the ranch—ambled out from the brush along the roadside. Near the end of the tour, we passed by a baseball diamond named Assault Field.

I also stopped by the King Ranch Museum on North Sixth Street in Kingsville. It's filled with artifacts and images about life on the ranch. In a section of the museum, I found a display of trophies won by King Ranch racehorses, including a series of julep cups from Keeneland Race Course. Keeneland, in Lexington, Kentucky, has a tradition of naming races after farms in the bluegrass, and the owner of the winner is presented with a silver julep cup. One of the cups won by a runner carrying the King Ranch colors was inscribed: *Escondidas, October 14, 1966, Glenary Farm Purse.* Glenary, a small horse-breeding farm in Frankfort, Kentucky, was built by my grandfather, and after his passing the property was willed to my mother, her sister, and her brother. Following my graduation from a college in Kansas, I worked on this farm for two years. In *Stymie*, Glenary serves as the model for the fictional Galileo Farm.

The Keeneland Library, the primary spot for researching all that has to do with the history of horse racing, proved to be a meaningful source. There, I read dozens of magazine articles from the 1940s and 1950s as well as interviews with lords of the racing world, including Eddie Arcaro, Max Hirsch, and Hirsch Jacobs. On one visit, I was informed that the library had recently acquired *Daily Racing Form* and *The Morning Telegraph* archives from the 1940s. A librarian and I were able to locate the July 3, 1948, and September 14, 1949, editions where Stymie competed in the Sussex Handicap and the Manhattan Handicap, respectively. I was able to look over the past performances for these events, like I would be able to for any race that had yet to be run.

On another road trip I happened to be in the vicinity of Stanton, Delaware, and one superb spring morning, I wound up sitting in the stands of Delaware Park, watching workouts. Compared to Belmont Park or Churchill Downs, Delaware Park is a modest facility. Though additions were made to the grandstand and clubhouse in 1958, I didn't imagine a horse race here would look dramatically different than in Stymie's time. Lost in thought, I watched until the oval was closed for daily maintenance. Then, I was on my way.

Sometime later, while in New York, from Grand Central I took the Long Island train to Jamaica, Queens. I simply wanted to be on the sidewalks where the old Jamaica racetrack once stood. After the track was demolished, in place rose Rochedale Village, which at the time (1963) was the largest housing cooperative in the world.

It was a Saturday morning, and the neighborhood streets were quiet. As I attempted to orient myself, try to find the exact spot where Jamaica had once been, I drifted out to the middle of a section of 140th Avenue where I could have easily been run over by a teenager and his rocketing Chevy.

He swerved, the car shrieked to a stop. Down rolled the driver's side window. Yo! You okay, man? he said.

Sorry! I said. I could've explained what I was doing, why I was there, but he blasted his horn and sped off.

* * *

I thank my literary brother Anthony Grooms for providing guidance on the realities for people of color traveling through the South in the 1950s.

* * *

I am also appreciative of Mercer University Press, *New World Writing Quarterly*, and the Pirate's Alley Faulkner Society.

* * *

The image of Stymie on the cover of this book was painted by one of my favorite artists, Lazarus Nazario.

* * *

While there was an obsessive focus on historical accuracy in *Stymie*, all the characters and everything that happens to them has been fictionalized.

* * *

This book is dedicated to the equine soldiers of my lifetime, and to Diana, who loves horses more than life itself.